I
CHOOSE
you

Other Great Love Stories
* * *

Falling in Love with You
41 real love stories guaranteed for a smile

My Love to You Always
42 real stories of enduring love

*Go to www.oaktara.com
for these and many other romances*

I CHOOSE you

38 ROMANTIC SHORT STORIES TO WARM THE HEART

COMPILED & EDITED BY
RAMONA TUCKER & JENNIFER WESSNER

OakTara

Waterford, Virginia

I Choose You

Published in the U.S. by:
OakTara Publishers, P.O. Box 8, Waterford, VA 20197
www.oaktara.com

Cover design by Yvonne Parks at www.pearcreative.ca
Cover images © thinkstockphotos.ca: Jeremy Maude

Compilation/edition copyright © 2012 by OakTara Publishers, LLC. All rights reserved.
Individual stories copyright © 2012 by the authors. All rights reserved.

ISBN: 978-1-60290-208-4

Printed in the U.S.A.

Contents

* * *

I Choose You: Introduction • *1*

The Lighthouse Challenge • CONNIE MANN • *3*

The Park Bench • SADIE AND SOPHIE CUFFE • *8*

The Promise Still Holds... • JENNY JOHNSON • *15*

Return to Eden • ESTHER SEATON-DUMMER • *22*

The Rescuer • JAN CLINE • *28*

Dancing in the Moonlight • SHARON BERNASH SMITH • *34*

Foreign Feelings • MARYELLEN STONE • *41*

Springtime Love Forever • JANET R. SADY • *48*

Love at Vila Veronica • MARLENE WORRALL • *51*

Right on Time • ELAINE BALDWIN • *58*

I'll Take Romance • KATHRYN HARTMAN • *65*

A Friend of Mine • LYNN GIPSON • *72*

To Love or Not • MARY CANTELL • *78*

Tehya and Rode • M.E. BORN • *82*

A Kiss on Michigan Avenue • DICKY TO • *89*

Angel on Fourth Street • SUSAN M. BAGANZ • *96*

Heart Choice • MILLICENT NJUE • *101*

The Value of a Penny • CANDICE SUE PATTERSON • *104*

The Unfinished Story • KRISTINA STORER • *110*

Young Hearts • BEVERLY LAHOTE SCHWIND • *114*

Chosen • LORI-ANN WHYTE • *120*

The Mechanic • BEATRICE FISHBACK • *127*

Her Lucky Break • DAVALYNN SPENCER • *132*

Not Just Another Casserole Lady • CHRISTINA RYAN CLAYPOOL • *139*

A Sunday Kind of Love • LYNN GIPSON • *145*

Cyber Love • JUDE URBANSKI • *149*

Earned Love • CHARLOTTE S. SNEAD • *156*

Please • JOANN DURGIN • *161*

Thirty Minutes or Less • CAROLE TOWRISS • *166*

The Gingerbread Box • JANET R. SADY • *171*

Mission of the Heart • LAURA HODGES POOLE • *176*

Twenty Years of Convenience • ALETHEIA VON GOTTLIEB • *183*

The Tea Set • ELAINE MARIE COOPER • *188*

The Right Partner • SARA GIPSON • *194*

A Star-Spangled Courtship • GAIL KITTLESON • *198*

Something More • TRICIA SAXBY • *202*

More Than Just Another Day • DIANE K. ELLENWOOD • *206*

A Christmas Party • ANNE-MARIE MOONEY • *210*

Don't Miss *Falling in Love with You* • *214*

Don't Miss *My Love to You Always* • *215*

About the Compilers/Editors • *217*

I Choose You

* * *

INTRODUCTION

> Once in awhile, right in the middle of an ordinary life,
> love gives us a fairy tale.
> —ANONYMOUS

> It takes a second to say I love you, but a lifetime to show it.
> —TERESA COLLINS

There's nothing better than curling up in your favorite chair with a cup of tea or coffee and a great love story, is there?

Nestled in this treasured volume are 38 of the best-of-the-best romantic short stories from our international search for tales that will curl your toes, make you smile, and inspire you. These surprising romances are guaranteed to mist your eyes and renew your faith in enduring love and magical moments.

The Lighthouse Challenge

* * *

Connie Mann

My sister insisted I was crazy to even consider it. After several heated discussions, I'd finally convinced her not to tattle to Mom. If our mother—with her overactive fears and excessive worry gene—caught wind of my plan, she would have tried to chain me to my bed to keep me away. Or she'd have resorted to guilt and frightening *what-if* scenarios. But this was something I had to do.

As I sat in my wheelchair in the gravel parking lot and looked up, up, up to the top of the lighthouse, I had to wonder if my beloved worriers might be right after all. Was I crazy to try?

No. I slapped a hand on the arm of my chair and straightened my spine. The physical therapist had said if I didn't get serious about strengthening my legs, I would spend the rest of my life in this chair.

Not acceptable. I wanted my old life back, the one before the car accident, where I spent weekends and evenings after work jogging on the beach, riding my bicycle, and even surfing with my nephews on occasion.

You can do this, I told myself. I looked up again and my heart pounded, the hands gripping my wheelchair tires slick with sweat. The first time would be the hardest, I knew.

There were few visitors to the St. Augustine lighthouse this sunny Monday afternoon, just as I'd hoped. I wheeled my chair inside and handed my admission fee to Cindy, the young woman manning the cash register. If she wondered about my chair, she never said.

I thanked her and wheeled myself into the tower. I angled my chair as close to the spiral staircase as I could and looked up. My mouth went dry, and I felt slightly dizzy as my gaze followed the metal treads spiraling higher and higher. Two-hundred-and-nineteen is a lot of steps.

I forced myself to take a deep breath. Okay, I wasn't planning to go all the way up, just the first 50 steps. I pulled myself out of my chair and steadied my legs as I marshaled my courage.

I had one shaking hand on the handrail when a gruff voice said, "There's no elevator."

My head whipped around, and I came face-to-face with a giant of a man. At least, he seemed that way to me. Tall and rugged, he looked like one of the craggy sea captains depicted in my favorite books. He even dressed the part; a sea cap perched on midnight black hair slightly streaked with gray at the temples.

My fragile courage threatened to desert me, so I raised my chin. "I don't need an elevator, thank you. I'm planning to walk."

His stern expression didn't soften one bit. If anything, it hardened as his gray eyes raked over my spindly legs. "It's a 14-story climb."

I swallowed. Hard. "I know. But I'm only going partway up today."

"Suit yourself," he said shortly. "But the lighthouse foundation isn't responsible for injuries." Before I could comment, he turned and strode back outside, disappearing into the light keeper's house.

Strangely, his gruff demeanor didn't discourage me. Actually, it was oddly freeing. Ever since the car accident, my family had insisted on making the smallest of choices for me. This man assumed I knew my own mind and left me to deal with my own decisions—and their consequences.

Determined, I pushed the chair out of the way and clutched the railing like a lifeline in a storm-tossed sea. *This is just like the treadmill*, I reminded myself, and slowly placed my left foot on the bottom tread. Then I dragged the right one up beside it. I slid my hands up the railing and then hoisted my left foot up to the second step.

By the time I'd counted off 10 steps, sweat dripped down my face. By 20, my legs were shaking, and by 25, I slid to the floor in defeat. I couldn't go another step. Breathing hard, I looked up towards my goal and then down towards the familiar chair. Both seemed impossibly far away. After several minutes, I grabbed the rail and pulled myself up. I'd walk down as far as I could and scoot the rest of the way on my bottom, if necessary.

I was halfway down when a loud squawk from above startled me. My head snapped up, my foot slipped, and my hands lost their grip on the rail. Suddenly, I was pitching forward headfirst. But instead of cold metal, I collided with a hard chest as the light keeper's strong arms swept me up and carried me down the stairs as though I weighed no more than a puff of smoke.

"You don't have to do this," I mumbled, grateful and mortified at the same time.

Sympathetic gray eyes pierced mine for a brief moment. "Best not to overdo the first day."

He placed me in the chair as though I were fragile china, touched a finger to the brim of his cap, and disappeared.

I came back the next day, and the same thing happened. And the next. As though he had some sixth sense, the light keeper appeared every day just as my strength gave out, ignoring my protests and offering nothing more than his quiet assistance—whether that meant carrying me or placing a protective hand at my back.

By the end of the first week, I was able to stumble back down all twenty steps by myself. I eagerly looked for him so he could share my excitement, but he wasn't there. Disappointed, I turned towards my chair and found a single red rose lying on the seat. Somehow he'd known today was the day.

The second week, I pushed even harder. I made it up to the 35th step before my legs gave out. As though my thoughts conjured him, he raced up the stairs two at a time and scooped me up. I snuggled against that now-familiar chest and realized I didn't even know his name.

"Nathan Brandt," he said, setting me in the chair. "But my friends call me Nate." He saluted, then strode briskly away again.

Our days fell into a lovely routine. At the start of each week, he'd ask, "How many steps?" and then give a curt nod when I told him the number. And at the end of every week, a little gift would appear on my chair to celebrate the victory. A water bottle I could wear around my waist; a mug that said, *Fighter;* a book on the history of the lighthouse.

As time went on, knowing more about this quiet man became as important as reaching the top of the lighthouse. The two were somehow connected in my mind, both equally important. I still didn't like that he had to carry me down the first day of every week, but I relished the opportunity to learn more about him. He never said much, just dropped little bits of his story like perfect seashells I gathered as we traversed those steps. He'd grown up near the sea; spent time in the merchant marines. I also learned he'd never married, had no family nearby, and his work at the lighthouse was important to him.

At long last I reached 50 steps and then, finally, the 100 step mark. As the count increased, my confidence returned in tandem with the strength in my legs. The days were getting shorter by the time the 175-step mark became my goal. I wanted to reach the top by Christmas.

I hadn't seen Nate that fall afternoon, but I was grinning from ear to ear after descending 175 stairs. I couldn't wait to see what surprise he had left for me, though what I really wanted was to launch myself into his arms and shout for joy. I'd almost made it!

But when I reached my chair, shaking, sweaty, and proud, there was no gift. And no sign of Nate. I wheeled myself into the gift shop. I was using the chair less and less, though I still needed it after my climb. "Where's Nate?" I asked Cindy, who was straightening some books near the cash register.

"Didn't you know?" she asked. "Mr. Brandt had a heart attack yesterday."

My heart pounded crazily. "Is he okay?"

Cindy shrugged, eyes concerned. "I'm really not sure."

All the way to the hospital, I gripped the steering wheel and prayed. And when I saw Nate, I stifled a gasp. Surely this shrunken man wasn't my sea captain? But he needed me, so I plunged into the room, cane in hand, big smile on my face.

"What are you doing here?" he demanded.

Once that bark would have scared me off. But not anymore. "You didn't leave me a present today, so I came to get it."

He grunted, but I could see pleasure mixed with the uncertainty in his eyes.

"Besides, as soon as they let you out of here, I've got this great therapy planned. You start by climbing 20 stairs…"

When he smiled slowly, that heart-stopping grin gave me all the answer I needed.

We didn't quite make it for Christmas, but one day in early spring, Nate and I slowly climbed the last of the 219 steps to the top of the lighthouse. We stepped out onto the viewing platform, the wind stinging our cheeks and threatening to blow us off our feet. We huddled together and scanned the horizon, triumphant, sweating and elated.

After a few minutes, Nate drew me to the other side of the light, out of the wind, and cupped both hands against my cold cheeks, his gray eyes tender. "Thank you, Claire. I couldn't have done it without you."

I placed my hands atop his. "Isn't that my line?"

He laughed, a full, rich sound that touched my heart. Then he lowered his head and kissed me gently. When he pulled back, the look in his eyes took my breath away.

"There may be lots more tough climbs ahead in this life. I'd be honored if you'd consider us tackling them as a team."

My eyes filled as his meaning became clear. "I would like nothing better," I whispered.

Then Nate reached into his pocket and drew out a beautiful diamond ring. "Here's your 219th-step surprise."

I gasped, then asked, "When did you buy this?"

His gray eyes twinkled. "After you reached step 50. I knew right then you were the only lady for me."

Author's Note: "The Lighthouse Challenge" is inspired by a true story. On a visit to the St. Augustine Lighthouse, I met a lady in a wheelchair who was absolutely determined to make it all the way to the top of those 219 steps. She started by sitting on the bottom step and moving herself up using her arms. She'd already conquered the first 50 steps the day we met her. I'd like to believe she made it all the way to the top.

CONNIE MANN, author and USCG-licensed captain, lives in Central Florida and encourages busy women through her blog: **www.BusyWomenBigDreams.com**. Her Florida-set romantic suspense, *Trapped!* showcases a gator-trapping heroine, while a trip to her father's native Brazil provided the inspiration for *Angel Falls*. The screenplay for her romantic comedy, *Catch of a Lifetime*, was made into a feature-length film. Connie is a member of Romance Writers of America, Volusia County Romance Writers, Central Florida Romance Writers and Faith, Hope and Love, RWA's inspirational chapter. Connie is also the author of *Parenting in the Home Stretch: Twelve Ways to Prepare Your Kids for Life on Their Own*. She has written dozens of articles, ghostwritten six books and was the editor of a parenting magazine. When she's not writing, you can usually find her out on the water.

www.conniemann.com
www.BusyWomenBigDreams.com

The Park Bench

* * *

Sadie and Sophie Cuffe

"I didn't want to come." It came out like a two-year old's tantrum, but second childhood aside, I didn't care.

"The fresh air will do you good. Instead of walking today, sit here. I'll do my mile around the lake, and then we'll go home."

I sat on the bench to put some distance between me and the stern visage of my only granddaughter, nothing but sinew and bone with an x-ray tan. *Giving the orders now, are we?* The thought crossed my tongue, but instead of opening my mouth, I closed my eyes and nodded.

"On second thought, maybe I'll sit with you."

My eyes popped open and narrowed. Hayley bent over me, nose poked into my business, her clavicle sticking out like plucked chicken wings.

"Go! I'm perfectly fine to sit here by myself, an old woman on a park bench enjoying her own company."

"But—"

"Go." I flicked my fingers at her. She frowned but took the hint and loped off, looking back over her bony shoulder once, as I knew she would. I waved her off and she hit her stride on the track, her honey-colored hair sculpted to her head like a gold leaf Olympic crown.

"Is this seat taken?"

I squinted up into the austere face of a man with hair whiter than my own.

"I guess not." I wasn't sure which was worse, this stork-like stranger settling down beside me or my granddaughter hovering. Fortunately, he pulled out the paper tucked under his arm and opened it wide.

I focused on the runners rounding the head of the pond, but, truth be told, couldn't pick out Hayley among the lean lot of them. My eyes gravitated to the printed page and stuck on the photo on page six. I knew him—Clark Kent glasses on a Clark Gable face.

"Would you like a section?" My bench mate crackled the paper at me.

I shook my head and let my hair flop over one red cheek. "Ah, no. I apologize. I was just looking at the picture." I pointed at the new business owner spread.

"The recently renovated downtown welcomes a new business of old books. Kingsley's Ransom is a treasure trove of antique, used, and hard-to-find tomes. Owner, Preston Kingsley—" He stopped reading and stroked the photo with his finger. "He looks the part, don't you think?"

"I think the goatee is a bit much."

He tipped back his head and laughed. "I hear his girlfriend thinks it's cool."

"Really?" I let the one word drip with as much disdain as a leaky showerhead.

"I've never met someone so passionate over a stranger's picture." He pinned me with a smoky blue stare. Mr. Cool himself without a goatee, but the crow's feet said he either had eye trouble or laughed enough to be good company.

I didn't have anything else to do, so I opened the conversation door, but kept on the safety chain. "He's not a stranger. I know the girlfriend."

"So do I."

"No! Seriously?"

"Now you sound like the girlfriend." He grinned, nice set of pearly whites and they looked to be original equipment. Not as old as I thought.

I snorted.

"Oh, you've met!" My granddaughter put her foot on the bench beside me.

I jerked my head up to catch her uncertain smile, right as the man beside me stood. He kissed Hayley's cheek, then extended his hand to me. "Not quite. Julius Kingsley. I've been looking forward to meeting you, Mrs. Fitzpatrick."

I clenched my fist in my lap for a split second. My granddaughter finished her leg stretch and glared at me, her eyes rabbiting toward the man's outstretched palm. I uncurled my fingers and clasped his hand. It was warm and strong like the smile he leveled on me. I'd deal with Hayley later.

"Gran, this is Preston's father." Hayley's voice had a bubble in it. I thought she'd outgrown the affectation...obviously not.

"I gathered as much. Nice to meet you, Mr. Kingsley." I stood so I wouldn't be such a pipsqueak in the land of giants. It didn't help my self-esteem, but it fueled my indignation.

"Call me Julius."

"You can call her Roma." Hayley patted my arm.

Since she was so chatty, I let them handle the small talk on the way to the car.

He opened the door with a relaxed gallantry that pricked a buried memory and brought a lump in my throat. I slipped in front of him and got in, blinking back tears. I felt old and dowdy and hated myself for caring how I felt.

On the drive back to the house, I glared at Hayley, but she didn't take a breath. Obviously her feet weren't the only thing that could run. "Preston and I are considering moving in together. Of course, then people will think we're engaged, and I'm not sure how I feel about that."

"You're worried about people thinking you're engaged? I'd rather have you stay single your whole life than live together. God has a word for that, you know."

We stopped at a light and Hayley held up her palm like a traffic cop. "Gran, stop it right there. I'm an adult. I make my own decisions."

"Wait a minute." I shook my head. I must be old, letting myself get sidetracked so easily. I didn't want to slip like this. I wanted to go out quick. I clenched the seatbelt and sent up an angry plea for God to take me out of here. *Haven't I had enough?* "You aren't moving in with Preston. You're ducking this morning."

She revved the engine and took off. "I've no idea what you're talking about."

"You never could hide your bubble-gum voice when you had a guilty conscience. I'm talking about that setup with Julius."

"Did you like him?"

"He's nice enough, I guess."

"He recently retired, and he's driving Preston crazy at the new shop. I thought maybe you could keep him occupied for a few days. Just until Pres gets up and running."

"You could've given me a little heads-up."

"If I had, would you have come with me?"

I thought about the question for the rest of the day, and I still hadn't answered it when we returned to the park the next morning for our daily ritual.

There he sat on *my* bench reading his newspaper. Pretty nervy, I thought.

Hayley hovered at my elbow. "I didn't do this, Gran. Want me to tell him to leave?"

"No, go on and run." We were whispering like silly school girls. I waited until Hayley took off, but she stooped down and tied her sneaker, all the while spying.

I sauntered over and sat down.

Julius opened the paper wide so I could see.

"No need to share. No pictures of anyone I know today."

He laughed, flicked the paper shut, and, with a wave of a magician's hand, slipped it into his gym bag.

"Are you here to run?" I nodded toward the bag.

He shook his head, and his white hair glinted in the sun. "I'm here to get the skinny on the kids. Preston may sell books, but my son is anything but an open book."

"There's nothing to tell. Hayley's a history professor. That says it all, doesn't it? Their romance, if you can call it that, is slower than the 100 Years' War. She's in love with the intellectual side of life, not the flesh-and-blood rush of it all. By the way, she doesn't get that from my side."

"Hmmm, I thought not." He patted the back of my hand. I would've moved it, but his didn't linger. "Well, I know Preston doesn't want to pressure her. He proposed once, but she wasn't ready, said she needed to focus on her career."

"I think you've been misinformed. It's your son who's dragging his feet. He said he just opened the shop and needs to focus on his new business."

He swiveled in the seat, and his long knees collided with mine. I pulled back into my corner, unobtrusively, of course. He might be rude, but I refused to follow suit.

"Preston's right to be cautious. My wife always cooked dinner for me, kept the house so beautiful. Even when she was sick, she put flowers on the table...." He gazed out over the pond. In profile, his chin quivered.

It was unfair of him to bring up the flowers, especially since I was working up some self-righteous indignation on Hayley's behalf. I tried to hold on to it. "You *are* a dinosaur, aren't you! There's more to life than dinner at six and clean socks. That's not what love is all about."

He turned and fixed his blue gaze on mine. His eyes glistened without a trace of a tear, and a twinge of admiration rose in me. He took my hand in both of his, without pressure or presumption. "It may not be your idea of romance, but it..."

He didn't finish. He didn't have to. I wanted to rave at him for transporting me back to Saturday nights in the living room, scorching popcorn over the fireplace, lying against each other and dreaming.

I clung to the park bench and today. "Look, it doesn't matter what we think about romance. We need to light a fire under those kids. They're not kids either, by the way. Hayley's thirty-three years old. By the time I was her age, I had a teenage son. Six years later I buried him in a flag-draped coffin. Life is short."

He nodded and gently squeezed my hand. "I got a later start, but I hear you. Let's conspire."

Hayley jogged up, puffing and grinning. Julius and I both slipped our hands away.

"It looks like you two are getting along," she cooed on the ride home.

"Maybe you and Preston should take notes."

She turned up the radio and focused on the traffic.

Why do people persist in plucking the petals off a daisy? Let the poor flower alone. It hasn't done anything to us...but it had.

Julius started bringing coffee and muffins to the park bench. Okay, he was a widower; maybe he didn't know how to cook breakfast. Then he offered to bring me home in his car. I agreed, only because it saved Hayley the extra drive before she went to work. But then he brought the daisies, and I shook my head.

"What?" It was the first time I'd seen that dear long face color up. He tossed the flowers on the bench and gripped my hand. "You're just like your granddaughter—one foot in the cement and the other in a pot of glue."

I yanked my hand from his big warm grip and he sat back, staring at me down his long nose. "What do you know? I don't have time for this. I only want to see my granddaughter happy and settled before I die!"

His face crumpled, and he wrapped his long arm around my hunched shoulders. "How much time?" he whispered into my hair.

I swallowed hard and turned my face into his striped shirt. I didn't ask how he knew. I'd seen the look in my husband's eyes when he had his stroke. No doubt Julius had seen it when his wife died of cancer. I sniffled into his shoulder. "Enough. God always gives us enough."

"Yes, He does." Julius smoothed back my hair and erased my tears with his gentle fingers. "What will we do with it?"

God bless a man who can wade with you but doesn't let you wallow. I smiled, a little shaky, but enough to let some hope in. "I always wanted to ride a bike. We never had the money when I was a kid, and I never took the time later."

"A bicycle built for two?"

I gripped his hand. "Hayley doesn't know, but I think she suspects."

He met my gaze, his eyes wet. "Your secret is safe with me."

Hand in hand we walked to the bike rental. "My girl needs a nice ride."

No bicycle built for two, but Julius picked out a red flyer for me. I touched the handlebars, instantly eight years old again. His strong arm steadied me on the seat. Off we went, Julius jogging beside me, white mane streaming.

"Should you be doing this?" I yelled.

"Should you? Pedal!"

The bike wobbled, and I was on my way. I looked back, saw him waving his arms, and snapped forward just in time to avoid getting tossed into a bed of tulips. The next day he rode by my side.

The robins came and built their nest in a tree by our bench.

I taught Julius to hula hoop. Well, I tried.

We ate ice cream cones and argued over a chess board.

He swept the scarlet leaves from our bench and laid his sweater over it to cushion my seat. I closed my eyes and leaned back in the weakening sun. His arm brushed mine, and I cracked my eyelids.

Julius knelt on the seat, knife in hand.

"What are you doing?"

"Keep your eyes closed, or you'll ruin the surprise." He grinned, and slivers of wood peeled off the backrest as he worked.

"Sir, you're defacing city property!"

We both jumped a mile, then laughed. The officer didn't crack a smile.

Julius nodded to the younger man. "I prefer to think of it as donating artwork to the city." I don't know how he kept a straight face. I didn't.

"I'll let you off with a warning this time." The cop confiscated the penknife and moved on.

"He could've at least let me finish."

I traced the R.F. + J.K. and the crooked heart that had no bottom. "It's perfect. You got in the important stuff."

The day of the first snowfall, he tucked the lap robe around me. The carriage driver took off, and he squeezed my hand. "Warm enough?"

I nodded, even though it was a lie. "Marry me, Roma," he murmured into my hair.

I shook my head no, blinking back tears.

He held my face in both his hands. "Come on! Life is short."

The next day he dusted off the snow, and I sat on the bench beside him. I traced his artwork with a gloved finger and said, "I do."

Hayley stood beside me, Preston beside his dad. *Thanks for just enough.*

*

Julius sat on the bench watching the towhead hula-hoop. "Roma, come sit." She skipped to the bench and squirmed up beside him. Her small finger traced the RF carved on the back rest. "That's me, Grampa."

"That's your gran, but you can hula-hoop just like her." He tipped his head back, eyes to the sky, and whispered. "I see you in her, and a little of myself, too."

SADIE AND SOPHIE CUFFE are sisters (yes, they're really siblings) who work a small farm in Maine. They bring the strength of a living sisterhood and an undying faith to their writing. They've authored inspirational e-books, but their octogenarian mom wants to know when they'll write a "real" book. Hopefully, soon! (If God wills.)

www.cuffesisters.com
www.cuffesisters.com/off-the-cuffe

The Promise Still Holds

* * *

Jenny Johnson

"Me? On Facebook? Really, Travis, if I'd wanted to keep up with those people in my college yearbook, I'd have done it before now. It's been 15 years, for heaven's sake. I don't need Facebook to connect with folks who haven't felt a need to get in touch with me, either."

"Mom, you never know who might be trying to find you. They don't know your married name. You don't live where you grew up. You'd be hard to track down."

"Now who would want to track me down, Travis Sawyer? It wasn't like I was a cheerleader or the homecoming queen with hunks lining up for dates, but, wait, I ran away and married your daddy so they've been waiting around all these years and now they've heard your daddy died so here they come. I'm almost middle-aged, son. I really don't think there's a demand for my presence online."

"What's a hunk, Mom?"

"It's what we used to call...I can't believe I'm having this conversation. Never mind. I'm beat. I have to go to bed. Don't stay up too late chirping with your friends."

"Mom, it's not chirp..."

"Kidding. G'night, honey. Love you."

*

That boy needs a dad. And a hobby other than trying to influence his mom to join the 21st century. He's a sweet kid for a 13-year-old. Thank you, God, for being his heavenly Father, now that his earthly one's gone. You've kept us going, Lord, when I didn't think I could, especially right after Steve died. That was hard, and moving on has been tough. But it's been two years and we're doing OK. I didn't expect to be able to say that again—ever. In truth, Psalm 68:5 (ESV) is personal for Travis and me, Lord. You are a "Father of the fatherless and protector of widows." Please keep us safe tonight. Amen.

*

My mom rocks, God. She's a little overprotective, but I can handle that because I know she loves me. I miss Dad. Can't believe it's been two years. At least now I can think about him without crying like a girl. Mom misses him, too. She doesn't say much, but I think that's why she works so hard. I know she has to make money for us, but even when she's home, she hardly ever stops. I think that's how she keeps from thinking too much about Dad. I never thought I'd say this, but I sure do wish Mom could find someone…OK, God. Can't say it. You know what I mean. And I don't think Dad would mind.

*

"Travis, I have to run to town. Do you and Terrance want to come along?"

"Thanks, Mom, but no. We'll just stay here. Can you bring pizza? We're starved."

"Sure, won't be long. Don't let anyone in that you…"

"We know, Mom. You tell us that every time…."

"Mom? Mom?"

"I think she's gone."

"Check out the window. Is the car still here?"

"No car. What's up?"

"She's going to kill me. But we're going to put my mom on Facebook."

"She's not on already? My mom lives in cyberspace. She's online more than I am."

"Mom says she doesn't care about keeping up with people from her past—like from her college. She says they haven't been beating down her door to find her in the 15 years since she graduated. I think she's afraid no one remembers her."

"Your mom's been out of college 15 years? She's that old?"

"She's not old, dumbhead; she's only 37."

"Why are you risking your neck to set her up a Facebook account? Is it worth being grounded the rest of your life?"

"I think she needs…it's hard to explain…my mom's the best, but I think…she needs….a…boyfriend. If you tell her I said that, I'll tell Janie McCarvey you have a crush on her."

"Lips locked! Do you know enough about your mom to set up an account? My mom's just my mom. I'd have no idea about the details."

"I know my mom pretty well and, anyway, I'm giving her a new identity.

Or I should say her old identity back."

"Travis, make sense."

"On my mom's Facebook page, she'll have the same name she had in college, before she married Dad, and way before me. And I'm putting up a picture I found of her right after she graduated. She looked great."

"Your mom's not bad now, Trav. For a mom. She has a nice smile."

"Yeah, but you don't see it as much as before Dad died. Anyway, I'm not putting up any more info about her, like where she went to high school or where we live or anything…just where she went to college."

"And where was that?"

"A small church school in North Carolina. And I'm putting her status as single, because now it's true."

"You're right, buddy. You're a dead man. What if people want her to friend them? What will you do then?"

"I'll stall."

"What's the point? Why set her up on Facebook and then not friend anybody?"

"I'll stall until the right person comes along, if he comes along. Look, Terrance, this is sort of an experiment. I've done my research. I have Mom's college senior yearbook. I've studied the names of people who signed it and what they said to her. I made her tell me about who her friends were in the book, especially the guys. I even asked if she had any boyfriends or anybody she had a crush on. That was way before she met Dad."

"So what did she say?"

"There was this one guy I think she liked. His name was Evan. She said they were just good friends. But the way she said it, I think she really cared about him."

"So, back to my question. What do you hope to get out of this Facebook thing? For your mom, I mean?"

"I'm really not sure. I'll just put it out there and see what happens."

"Travis Sawyer, you're my best friend. I'm going to watch you do this, and then I'll help you write your obituary."

*

Just make it to your car. Walk with intention…not too fast…casual but with purpose. Act like this happens to you every day. Take your time. You're in control. Breathe. Start the car. Smooth. Back out carefully. Watch. All you have to do now is wave, smile, and drive away. It's over. You're fine. You said no, but you didn't hurt his feelings—you hope. He's a nice guy...a believer...good-looking...goes to your church. He only wanted to take you to dinner sometime. What's the big deal? Only a simple meal together. Might be fun.

But just didn't feel right. Was that a mistake? What if it was the right thing? I could ask the pastor what he thinks. Maybe I should call...

Stop it! Just because he's cute and asked nicely doesn't mean you have to say yes. You don't have to date anyone you don't want to. Period. It's OK to say no. You don't have to do anything until you're ready. Or ever. No pressure. You and Travis are fine the way you are. Sure, he needs a dad, but neither of you is desperate. Desperate is no good reason. You made the right decision. Take a deep breath and drive home.

*

"Uh, oh. I hear a car. She's home, Trav. If I were you, I'd get out of there and erase your history, fast. You can go back later and shut down her account when sanity hits you."

"No problem, Terrance. I'm done here. I set her up a new email account and a Facebook profile. That picture's a nice touch, if I do say so. What do you think?"

"I think I hope you know what you're doing. This idea could be toxic."

"Not really, Terrance. I can pull the plug any time. Mom doesn't even have to know for now. Like I said, it's an experiment. Let's go see if she got the pizza."

*

"Thanks, Mom. You're the best. Terrance ate six pieces before he had to leave. Is something wrong? You're acting a little weird."

"Honey, let me ask you something. I know we haven't talked about this, but how would you feel about me going out if someone asked me?"

"Out? You mean, like on a date?"

"Well, sort of, I guess. Yes, a date. Just out for the evening. Back early. That sort of thing."

"Would I have to have a babysitter?"

"No, unless you considered Terrance a babysitter. He could come over. So, what would you think?"

"I think it would depend on how you feel and on who the guy is. Why? Did somebody hit on you?"

"Travis, I certainly wouldn't put it like that. But someone did ask me if I'd like to go to dinner. Why are you looking at me like that?"

"Who was he? Some old guy? Somebody from work?"

"As a matter of fact, a very nice man from church."

"What did you say? Mom?"

"No. I said, 'No thank you.' I couldn't do it, Travis. I was flattered he asked, but I couldn't say yes. Maybe I'm just not ready yet."

"Or maybe he's not the right one."

"You could be right. Anyway, I shouldn't worry you about it. I just wondered how you'd feel when…if…I ever did say yes. To a date, I mean."

"I think it would depend, Mom. I think it would all depend. Got homework. Got to go study. Thanks again."

*

God, maybe Terrance is right, and this Facebook thing is one of the dumbest ideas I've ever had. But for some reason, I don't think so. If it is, then you show me and I'll take it down. Just don't let Mom get hurt. Or me either, for that matter. I'm trying to help her, God. If I'm running too far ahead of you, slow me down, please. Amen.

*

Father, today totally made me uncomfortable. I'll admit I'm lonely. But something held me back from wanting to go out with that guy from church. Don't let me stand in my own way of happiness, but also don't let me get anxious and jump into anything that's not right with you. And there's Travis. He seemed a little strange with my question to him. I don't want to get into any relationship before Travis is ready. You're sufficient, Lord. You always have been. Give me wisdom.

*

OK, I promised I wouldn't check Mom's new Facebook page for at least three days. Now it's time, but I'm scared to log in. Didn't know it would be this hard. Maybe I should just…no, I have to man up and follow through. I may be way out of my league here.

Yikes! Twenty-five requests for friends already. Mom would be surprised at this. Let's see if I remember any of these names from her yearbook…at least the first names. No…don't remember her. That name sounds familiar. I think she was one of mom's good friends. So was this one. Let me just run through the rest of these, but I'm not friending anybody yet. There's a guy. Don't remember his name. Let's see…whoa, he looks strange. I'd never friend him for Mom.

Hold it. Wait a second. I remember that name. Evan Clarke. No waaaayy. Is that the guy Mom talked about? Where's that yearbook?

Where'd I put it? I should've cleaned my room like Mom said. I know I had it...here it is.

There was this one note in the back...should be right here someplace. Here...**Evan C**. Has to be the same guy. How many Evan C.'s would there be at her little college? This is definitely the same one. It says right here:

> *To Laurel E.—*
> *If I ever marry, it will be 2 U.*
> *Evan C.*

I'm not believing this! For sure he has to be the same one I think Mom really liked. She said he was her best friend, but he never dated. Mom said he was focused on his studies and finding out what his life was supposed to stand for. The last time she saw him, he was getting on a bus to spend the summer after graduation working in migrant camps as a missionary.

I know this is the guy. I'm going to friend him. OK, now I'll just wait and see what...who am I kidding? This won't work. I can't friend him without sending some kind of message. What would Mom say to him after 15 years? I don't have a clue what to write.

But I do know what Mom would say to me. She'd say I've really gone too far here. That I must be nuts, and I've got no right to do this. I've got to go talk to Mom.

*

"Travis Mayfield Sawyer, you did what?"

"I did, Mom. Believe it."

"No, I know you did not! You did not put your mom on Facebook without my permission! I told you I wasn't interested...that I didn't care about...I can't believe you would do that!"

"Mom, I'm so sorry. I love you. I know it sounds crazy, but that's why I did it. The truth! I can explain, but if you want me to pull the plug, I will, right now. I did put up the page. I promise I've only friended one person. But Mom, I think I need to tell you one thing before you say anything else."

"Travis, this is serious. What could you possibly say that would cause me to change my mind about locking you in your room without your computer until you are at least 30?"

"It's him, Mom. He asked to be your Facebook friend."

"He who? What are you talking about?"

"Evan Clarke, Mom. I'm sure it's the same guy you told me about. He wanted you to friend him, and I did."

"I don't believe you. This is a joke, right?"

"No joke, Mom. See for yourself."

"This isn't funny, Trav. If you're kidding around, you don't know…"

"Look, Mom. He's already sent you a message. Here, read what it says."

Laurel, it's been a long time, but the promise still holds.
I'm ready…are you?

"Mom, I think he's talking about what he wrote in your yearbook! He's asking you…Mom, are you crying? No, look, I'll explain everything to him. I'll apologize. I was just trying to help. Mom, please…what?"

"Travis, the last thing Evan said to me when he got on the bus the day he left was, '*Don't wait for me, Laurel, but if it's meant to be, I'll find you when the time is right.*'"

"He did it, Mom. He found you!"

"He had a little help. I love you, Travis Sawyer."

JENNY JOHNSON is a writer with a double life. As a semi-retired university professor of Special Education, she continues her professional education publishing. While using her pen name, she indulges her "never-too-late" list by writing faith-based romance and other for-fun projects. Her first romantic suspense novel, *The Taxi,* was published in 2012 (OakTara).

http://www.jennyjohnsonauthor.com
http://jennywjohnson.blogspot.com

Return to Eden

***

Esther Seaton-Dummer

It was a sweltering day in August. Twenty-six-year-old Eve Devonshire drove into her quaint little hometown of Eden, Oregon. Nestled in the northern coastal range, the town is a mixture of timber and pastureland the homesteaders had carved out long ago. It took her back in time, to another era where everything was innocent, but today she felt soiled. She was coming home to heal.

Her parents, Dan, a tall, sinewy man of strength gained from hard work, and Marie, small of stature but of the same strength, loved their homestead nestled in the hills just outside the city limits. But more than hard work had strengthened them; it was their faith in God that had built them into the people they had become.

When their only child was born, the whimsical idea of naming their daughter Eve, because of their town's name, became a reality on February 14, 1986. She was a beautiful baby with a head full of wavy golden hair and the delight of her parent's hearts.

Eve grew into a striking young lady with her faith blossoming as well. While in a small town there might be a few suitors, Adam Vermont was always around from as long as she could remember and canceled her interest in anyone else. She assumed, as he did, that they would someday marry and live in Eden. She was often teased about *finding her Adam and living happily ever after in Eden.*

As Eve rounded the corner with her little Volkswagen Beetle onto Oak Tree Lane, a gravel road only a mile from her family's home, a tabby cat followed by a small terrier-looking dog, followed by a large shepherd-mix dog, followed by a man with his arms wildly pumping, all ran onto the road. Eve hit her brakes, skidding on the loose gravel, barely missing the strange menagerie.

The man, about age 26, dressed in jeans and an unbuttoned plaid shirt flapping as he ran and flip-flops he could barely keep on his feet, turned her way, frozen in time for a second. His sun-streaked light brown hair, long enough to tuck behind his ears and touching his collar, was disheveled, wet with sweat he was obviously working up. He looked at her with vivid green eyes flickering with questions before running on after the string of animals. They all disappeared into a thick stand of trees that led to the Eden River that ran behind the family farm and traced its way through the countryside into Eden.

Eve sat there wondering if she had just witnessed what she thought she had and tried to bring her fluttering heart back down from her throat and calm it. The man resembled a grown up version of her childhood friend, *but that couldn't be, could it?* She'd heard that Adam Vermont had moved out of the area when he married some Easterner. She had heard he was working for corporate America and living the high life in New York City. From what she had heard about *the man*, Adam, he would never be found wearing the farmer's clothes this man wore and chasing animals around the country.

A funny song from her childhood came to her: "The Farmer in the Dell..." She hummed it, envisioning the animals in the circus that had just passed before her eyes, substituting them in the stead of the rat, cat, and dog.

Shaking herself, she drove on down the gravel road, skitter-bugging in the ruts of the dusty lane.

What a strange thing to see and what a strange man.

What she remembered about *the boy*, Adam, was that he was as rustic and earthy as the farm he grew up on. Eve and Adam had spent their childhood together, with their friendship deepening and flourishing in their teen years. They had made a vow that when they got old enough, they would get a farm, marry, and live in Eden. They were part of a group of kids who were organically grown in this piece of God's green earth and they loved it. Adam had been her first love, but time had eroded so much....

Stop it, Eve. There's no point in going there. You had your chance and you blew it.

Eve shook the memories loose and turned into her parents' driveway. It was an old, typical farmhouse, with a big barn out back and fenced and cross-fenced pasture land where a head of cattle roamed. The smells of the farm hit her fully when she opened her car door with nostalgia not far behind as she was suddenly overwhelmed with longing for the life she once had.

It had been eight years since she had left to go to college in Florida. Her vow to come back had disappeared into the life she had adopted living in the fast lane of Miami, Florida. And that fast lane had held many bad choices. Her heart was buried deep within a tomb of regret.

The long drive home had given her time to inventory her life, laying it all out, sparing her heart no pain. She systematically remembered the disaster her life had become and thought of Sammy. He had offered her a life filled with promise, but then the restraints of her faith slipped free of her heart and she ate the forbidden fruit.

Eve thought about how far removed she was from the roots of the family tree in Eden. Her family lineage dated back to the founding of this little town. The cemetery was filled with her family members—from the great-greats to the greats and on and on...

As she slid out of her car, her father and mother ran out and smothered her in their strong arms, whispering in her ears, "Welcome back to Eden, Eve." Tears of relief and shame mingled down her cheeks as she received their confirming love and acceptance. She was home.

Heading inside, she saw the time capsule of her home. Everything was as it had been, and it comforted her. The creaky steps to her old bedroom resounded in a symphony of welcome. She slowly opened the door as if it were a present from the past and was not disappointed. The room of her childhood wrapped itself around her heart.

She spent the afternoon unpacking and settling into what would be her refuge until she could find herself again. She knew the search would be painful but hopefully healing.

Later that night, after her mom's fried chicken dinner with all the trimmings, she and her parents settled into the comfortable, old living room furniture of the past and nestled their hearts together for a warm chat. It was filled with memories and questions and hope. They reminisced, going over her childhood, school friends, and finally, Adam.

Her dad's eyes probed her soul as he spoke. "Eve, Adam really messed up his life, and I'm not sure if he is ever coming back."

Eve was disappointed to find that the running man couldn't have been Adam. She had hoped...

The week worked its way into the weekend, where the subject of church came up. It had been years since Eve had attended any worship services. Her faith, which she thought was strong when she left home, had been severely tested by college life, friends, and secular professors and the choices that had been made bit by bit.

Now, as she sat talking to her parents, she knew that if she was coming home to Eden, it would mean a full return. It would be impossible to live here *partway*. She told her parents she'd be attending church with them. Another of their redeeming hugs drew her in.

Sunday morning she got up early and dressed in a nice, cool summer dress. Slipping her feet into sandals, she grabbed her purse. If she remembered right, there was no air-conditioning in the ancient, little white church that had stood on the corner of Fifth and Pine Streets for years.

She went downstairs and ate breakfast with her mom and dad. Mom's customary pancakes, eggs, and bacon brought an attack of delightful nostalgia. The smell of the breakfast was almost as sacred as the fact she was going to church this morning; it all went together.

Her dad, mom, and she went out to their car and drove down Oak Tree Lane, turning the corner onto the paved road toward town. In a moment's time they were there, pulling up in front of her hometown church in Eden. Her heart was moved as she took in the sight of the worshippers of several generations—grandparents, moms, dads, and kids—filing into the church.

As they entered, she was shocked to see the preacher, Pastor Mike Marks, was the same one as when she left. He made his way to her with a wide smile. "Welcome back to Eden, Eve."

Her heart was a mixture of awe and shame that she was back but not the same girl as the one who left, yet his words nurtured her soul someplace deep.

The singing was wonderful, but it was Pastor Mike's message that captured her fully: "Today, my message text is taken from Luke 15:11-24, the story of the Prodigal Son...." He detailed the steps of leaving and the steps of return, then opened the altar to those who wanted to return to God. Her heart was quickened to take that bold step of commitment and return completely to her heavenly Father.

As she stepped out into the aisle, she collided with someone. It was like a car wreck as their two bodies rebounded off each other, both in such a hurry and so focused on getting back to the Father that neither had eyes for anything but the altar.

Eve turned to see who she had bumped into and was taken aback by the sight of the same man who had run in front of her car. Both were flustered beyond words as they found themselves walking in tandem to the same altar. She could hear people begin to sniffle all around her as they walked down the center aisle and stood before Pastor Mike for prayer.

The greater shock was when Pastor Mike said, "Adam and Eve, welcome back to Eden, and welcome back to the Father. You have come home today."

And then he prayed for them, asking them to make that commitment to serve Jesus all the days of their lives.

After the prayer time was concluded, if there wasn't a fatted calf being prepared for a feast, it could have fooled Eve. Of all the hugs, kisses, handshaking, backslapping moments, this was the best. Eve knew she was home from a long, fruitless journey into a sin-sick world where no absolutes existed. She had a hundred questions for Adam. Her eyes searched for his and had no trouble finding them.

Tears glistened in his eyes as he mouthed, "Welcome home to Eden, Eve."

Later, at home, she asked her dad about his statement about not knowing if Adam would ever come back.

"I wasn't talking about a physical return," her father said, "but a spiritual return." He then said Adam had come back to Eden six months ago and bought a little farm not too far from theirs, but until today he had made no move to truly return. Her father was overjoyed by what God had just done in both their lives. "I've seen miracles"—he chuckled—"but this takes the cake.

As he was talking to Eve, a knock sounded on the back door to the kitchen.

"I'll get it, Dad." Eve opened the door to see Adam standing there, flanked by two dogs—one small terrier mix and one large shepherd-mix. Lagging behind was a tabby cat. Her mouth opened and, for the life of her, she couldn't shut it. So, he truly was the Farmer in the Dell...

His first words were, "It was the squirrel."

She smiled and stepped outside into the sunlight as past history was shoved aside by the promise of tomorrow. The two prodigals joined hands, as if they had never parted, and walked to where Eden River flowed gently through the farm. Here they had made memories and enjoyed many childhood years. It was here their young romance had begun to bud, and here they had shared their tentative first kiss.

It was also here that Eden had told Adam good-bye just before she left for college. She could still remember the sadness in his eyes as he stood under their tree where they had carved their initials, which served as a witness to their promise to return to this spot again.

Now, in this sacred place, they spoke of their individual journeys. They wept together for the lost years, but rejoiced in the returning.

Adam had not married the Easterner, could not bring himself to do it. He had remained single but had become engaged to a bottle of booze. He told her of his pigpen and of his awakening. He told her of the gentle voice that kept compelling him to return *all the way home*. He told her of how he had rushed into the church earlier, ready to truly return to God and Eden.

And Eve told Adam of her walking away from God and all she believed for the pleasure of sin for a season that had left her empty and hungry to return. She spoke of her shame and deep regret and wasted years, but that God had also drawn her to fully surrender.

And in the same way that God had redeemed them to Himself that morning, He had also brought them both on a collision course of destiny yet unfulfilled for their lives. He knew they were both better together than they could ever be apart.

Adam and Eve finished their confessions. Then, with a deep breath of grace and anticipation, they gazed into each other's eyes. A joy of wonderment and realization washed over Eve. She saw tears in Adam's eyes as all the sorrows of the past were washed away. Her eyes also misted as she realized the grace of God in all that had happened.

Adam dropped his lips to meet hers and sealed their full return with a kiss—a kiss that would resonate for a lifetime—in Eden.

ESTHER SEATON-DUMMER has co-pastored Gateway Worship Center in Clatskanie, Oregon with her husband, Loren, for the past 20 years. Teaching and writing are her passion. She is the author of *Outside the Box Faith* series, including *Elusive Faith* and *Bedrock Faith*.

    http://www.outsidetheboxonline.com
    http://www.gatewayrevival.org

The Rescuer

* * *

Jan Cline

Maggie turned from the store window and looked down. Jonathan had disappeared. She scanned the sidewalk and caught a glimpse of his blue coat close to the street corner.

"Stop him! Stop that little guy!" Shaking, she launched forward, tripping over the purse and package she had dropped. She gathered her belongings and weaved through the crowd. The blue coat, barely visible, floated among a sea of moving bodies. Suddenly, she lost sight of it. In a panic she shoved her way past one last group of pedestrians until she stood face-to-face with the rascal in the arms of a tall young man.

"Jonathan! You scared Mommy. Come here to me." She didn't know whether to spank him or smother his little face with kisses. "Thank you, sir." She pulled Jonathan into her arms.

"You should be more careful. They tend to disappear when you least expect it."

Heat flooded her cheeks. "I'm usually very careful. I just stopped to look at something in the window—"

"I understand. I have one of my own." The wind blew strands of the man's black hair onto his forehead. Maggie examined his face. A day's growth of beard surrounded full lips. His manner inspired a certain familiarity she couldn't pinpoint.

Jonathan broke her stare with a wet kiss.

"He looks happy now. I'll be on my way." The young man took a few strides down the street and then spun around. "Oh, and he told me he doesn't like wearing that little blue coat. Coats are for people, not dogs." He flashed a charming smile and lingered a moment before disappearing into the crowd.

"I don't need advice about my own dog, thank you," Maggie mumbled as she snuggled Jonathan under her arm. She glanced at her watch. Time to go home to the stack of work. "I need a cappuccino." She grasped his little face in her hand. "You stay close."

Together they dodged cars to cross the street and sat at an outside table in front of a busy coffee shop. She drew Jonathan close to her chair and took a long look at his blue coat. "You like your coat, don't you, Johnny?" She strapped his leash to the table leg. Jonathan yipped playfully and lay at her feet.

The biting breeze prompted Maggie to wrap her scarf tight around her neck. She loved the smell of fall. A hint of chimney smoke collided with a whiff of espresso escaping from the open door of the coffee shop.

A man's voice chimed behind her as she studied the drink selection on the menu. "May I take your order?"

"Yes, I'll have a double-shot mocha cappuccino. Extra whipped cream." She held up the menu but dropped it when she recognized the face. It was the same man who had rescued Jonathan. Her eyes found his nametag: *Michael.*

"Well, hello again." He looked at the scribbling on his pad. "Extra whipped cream? It's pretty fattening, you know. You'll need to stay in shape to run after the little guy." He leaned down and tapped Jonathan's head.

"Are you following me?" She glanced around to make sure no one heard.

"How could I be following you when I left the corner first? Jonathan nearly made me late for work. I'll bring your order right out." He scooped up the menu and hurried away.

How rude. Still, he was cute. His soft brown eyes sparkled.

"Here you are. Cappuccino. Extra whipped cream." Michael lifted the steaming cup from a tray and set it in front of her. "Can I get you anything else?"

"No, thank you, and here you go." She pulled out cash from the bottom of her messy purse and held it up. "Keep the change."

"It's on me today. To thank you for the privilege of rescuing Jonathan."

"Oh, no. I can't let you do that. And besides, what would your boss say?" She waved the money in the air.

"I am the boss." He winked and moved toward a nearby table.

She stuffed the money back in her purse and leaned down. "Did you hear that, Johnny? He's the boss."

Jonathan answered her with a snort.

She leisurely sipped her cappuccino. The clock tower across the street clanged four o'clock. She peered at the door while untying Jonathan. "I think we should go say thank you."

Scooping him up, she marched toward the door. The aroma of fresh brewed coffee and baked biscotti filled the shop. The room seemed to pull her in, and she blinked away a slight fuzzy feeling. Not now, not another dizzy

29

spell.... The sensation subsided just in time to hear a rebuke from a young woman coming toward them.

"I'm sorry, but animals aren't allowed in here." She smirked and held the door open for Maggie. "We can serve you outside."

"It's all right, Julie. I know this customer," Michael interrupted.

Maggie leaned to the side to watch the girl walk away, but he stepped in front of her. "Did Jonathan enjoy his cappuccino?"

"Yes...I mean I did. We just came in to say thank you again." She turned to leave, but he caught her arm.

"By the way, my name is Michael, and you're welcome." That charming smile again. "You haven't told me your name."

"It's uh—Shannon. I mean, Maggie." Was her face red? Why was she stammering?

"Well, is it Maggie or Shannon?" He frowned.

"It's Maggie Shannon." *Settle down, Mags.*

"Well, it's nice to meet you, Maggie Shannon. I hope you'll come back soon." He patted Jonathan on the head and walked toward the counter. "And I do mean soon, okay?"

Maggie's knees shook as she stepped through the door. *Move, stupid. What's wrong with you?*

Once outside, she put Jonathan down. The cloudy day had turned drizzly. "Let's get home before we both get wet."

*

The rain pelted the window as Maggie towel-dried Jonathan's matted fur. Her mind wandered to the coffee shop, picturing Michael's face. He was the first good-looking man she'd met since returning home to live. At least she was told this was her home.

"What do you say we go back to the coffee shop tomorrow, Johnny? I'll have to cash my paycheck first." She rummaged through her purse to find her check. "Lipstick, wallet, mirror, lipstick, gum." Her stomach knotted as she checked her trench pocket and all her packages.

"Stay calm." She dumped her purse on the table, unzipping each compartment. The check was lost. She slumped into the chair, tears stinging her eyes.

A knock on the door startled her. Johnny bounded out of his bed and ran around barking and dancing. She pulled the door open to the end of the chain.

"Hello." Michael looked her up and down with a childish grin. "I hope I'm not intruding. I think I have something of yours."

Maggie had the sinking realization that her wet hair, tattered robe, smudged makeup, and bunny slippers made her a charming sight. "Oh, Michael. Hello. You have what?"

"I have something that belongs to you."

He held out a dampened envelope with a black shoeprint on it. She snatched it from him and opened it. It was there. Her paycheck. "Thank you so much," she said, holding it to her chest. "I must have dropped it when I reached in my purse to pay you. It's so nice of you to return it." She tucked her robe up under her chin. "How did you find me?"

"Your address is on the envelope. I would have called, but there was no phone number. Well, I'll be going now. I'm glad I was the one to find it." He knelt to pet Jonathan, who promptly jumped into his arms.

"He remembers you all right." Maggie knelt to join them. "I would ask you in but—" She tugged at her robe again.

"Oh, I understand. I really should get back to the shop. A pipe broke behind the juice bar after you left. It's a mess. It's just me and the mop. The life of a coffee shop owner. But we'll be open for business tomorrow if you care to stop by." He stood and backed away. "Bye now."

Maggie's heart fluttered as she watched him stroll down the hallway. She slipped back inside. The mirror beside the door confirmed her worst fears. She ran her fingers through her damp hair. "He must have thought I was a mess."

She stood and shuffled to the window. The rain had stopped. She thought about Michael having to clean the coffee shop by himself after working all day. What a shame there was no one to help him.

She tugged on Jonathan's ears. "You know, I can sleep in tomorrow. I could go down there and help the poor guy. It's the least I could do. After all, he did save you from disaster." The pup tilted his head. It was settled. She ran to the bedroom, dressed, and fixed her hair and makeup. "I won't be long, Johnny. Go back to sleep."

*

Maggie spotted the coffee shop ahead and quickened her steps. Peering through the window she saw lights in the back of the shop. She knocked on the glass door. The figure of a man came forward.

I don't even know this guy. What am I doing here?

Michael unlocked and opened the door. "You took my hint, I see. Come in, Maggie." He led her to the juice bar and handed her an apron.

"Were you really expecting me?" She reluctantly took the apron and tied the strings in the back. The aroma of coffee nagged at her.

"Well, let's say I had high hopes. You seemed like someone who would help a person in need." He picked up a bucket of water and a mop. "I need to empty this. If you want to start restocking the glasses and plates, that would be a great help." He whistled as he pushed through the swinging doors.

"What's that tune you're whistling? I think I know it from somewhere." She picked up a tray of clear juice glasses and wiped the water spots.

Michael stepped through the swinging doors and smiled. "It's called Wine and Roses. A favorite of mine."

"Nice song." *What is that sparkle in his eye?* "Is this where these juice glasses go?" Her face flushed when he met her gaze.

"Yes, and the bowls go—"

"I know, over here in this cupboard." She placed the bowls on the shelf, then turned to see Michael staring at her. "Wasn't that right?"

As he nodded and dropped some rags in the sink, a memory flashed. She had been there before. She winced as a familiar headache stabbed.

"Are you all right, Mags?" A frown wrinkled Michael's brow.

"Just one of my headaches. I had this feeling as if—did you call me Mags?"

"Did I?" His face drained of color.

"Yes, you did. Why did you call me that? No one else...I mean—wait."

"Here, sit down. You're pretty pale." He pulled a bar stool over.

"What's the matter with me? This only happens during my therapy sessions. So much for making progress. Sorry. I shouldn't be telling you this. I don't even know you. I should go." She stared at the door. *Just go.*

Michael interrupted her panic. "Are you sure you don't know me, Mags?"

His gaze seared through her. "But I feel as though I should know you. I felt that way on the street corner this morning." The pain in her temples increased. "Michael, I'm scared. I need to go home."

He sat beside her, his arms outstretched. "Maggie, take my hands."

Without hesitation she placed her cold palms in his warm grasp.

"Maybe I shouldn't have pushed you into this, but I couldn't wait any longer." Michael's voice quivered.

"What are you talking about? Wait for what?"

"For you to come back. It's been so long, I thought you were lost forever."

What does he mean? She closed her eyes tight. He squeezed her shaking hands. "I've been here before, haven't I?" She yanked away and opened her eyes. "Is there a room behind the kitchen with green easy chairs?"

Michael's lips parted into a smile. "Yes. Do you remember anything else? Please remember, Mags. Come back to me. I love you. God has a plan for us."

Maggie jumped up and backed away. *Love?* Dr. Connor warned her about the possibility of something or someone triggering her memory. Was it happening now? She had prayed for this.

She tried to envision herself behind the coffee bar. A flood of vivid memories rolled over her like waves. She couldn't tell if they would drown her or wash her clean. The throbbing in her temples stopped. She ran her hands across her apron and remembered wearing one while serving lattés. Michael was in her vision. She belonged to this coffee shop, and she belonged to Michael. *God, can it be true?*

"Maggie?" She heard him call her name but waited for a few moments to answer. She had to be sure. There had to be peace in her heart before she could—yes, there it was. Peace. "Yes, Michael. It's me." When she faced him, he put his arms on her shoulders and drew her close. His kiss was soft and tender. Everything felt comfortable and right. Tears that had been held behind an emotional dam now burst.

"Thank you, Michael, for pulling me back from my darkness. I had given up trying. I knew someone was out there waiting for me, I just didn't know where to start looking for my past." He wrapped his arms around her, and she relaxed in another wave of familiarity. "I've passed by here many times but never made a connection. Being with you and the smells and sounds brought it all back. Like 'Wine and Roses.' Our favorite song?"

"Yes." Tears brimmed in his brown eyes. "I was going to propose to it the night of your accident. It's been a long year without you. But I abided by the doctor's request. I stayed away."

"Dr. Connor said this would happen someday. You'll have to fill me in on my lost months."

"I'll tell you what I can. I don't know much. I've just been waiting."

"I guess Johnny wasn't the only one that needed rescuing today."

Michael nodded as he untied her apron. "Let's go home and tell him the news. No more watching the two of you from afar."

He locked the door behind them. "And Mags, the little blue coat has to go."

JAN CLINE is a freelance writer, author, and speaker from Spokane, Washington. She is founder and director of the Inland Northwest Christian Writers conference.

    www.jancline.net
    www.inlandnwchristianwriters.com

Dancing in the Moonlight

* * *

Sharon Bernash Smith

The accident had taken more than her leg. Every last ounce of courage she'd ever possessed was now a distant memory. All the get-well cards and months of rehabilitation could not restore the freedom-loving spirit that Laura Hastings once possessed, especially on the back of a horse.

"I think going to the stables will be good for you, Laurie, you'll see." Her mother reached over and patted her arm.

"Mmm." Thinking of the stable caused her stomach to lurch, while painful memories swept like prairie wind through every corner of her mind. Fear made it impossible to stop them.

Barrel racing had been her passion since she'd turned 10 and began entering pee-wee competitions. From the start, her uncanny ability to become one with the horse was deemed a gift by anyone who'd been privileged enough to watch her ride. It'd been Granddad Monty who mentioned it first. "Girl, you musta been born on the back of a horse, 'cuz I never seen nobody, male or female, ride like you." Every word he spoke fueled a deep inner desire to fulfill her cowgirl destiny. How she grew to love the word *destiny*.

As the years went by, the "gift" was honed until Laura became Montana's top barrel racer. Blue ribbons and trophys filled her bedroom, tangible rewards highlighting the benefits of hard work and sheer grit. The biggest reward came when she received a full ride scholarship to the University of Montana in Bozeman, three years ago. It was four months into her senior year when Laura's destiny changed forever in one split second.

A green broke filly had been donated to the equestrian program, and Laura had been working with her for several days, focusing on the animal's over-reactive response to sudden stimuli. It had taken a lot of gentle handling, but the little bay's confidence was building daily.

They'd been warming up with several trots around the riding arena when a sudden gust of wind blew open a metal gate directly in front of the horse and rider. Beside herself with panic, the little horse whirled around twice, slamming Laura against the wall both times. The crack of her right femur shattering was audible, but she hung on, trying to calm the animal beneath her.

It might have worked too, but the instant someone ran to help, the horse panicked again... rearing and twisting at the same time, throwing Laura to the ground, where she watched in horror as a thousand pounds of horseflesh fell directly on top of her.

Five and a half hours of surgery could not repair the damage that had been done in mere seconds, and Laura's leg was amputated below the knee. Her first words spoken through mind-numbing pain had been, "I'm going to ride again." She'd meant them at the time, but that was before...before reality and fear became unwanted 24/7 companions.

A strong woman of faith, Laura began praying the minute she'd hit the ground, yet the shadow of fear stalked her relentlessly. In the beginning, physical therapy had been encouraging, and everyone seemed to think she'd be able to resume her equine studies. Everyone but her. Reality slapped hard and fast whenever the mirror reflected the altered remnant of what had once been a top athlete's body.

Today's trip to the campus stables had been the therapist's idea, and initially, Laura had been all for it. But now, the closer they came, the less courage she had. Every heartbeat pounded out one word...*fear...fear...fear!*

A welcoming committee of sorts stood in the freezing Montana cold. Fellow students rushed the car and opened it with enthusiasm. "Welcome back, cowgirl." Her roommate, Jesse, bent into the car with a hug. "Do you have a wheelchair?" she said, looking in the back of Laura's jeep.

"Nope, using crutches now...makes for great abs, you know." Laura laughed. Taking in the crisp air mixed with familiar stable sounds and smells gave her a needed boost.

Her mom was standing on the passenger side, ready to help. "Mom, you're hovering," she said and winked. "I'm good at this, remember?" Once out of the car, she pulled her stocking cap further down over both ears. "Hope the arena isn't this cold."

Inside, she willed herself to breathe...*in...out...in...out. Lord, please give me the courage I need.* Jesse was saying something to her. "I'm sorry, Jess, what'd you say?" Her voice came out strained, but she managed a smile.

"I said, I'd like you meet the new wrangler. Laura, this is Chase Bennett."

"Nice to meet you, Chase. I'd shake your hand, but I'd probably fall flat on my face." She laughed, but he didn't.

He said, "Thanks," tipped his Stetson, and left.

"Well, I can see I made a great first impression." She watched him walk across the arena, noticing his awkward gait.

Jesse saw Laura looking. "Lost his leg in Iraq."

Laura's head snapped around. "Oh, now I get it. This must be match-up-a-freak day!" Her anger spilled over, making her arms weak. She made her way to the bleachers and sat down.

Jesse scooted in beside her. "Laura, come on; you should know me better than that. Chase just happened to come in, honestly."

Laura saw the truth in Jesse's eyes. "Sorry. Guess I'm on edge. Please forgive me?"

"Done deal, girlfriend." Jesse edged closer. "But, you have to admit, that's one good-looking wrangler."

"I'm not sure; I haven't seen him on a horse yet."

Jesse laughed. "Well, FYI...he rides very well. Which should be an encouragement to you, I might add."

"Maybe, but I'll bet he didn't lose that leg from a horse falling on him." She raised both hands in mock surrender. "Hey, just sayin'."

"Just sayin', I heard he lost it when his Humvee rolled over after being hit by mortar fire."

"OK, stuff a rag in my mouth so I can't divulge any more of my stupidity." She exhaled. "Even I'm tired of my pity parties."

Jess smiled. "If I were you, I'd be having the same party." She jumped up and offered a hand to Laura. "Let's take a look around at the new horses."

Every step seemed a victory in itself to Laura, and she couldn't help smiling as they approached the arena again.

A rider was working a big black gelding in the middle. It was Chase. Her heart pounded, and she gripped the arena side to steady herself against the onslaught of memories. *Lord, help me...*

"Are you all right, Laurie?" Jesse asked.

"Sure."

"Well, you don't look it. Let's sit for a while." She helped Laurie up a couple of steps so they could see better.

"You're right, Jess, that guy's a great rider. I wonder how long it took before he could ride like that with a prosthesis?"

"I have no idea." She jumped to her feet and whistled. "Let's ask him." Chase looked up and waved. She motioned him over.

"Hey there, ladies. How was your tour?" He tipped his hat again.

Corny, Laura thought.

"Fine thanks, but my friend here has a question for you."

"Sure." He dismounted easily.

Laura felt her face getting warm. Chase removed his hat and smiled. His eyes were the color of steel, nearly matching his hair. How odd for a young man to have gray hair. A four-inch scar marked the right side of his head.

He waited for the question, his eyes never leaving hers.

She cleared her throat. "We, uh, that is, I'd like to know how long it took you to learn to ride again after you got your prosthesis?"

He grinned. "Again?"

"Yes. How long was it before you rode again after you got the new leg?"

Chase walked closer. "It's a long story, and I need to take care of the big guy. How 'bout I meet you two in the cafeteria in about 30 minutes or so?"

"Sure," Jesse said. "See ya then."

After Chase walked away, Laura turned. "Wait just a minute, Jesse. Who said I wanted to have lunch with that guy?"

"Well, of course you do, Laura. It's written all over your very reddish, albeit beautiful, face." She threw back her head and laughed.

"I don't think you're funny, just so you know." She was exhausted, but kept up with Jesse's pace.

"I'm only being truthful...just so you know."

*

Laura checked her watch for the third time. "How rude! He asked us to lunch and now he's a no-show." She sipped cold coffee, making a face.

"Come on, he's only a little late. Look...there he is now." She waved him over.

"Sorry I'm late; there was a problem with one of the other horses, and they needed my help. I'll make it up to you if you let me buy."

"Thanks," Laura said sarcastically.

"Oh, good. Can I carry your tray, Laura?" He made eye contact again, and she couldn't say no.

When they'd settled into a booth, Chase said grace and Laura relaxed a little. She'd just met him after all, so why had she been so rattled? They made the usual polite conversation before Chase got to the question Laura had asked.

"You wanted to know how long it took me to ride again after I got my prosthesis, right?"

"Right." Although she really did want to know, she'd already made up her mind to never get on the back of another horse...ever.

"Truth is, I never rode before I lost my leg." Sighing, he shoved his plate aside.

Laura looked at Jess to make sure she'd heard correctly. Both of them were speechless. *What?*

He didn't wait for a reply. "See, I grew up in Billings, just me and my mom. She worked full-time and I was a latchkey kid, which left lots of time for me to fill. I loved to read and probably finished every Zane Gray novel ever written. No one my age would be caught dead reading one, so I kept it to myself."

Laura was listening to every word, but her mind lingered on the part about him never riding before his war injury.

"I wanted, no, *yearned* to be a cowboy. I mean, really, growing up in Montana, it must have been in my DNA."

"So why didn't you ever ride then?" Jesse asked.

"We lived smack-dab in the middle of town, and like I said, my mother worked full-time just to make ends meet. There wasn't a way to make my cowboy dreams come true, so eventually I gave up on them. In high school, I got in some trouble, but a Christian school counselor talked me through my bad boy stage and I graduated. Right after, I joined the Army and ended up in Iraq. One hot day, I went out on a recon mission and woke up in a helicopter without my leg."

Laura shivered.

"I thought I was going to die, but when I didn't, I made a vow to fulfill my dream of riding and so…"

"…so?" Laura said. "Just like that, you lose a leg, get a prosthetic replacement, and jump on the back of the nearest horse?" She slapped the table.

Chase laughed. "Whoa, not so fast. It took six months in the hospital to recover from the rest of my injuries." He paused, meeting her eyes again. "But nothing after that could stop me." He reached across the table and touched her hand for emphasis. "Nothing."

She was crying…and not sure why. "Well, how absolutely brave of you, Chase. And God bless you for your faith." She went to get up but dropped a crutch and stumbled back into the booth.

Chase was up and on his feet, offering a steady hand to help.

At first she refused, but then she gave in and reached for him. "Thank you," she said, wiping at her face.

"Just so you know," he whispered into her ear, "I was petrified when I got on that first horse." He stepped back and winked. "I've got to get back to work, but I'd like to call you?" His smile was lopsided.

She gave him her number, and they talked every night for the next two weeks. She'd never shared all her feelings of fear and anxiety with anyone but the Lord. Yet all of it poured out in each conversation with this man she barely knew.

During this time, she was making good progress with her own artificial leg. But each new victory brought torrents of tears. It was always painful, and once she threw the thing toward the therapist. When she looked up, Chase stood in the doorway, shaking his head.

"How long have you been watching?" Sweat poured off her like a proverbial racehorse, and even though she wanted to throw the leg again, when he walked over, she collapsed against him. It was crazy because they barely knew each other, yet his arms were the reassurance she needed. He understood.

It was his encouragement that put her in the arena three weeks later. When she saw him walking towards her leading a beautiful pinto, her heart raced with fear, but determination would win.

"Ready, cowgirl?" She smiled, and he helped her up a ramp placed next to the horse. Swinging the prosthesis awkwardly to the other side of the saddle, she guided the "foot" into a stirrup. Readjusting herself, she nodded. "Ready," came out a whisper.

"I believe in you." Tears stained his face, matching hers. He winked and patted the horse's rump.

Nudging the horse, she entered a dream wide-awake… awake to the gift of God's restoration. Victory!

Once around was enough for the day, but Laura rejoiced in this triumphant beginning. Chase took the reins and helped her slip off onto the ramp. He swept her into his arms, allowing victory's sweetness to soak his shirt.

When she pulled away to gaze in his face, she knew he understood perfectly.

"Let's celebrate," he said.

"What?"

He helped her down to the sand. "Wait here." He walked to the outer wall, flipped off the lights, and returned, standing in moonlight streaming down from the huge skylights.

"Chase, what are you doing?"

"We're going to celebrate…with a dance."

"Without music? Crazy man!"

He took out his iPod and pulled up a song.

"I can't dance, Chase."

"You couldn't ride either." He turned up the volume.

"I hope you never fear those mountains in the distance
Never settle for the path of least resistance...
Give the heavens above more than just a passing glance
And when you get the choice to sit it out or dance
I hope you dance."

He reached out...waiting until she fit perfectly in his arms...before dancing in the moonlight.

SHARON BERNASH SMITH is the author of *The Train Baby's Mother,* a Holocaust story, *Old Sins, Long Shadows* (Book Two in The MacLeod Family Saga), and coauthor of *Like a Bird Wanders* (Book One in The MacLeod Family Saga), as well as three Christmas anthologies: *Once Upon a Christmas, Always Home for Christmas* and 2012's release, *Starry, Starry, Christmas Night.*
    www.sharonbernashsmith.blogspot.com

Foreign Feelings

* * *

MaryEllen Stone

When 1945 began and Addie turned 19, she had hoped for better things.

But this morning Addie's father announced he would take advantage of German POWs being brought in to help with sugar beet crops. "Prisoners'll be here after breakfast," he announced, leaving her to prepare for their arrival.

Now midmorning, straining under the weight, Addie carried two buckets of water to the field. Carefully setting the pails down, she dipped from one, filled a tin cup, and offered it to a German soldier.

As he stood up from thinning plants, sweat poured off his forehead. "Danke schön." His eyes—sky-blue—searched hers.

Addie scanned the field for her father. Her muscles relaxed when she saw him scrutinizing rows with his back to her. She knew he was too busy counting heads, still nervous because this morning's truck had simply rolled up and dumped off 21 Nazis. The driver told her father they couldn't spare a guard but assured him POWs were carefully screened on the East Coast. Big-time Nazis had already been weeded out.

Nonetheless, Addie remembered her father's admonition not to talk to the enemy. She did not look again at the soldier's face but snatched the cup from his hand and moved quickly to the next man bent down pulling up roots. She could feel a gaze fixed upon her. She knew they were the eyes of a man who had killed Father's people in Europe.

"You're a Jew," her father had said on more than one occasion. "Never forget your heritage."

If her father had his way, she would marry a Jew—Benjamin Rosen, one of the hardest workers this side of the Rockies. But on her deathbed two years ago, Mother had encouraged Addie to make her own decisions about things, in particular, her future mate. And her faith. Regarding that, prior to passing, Mother had become a Christian Jew, arguing with Father that Jesus was a Jew.

Addie shook her head. How could she make sense of her life when all she did was work from sunup to sundown? Shielding her eyes from the sun, she studied its position in the sky. She must hurry back to start the noon dinner.

Inside the coal shed, she shoveled the black lumps into a scuttle, banging it against her leg on her way to the kitchen. At the stove, she inserted the iron lifter into the black plate and dumped in coal. Addie had mouths to feed. Twenty-three in all. Two Steins and twenty-one Germans.

*

It was almost twelve o'clock. She'd been pumping water into the sink, cleaning, peeling, and baking for several hours, and she was tired.

A knock at the screen door startled her. The face of the enemy with the probing blue eyes peered through the screen. "Herr Stein tell me help…mit…tables."

Addie's mouth went dry. She was angry at the intrusion—and at the leap of her heart. She untied her apron and slammed out the door. In a huff, she arrived at the tool shed, where she pointed to sawhorses, three long planks, then to a shady spot under a mammoth oak tree. While the soldier set up makeshift tables, Addie upended buckets. She instructed the prisoner to lay boards across them for seats. It would be a tight fit, but they were the enemy. Addie was sure they hadn't given even this much kindness to their victims. Nazis probably didn't serve their POWs three times a day.

From the corner of her eye, she noticed her father watching from the edge of the field. Glad she hadn't looked at or talked to the young German, she hurried toward the house. From the porch where her father could still see her, she gestured inside, ordering the soldier to carry the kitchen table outside for a serving station.

"Fritz."

Addie whirled.

"Fritz." The German pointed to himself.

Addie felt her face flush. "Take these out and set them on the table." She made a sweeping gesture to glasses and silverware, plus roaster pans on the tall black-and-silver-plated cook stove. As well, she motioned to a stack of 18 mismatched, chipped plates. The remaining number of prisoners would have to eat from pie tins.

With his arms full, Fritz backed through the screen onto the porch. Addie ran from the room.

Before her bedroom mirror, she gasped at the coal dust streaked across her cheek and poured water from a pitcher into a bowl. Splashing her face,

Addie was able to cool the heat of the moment. After rearranging her hair into a bun at the nape of her neck, she returned to the kitchen.

With a glance out the window, she saw the error of her ways. Men stood around the crude temporary table and benches—waiting.

"Addie! We haven't got all day." Even from the house she could see that vein protruding on her father's forehead.

Hurriedly, Addie took her place behind the serving table. As the men approached, she dispensed either a spoon or fork. They could not have both. Nor could they have milk. Water would have to do.

Fritz reached toward her hand for his spoon. Instinctively, Addie pulled back. Her stomach somersaulted. She had already offered silverware to the other prisoners. Fritz was no different than any of them. She was frustrated at the irritation this one German stirred within her.

At once, her father was at her side. "There a problem here?" He drilled a gaze into the Nazi.

"No, Father." Addie's throat constricted. "Th…this spoon is dirty." She snatched the hem of her apron and thumbed the tableware.

Father grabbed the utensil and thrust it into Fritz's chest. "Move along." Her father shoved Fritz forward and glared at her.

Heat flooded Addie's face. Fritz hadn't done anything wrong. At least not today. She was confused. Why should she defend an enemy?

More than once during dinner, Addie felt Fritz's eyes studying her. When she was certain he wasn't looking, she stole glances at him.

Lying awake at the end of the long day, Addie pictured the German's countenance. His eyes seemed kind. Surely he had never killed. His smile offered warmth. His movements were helpful and gentle, not threatening.

Rolling over, she squeezed her eyes shut against the image. She mustn't think untrue things. He was the enemy and a prisoner of war because he had killed defenseless Jews. Some even talked of women and children being killed. "Gassed," they'd said. Addie turned away from things her mind refused to believe.

*

When the alarm clamored at four in the morning and stuttered to its final tinny clang, Addie's head felt thick, and her arms and legs as heavy as brim-full cream cans. She forced herself to rise and slip into her gingham dress before dashing to the outhouse.

Finished there, she quickened her steps in the dark toward the coal shed. The scuttle filled, she latched the door shut and headed for the house.

"Help...you." The voice was familiar, yet alarming. "Please." A hand reached out of the darkness, took hold of the pail, and lifted it from her.

Afraid to linger, Addie hastened toward light peeking from the back door. Fritz followed her into the kitchen and immediately set about scooping clinkers from the cast-iron stove.

Still frightened, now because of what her father would say or do, Addie grabbed a pot, lowered it into the sink basin, and pumped water for all she was worth. Her heart raced past her thoughts. She had to rid her kitchen of this German. "Out!" She pointed to the screen door.

Fritz smiled, bowed, and left.

After breakfast, looking out the window from the kitchen sink, Addie stiffened with fear. Father had pulled Fritz aside. When Father turned and marched toward the house, she stopped breathing.

Inside the back door, he halted, clamping his arms across his coveralls.

Swallowing to unstick her tongue from the roof of her mouth, Addie willed herself to lock eyes with him.

"That Nazi's only one can speak English. He gets the other prisoners set up, he's to come back here and help." Father screwed his index finger into his ear. "Can't be wasting time waiting around for grub." He scraped brown wax from beneath his nail, then tromped off. Small clumps of dirt from the treads of his boots left a trail in his wake.

*

By the time she finished washing breakfast dishes, Fritz was on his way back from the field. She watched him stride with confidence. As he neared, Addie's heart beat faster. She tried to take her eyes off his face. Handsome. Kind eyes—the likes of which she'd never seen.

At the door he rapped lightly with his knuckles, even though she was sure he saw her at the sink only six feet away. As he stepped inside, she nodded to a gunnysack in the corner. "Start by peeling potatoes."

Fritz nodded in return and hoisted the burlap onto the table. "How many years you have?"

"Years?"

Addie blinked. "You mean how old am I?"

"Yah."

She laid a paring knife beside potatoes spilling from the sack. She eyed a butcher knife on the counter. Shaking off the possibilities, Addie replied, "Nineteen." Now it was her turn to question. "How many men have you killed?"

The moment the words came out of her mouth, Addie tensed. Maybe that's what had been bothering her. She had to know.

"Me...nein kill."

"Nine?" The answer, like a dagger, penetrated her gut. She staggered backwards, gripping the counter's edge.

"Nein kill." Fritz shook his head while holding up both hands, fingertips circled to meet each thumb.

Swallowing a musket-ball-sized lump in her throat, Addie grasped for the truth. "Zero? None?"

"Yah, iss so."

Air filled Addie's lungs, then emptied in a gush.

"Dis farm, like mine." Fritz gestured out the window.

"You live on a farm?"

"Yah. In Germany."

"What do you grow?"

"Many sings."

"Sings, huh? Like songs? You grow songs." Addie laughed at the thought of music sprouting out of the ground.

"Nein songs." Fritz thrust his tongue to the top of his teeth and forced a thick "th." Still, it came out, "Sthings."

Addie giggled at the effort but stopped herself short, lest she silence him. She wanted to know more. How many in his family? What did he hope to do after the war? Did he have a girlfriend back home? At that question, Addie checked herself. Why should she care? But already her emotions were sneaking down a forbidden path.

The morning flew by as Fritz told of his little sister and how she loved to follow him around. He spoke of his dog—no, not a German shepherd. Tears filled Fritz's eyes as he talked of his Oma and Opa. At this, Fritz shifted the conversation back to Addie. She was glad of it, for she could hardly stand the sadness in his face. Soon, they were laughing over his attempts to teach her a song and at her efforts at pronunciation.

Addie had not known such companionship. At the end of the day, after two cooking sessions with Fritz, she glowed from the energy surging within her. Although far from tired, she could hardly wait to go to bed so morning would arrive.

*

Scurrying about the kitchen, Addie glanced again and again out the window into the dim light of dawn. Where was Fritz? Had she said or done something to put him off? At the thought, her head throbbed. Running every minute of yesterday through her mind, Addie examined and re-examined where she might have messed up.

The screen door squeaked. Her stomach flipped.

Fritz brushed by, barely touching her arm. Electricity charged through her. Had he meant to touch her?

"Sleep much." Fritz rubbed his eyes.

A sigh escaped Addie's lips.

The morning sped by. The afternoon went even faster. Addie wanted to stop time—to hold it in her hands and tuck these once-in-a-lifetime moments away in her heart.

*

Throughout the next week, every day enchanted Addie and thrilled, yet tormented her. For the first time in her life she actually felt alive.

Watching the sugar beet fields draw near to proper thinning, Addie dreaded the inevitable. Her chest grew heavy, as if a gravestone pressed upon her heart. It was hard to carry out daily tasks through tears swamping her eyes. After tomorrow, she would never see Fritz again. She didn't know what dying was like, but it had to be easier than this.

Tomorrow meant good-bye forever.

In bed, Addie heard someone at her open window.

Fritz whispered for her to join him.

She grabbed her robe and crawled outside. They stole away to the haystack on the other side of the barn. A crescent moon and the Milky Way dimly lit and webbed the sky.

Fritz gently pressed his hand in hers. Conflicting responses whirled through her. She withdrew her hand. He touched her cheek with the back of his hand and leaned his face into hers. His warm breath caressed her forehead.

As if discerning her innocence, Fritz turned his face toward the sky. She heard his heavy sigh, sensed his will for self-discipline.

Silence and stillness filled their time and space.

Addie rested her head against Fritz's chest and listened to the wild beating of his heart. Hers raced in rhythm. This fleeting emotional connection would have to be enough to last her a lifetime. They talked far into the night.

*

Just before dawn, Addie crept into the kitchen to prepare the final breakfast.

As the rising sun spilled orange across the eastern skyline, Addie heard a vehicle door slam. The transport was too early! She found it difficult to breathe as she watched the Germans pile into the back of the army truck. Finally, filling her lungs with air, she sneaked out the back door and ran to the barn where she clambered up the ladder to the hayloft window. She searched frantically for Fritz's face among the mass of bodies as the vehicle rolled down the dusty driveway. She had to see him one final time. She must imbed his face in her mind forever.

A hand rose into the air in the middle of the troop.

Addie lifted her hand. In the yard below, her father turned to look up. She fell back and crawled to where she imagined Fritz had slept in the hay this past week.

She closed her eyes and pondered: *Would Jewish tears for a German heart be enough to wash away the spoils of war?*

If only Mother were here to help her through this pain....

Suddenly, Mother's words echoed in Addie's mind: *Jesus loves you. He will bear your pain.*

Addie didn't know how this could be, but she began to pray as she wept.

MaryEllen Stone, M.S. Ed., is a keynote speaker, retired college counselor with Faculty Emeritus status, and author of *Run in the Path of Peace—the Secret of Being Content No Matter What.*
http://maryellenstone.com

Springtime Love Forever

* * *

Janet R. Sady

> In the spring a young man's fancy
> lightly turns to thoughts of love.
> —Alfred Lord Tennyson

Lillian's face filled Robert's dreams and filtered into his thoughts as soon as he awakened. Today was the anniversary of when they first met. He had big plans for this evening, but he wanted to surprise her early this morning. Robert thanked God every day for sending this wonderful woman into his life.

Robert fried two eggs—over easy, just the way he liked them. Bacon and Texas toast rounded out his breakfast. The Texas toast came from his freezer. Robert didn't fancy himself a cook, but he thought his coffee was pretty good. He poured a cup into his travel mug to take with him.

He sat in his recliner to read his devotions for the day. The Bible lay open to one of his favorite passages that described Lillian so well. Proverbs 31:10: "Who can find a virtuous woman? For her price is far above rubies." Yes, that certainly was his Lillian. He would be eternally grateful for her precious love.

After a shower, he dressed in the blue cashmere sweater she liked, and splashed her favorite aftershave on his cheeks. Lillian liked for him to smell good. Thoughts of her made Robert hurry.

Where was that poem he had written for her and the book of devotions he had bought at the Christian book store yesterday? He found them on the counter with his keys. She'd think the poem corny, but it would be worth the effort, if it made her laugh. Robert loved to hear Lillian laugh. The sound brought joy to his heart and filled his mind with the memories of the wonderful times they had spent together.

He locked the door and headed for his Subaru. Daffodils bloomed around the lamppost in the front yard. He stopped to cut a dozen with his penknife. Tonight, he would take red roses, but she'd be just as thrilled with the daffodils this morning. Robert turned right toward Interstate 80, and his much traveled route to Dubois, Pennsylvania. The distance always seemed way too long as he anticipated seeing her.

Robert parked as close to Lillian's building as he could. When he entered the building, he thought about calling her first but decided he wanted to surprise her. He knocked softly on her door and, when no one answered, let himself in. She lay curled up in her bed still asleep. He watched her for a few minutes. enjoying the sight. She looked like the young woman he'd first met. Then, not being able to restrain himself, he gently traced the curve of her cheek with his thumb. Lillian stretched, opened her eyes, and smiled.

"Bobby, what are you doing here this morning? I thought you weren't coming over until tonight." She sat up, looking a bit confused. "I didn't sleep through the whole day, did I?"

"Hello, beautiful. No, no. It's still morning, but I couldn't wait to see you." He loved it when she called him Bobby.

Robert sat on the edge of her bed and gathered her into his arms as he kissed her lips. He closed his eyes and allowed the familiar pleasure of her softness next to him to permeate his body. After a while he kissed her hand and stroked her face as she smiled and returned his kisses.

"Lillian, my love, do you know just how much I love you?"

"Yes, Bobby, I think I do. You tell me every day. And you know that I love you just as much."

"I wrote you a poem and brought a book of devotions. There's devotion for every day."

"You wrote me a poem? Well, read it to me. I can hardly wait, and I'll enjoy the book later. Thank you. You are such a sweetheart, and so thoughtful. What would I ever do without you?"

"Well, you don't have to worry about that, because as long as God gives me breath, you're the one I'm going to spend the rest of my life with."

"Oh, my dear Bobby." Lillian grasped his hand in both of hers. "Now, let's hear that poem you wrote. I know it has to be good since you're such a romantic."

To My Best Girl

Love is like a red, red rose.
How it happens no one knows.
I love you, and you love me.
We're as happy as can be.

No one else can take your place
I sure do love your precious face.

Robert heard the laughter escaping from behind Lillian's hands as she put them over her month in an attempt to cover her laughter. He laughed, too. "Pretty corny, huh? I thought it was one of my better ones."

"Yes, it is corny, but I love it. You are such a sweetie."

"I hate to cut this visit short, but I've got to leave. I have an appointment at the dentist, but I'll be back tonight for our celebration dinner. 'Ah, parting is such sweet sorrow.'"

"Get going—you're just as corny as ever."

Robert kissed Lillian with one long, passionate kiss. "Remember, I love you."

"Love you, too." Lillian held his hand and gazed into his eyes.

"Until later. The day will pass so slowly, but I'll have tonight to look forward to."

"Me, too."

Robert picked up his cane and shuffled to the elevator and pushed the button. Lillian's nurse came around the corner at that moment. "Oh, Robert, I thought you were coming tonight for your anniversary celebration."

"I am, but I just wanted to see her this morning."

"We'll have a special dinner for you and Lillian tonight in the activity room around six. Will that be okay?"

"Yes, that will be great. I'm bringing red roses for the table. You don't have to serve us dessert as I'm bringing Lillian's favorite cream puffs. So I guess I will see you later."

Robert stepped onto the elevator, and it descended to the lobby of the nursing home complex. On his way down he said, "I'll be back tonight and tomorrow and every day—'as long as we both shall live.'"

JANET R. SADY is an award-winning author, poet, story teller, and motivational speaker. She has published in devotional books and other anthologies, newspapers, and magazines, including *Falling in Love with You, Country Woman, Loyalhanna Review, True Story, Alamance.* Janet is the author of *The Great American Dream, God's Lessons from Nature, God's Parables, The Bird Woman,* and two children's books.

jansady422.wordpress.com

Love at Villa Veronica

* * *

Marlene Worrall

He was tall, his build athletic. He was probably a tennis player…or maybe a golfer. His eyes were smoldering burnt chocolate. My heart fluttered when I encountered him, which was every morning at breakfast. Seven-o'clock sharp. I was sure he was a guest at the Hotel de Varenne like I was.

It was April. The weather was idyllic, even balmy at times. Paris crackled with life, its streets filled with lovers, young and old, enraptured with life and love.

I longed to be one of them. I nibbled on a croissant and savored the fresh pineapple. I downed several cups of Mocha Java as I planned my day of sight-seeing. I couldn't wait to see the Eiffel Tower.

I hadn't met the handsome stranger, but he was becoming a familiar face. He spoke English with a divine French accent. I yearned to meet him.

This morning, he settled at the table next to mine. He glanced up occasionally as pairs of women in short skirts and long legs strolled by. He routinely immersed himself in the *Paris Times* for the first 15 minutes or so, sipping espresso before he dug into his breakfast.

He always dined alone, though the good Lord knew, plenty of women checked him out every morning at the café. Some smiled flirtatiously at him, while others attempted to converse with him—all to no avail. The man seemed oblivious to the effect he had on the female population. He had a commanding and dashing presence. Making a play for him wasn't likely to work, so how could I connect with him? There was always the chance he might dine alone in the brasserie, notice me dining solo, and insist I join him. *A girl can dream.*

What *would* my modus operandi be? Well…I would lift up a prayer to the Almighty. I didn't like being a widow. There was nothing wonderful about exploring Paris alone. Life was meant to be shared. I walked around the City of Lights every day, thinking about the handsome stranger. *Lord, he would be so perfect for me.*

Silence. I knew by this time that when God didn't speak an action word into my heart, I was to wait. I reined in my emotions and tried to be patient. My two-week vacation was fast coming to an end. Soon I would be flying back to Seattle and resuming my life as a realtor. Then the handsome stranger would be merely a pleasant memory. With one day to go, I relinquished my hope of meeting him.

I took a long stroll on a cobblestone street that meandered in ever-broadening circles. The more I tried to find my way out of the maze, the more confused I became. I glanced frantically around, hoping a taxi would appear. No such luck. I studied my map book, trying to figure out where I was and what route would take me back to the hotel. I had lost all sense of direction. I had no choice but to keep walking, while continuing to refer to the map, hoping something would click in.

Like a mirage, the Frenchman from the Hotel de Varenne suddenly appeared. He grinned at me. "You look lost, young lady. May I help you find your way back to de Varenne? "

My knees turned to water. I glanced up into his handsome face. I noticed then that his hair had premature gray flecks. It only added to his panache.

His grin broadened. "I've seen you many times at Hotel de Varenne. You *do* stay there, don't you?"

"I do...yes. "

He extended a bronzed hand. "Alfonso Bouget. So nice to meet you."

"Sondra Davis. Nice to meet you, too."

"Sondra, it's this way." He gestured in the opposite direction of where I was headed. "I'll walk you there."

A gentleman.

He led the way back to the hotel. He was urbane, but I sensed a sorrowful heart.

"Are you visiting from the country?"

"My home is in the South of France."

"Nice."

"So you just enjoy visiting Paris?"

"Not exactly. I'm recovering from shock."

"What happened?"

"Car crash...horrible, deadly...my wife..." He turned his head away, and I knew he was fighting overwhelming emotions.

"Oh...I'm so sorry."

I don't know what came over me then, but I reached over and hugged him. As I did, I felt that I'd been *led* to do it. It broke the ice. He opened up and began talking to me as though we'd been friends for a long time.

"Thanks, I really needed that. I checked into the hotel ten months ago. I couldn't bear to remain at the villa with all the memories."

He must be very rich.

We walked in silence for about 10 minutes. Just as we arrived at the hotel, he turned to me. "Any chance you would consider joining me for dinner tonight?"

My knees buckled, and giddiness bubbled inside me. I felt like leaping for joy! *He invited me for dinner! Thank you, God.*

"Yes, that would be lovely."

"Would seven work for you?"

"It would." I resisted the urge to jump up and down like a kid on a trampoline.

"Shall we meet in the lobby?"

"Sure. "

The emerald green dress I'd just bought would be perfect for our dinner date. I'd spotted the silk sheath with its long matching scarf at a couturier. I'd slipped into it, admired it in the three-way mirror, and knew I had to have it. I mustered up the courage to cast a furtive glance at the price tag. I nearly fainted. It would make a huge dent in my bank account.

Alfonso was waiting in the lobby, pacing, when I arrived. He grinned when our eyes locked. *If only I wasn't leaving tomorrow. How ironic to spend 13 days alone in Paris and meet Mr. Wonderful just as I'm about to leave.* My heart beat frantically. I was Cinderella at the ball.

He looked incredible in a snappy gray silk–nub sports jacket with a crisp, white shirt revealing olive skin. The chemistry was tangible.

We dined in the garden restaurant surrounded by cherubs perched on marble fountains, water sprouting from their fat bellies and cascading into the fountain. Elegant tables were shaded by gold and white silk umbrellas.

"Where in the South of France do you live?"

"Ever been to St. Tropez or Cannes?"

"Yes, but only briefly. My husband and I took a cruise from Cannes to St. Tropez. I've never seen anything more breathtaking in my life."

"Ah…so you have been in the area. Well, my dear, I have a massive villa. It's perched high on a cliff overlooking the Mediterranean. It's called Villa Veronica, after my late wife. "

"When are you planning to return there?"

"I shall go for a visit…but only if I have houseguests. When Veronica was alive, the villa brimmed with one of God's greatest treasures—friends. "

"Have you considered renting it out?"

"Yes, perhaps in the future. The household help goes with the villa, so that makes it easy. "

He was in an entirely different league financially than I was. Still, as a realtor, I was used to selling houses in the multi-million dollar range. In fact, I specialized in high-end properties. There was no reason for me to be intimidated by his wealth.

"I'm a realtor. I have a passion for houses. I tend to fall in love with most of my listings...it's my secret to selling them."

"Would you consider being my house guest at Villa Veronica? Perhaps you will fall in love with it."

"Ah. But you see, Alfonso, I can't take listings in France. So, if I *do* fall in love with it, it will be in vain."

"Well, I value your opinion. After all, I designed the villa. I poured my heart and soul into it."

"Then I consider your invitation a gracious compliment."

"And so you should."

The waiter arrived with the food menu but no wine menu.

"Do you like Beaujolais?" Alfonso grinned.

"You choose the wine."

He motioned to the Sommelier, who nodded. "Beaujolais, please, Eldon." He turned to me. "I have a private cellar here —one of the privileges of being an owner."

"Really? You're one of the owners of this hotel?"

"I'm an investor and a retired architect and builder. I built some large villas for my clients on the Riviera."

"How marvelous."

"It was a good livelihood. I retired at 48, pretty much burnt out. Then I invested in hotels."

"What an illustrious career."

Violins strummed romantic tunes on the patio. I stared into his eyes, mesmerized.

"You're very beautiful."

"Thank you." *Silently, I thanked the Creator.*

People said I looked like Doris Day. If only I could sing like her. I felt like serenading him.

"I'd like you to be my guest at Villa Veronica."

I was so thrilled I could barely speak. "When are you thinking?"

"Right away. Fly with me back to the Riviera. Julian and Ameilia will pick us up at the Nice airport. I'll take care of the travel arrangements, of course."

"Well, really, Alfonso, it's too short of notice. I should get back to work. My friend Jan Olson is looking after my listings, but I don't know if she'll continue…"

"Perhaps another time, then…"

Wait, no! I didn't mean it. "I…I'll have to call her."

Dinner arrived. The fresh trout was served with a potpourri of fresh veggies. The sommelier poured the vintage Beaujolais into fine crystal glasses. Alfonso proposed a toast. "To us."

"Call your office when you get back to your room and ask your colleague to cover you for another week."

I abhorred men telling me what to do, but found it exciting with Alfonso. In fact, I loved it. Not to mention the adrenaline I felt, knowing he was pursuing the matter. I smiled at him, my flimsy objections decomposing to mush. "Sure."

Jan agreed to continue looking after my real-estate business, so I could extend my trip.

*

Julian and Amelia were gems. They were waiting at the airport in a sleek Vandenplas Jaguar. Julian drove us down the winding road along the French Riviera until we came to a road that spiraled upwards into the hilly region. Passing magnificent villas, he finally pulled into the driveway of the opulent Villa Veronica.

It beckoned to me as though I belonged here. It was white, stately and majestic. The Alvarezes went on ahead with our bags. Alfonso clasped my hand and led me to an enormous patio. I stopped, dumbstruck, and gasped, viewing the most magnificent sight imaginable—the cerulean blue of the Mediterranean, sparkling beneath a perfect blue sky.

"Let me show you to your room." Amelia escorted me up the stairs.

My room featured a balustrade jutting out over the water and had a wrought-iron table with chairs and a pair of chaise lounges. I stepped onto it and was overwhelmed by the breathtaking view of the Mediterranean. A bevy of luxurious yachts gleamed in the sunlight cruising across smooth waters.

I *never want to leave!*

"Lunch will be served at one on the patio." My door was ajar, so Amelia popped her head in to make the announcement.

This is going be the vacation of a lifetime.

"Thank you, Amelia. After lunch, I trust Alfonso will give me the grand tour."

"You will win his heart if you love Villa Veronica. It's his masterpiece. We were sad when he checked into de Varenne, but with you here, he is happy and the villa is brimming with life again."

I stood on the balcony watching the waves lap lazily against the shore, enchanted by the panoramic view. *I don't ever want to leave.*

Lunch was amazing. Alfonso and I gazed at each other like love-struck fools as we dined on bluefish with ratatouille and Caesar salad. Amelia was a chef extraordinaire.

"Where does Amelia shop for this wonderful fresh food?"

"She drives into the village and buys the catch of the day, and whatever vegetables look fresh."

What an idyllic paradise. I could give up selling real estate for this.

We sipped a local white wine and munched on Brie and crackers with grape varieties for dessert.

"How about giving me the grand tour, Alfonso?"

"Ah, yes. I thought you'd never ask. I see you know the way to my heart."

"You mean it's not through cooking?"

His features took on a serious mode. "We have Amelia. You'll never have to cook."

Good, because I'm a lousy cook. I've always been too busy selling houses to take the time to learn. Was he saying he wants me around?

I adored the curved porticos. I had only seen arches and doorways like this in pictures, never in real life. The white marble floor sparkled. I loved the theme of white, lemon yellow, and lime green. The floral chintz sofas were superb.

He toured me through the house. Villa Veronica had a distinct personality. I loved the library and art gallery. I was a voracious reader and had a great appreciation for paintings.

Alfonso observed me as I studied an oil of a villa.

"Where is Villa Bianca?"

He grinned. A mischievous look crossed his face. "You know, it's interesting. I have over 20 paintings of villas in the gallery, but you focused on this particular one."

"Why is it interesting?"

"Because I designed it—and I own it. It's considerably smaller than this one. I used to live there before I met Veronica."

"Where is it?"

"Walking distance. Maybe we'll wander over later. Bianca lives in the villa. She's my aunt—a true eccentric."

"I love eccentrics."

I glanced at him. Our eyes met. I was transfixed. He leaned down and kissed me. I didn't stop him. I couldn't have if I'd wanted to. His kiss was tender but passionate. Excitement screamed through me. I knew I could never go back to my mundane existence. Alfonso and his lifestyle were a perfect fit for me. I responded with a depth of passion I never knew I had.

"Marry me, my darling. And I'll make you the happiest women on earth," Alfonso said, when we finally drew apart.

Lord, I had no doubt whatsoever that he could do that.

He pulled out a canary yellow, square-cut diamond from his pants pocket. It was dazzling.

I stared at him, stunned. When I finally caught my breath, I said, "Yes, Alfonso, I'll marry you, and *I* promise to make *you* very happy."

God had given me a banquet while so many people who don't know *Him* are starving.

"I'll call Nancy, my former assistant. She knows everybody. She'll put together a fabulous reception. There's a little church down the hill. We can say our vows there."

"Perfect."

MARLENE WORRALL has published short stories, articles, and a nonfiction book titled *Gold Nuggets*. Her real-life short story, "Love on the Malibu Seashore," is featured in OakTara's anthology *Falling in Love with You*. A veteran actor and singer in stage and film in the U.S., Canada, and the UK, she was featured in the original London, West End cast of *Promises, Promises*. Marlene has also been a speaker, ghostwriter, novelist, and screenwriter for about 15 years. An avid tennis player, she enjoys living near the ocean in a charming seaside town in British Columbia and winters in Southern California.

MarleneWorrall.blogspot.ca

Right on Time

* * *

Elaine Baldwin

5:09 a.m.

I'm wide awake and have been for hours. I should get up and do something…anything. Instead I sink further into my pillow and pull the chocolate duvet up to my chin. It's September 29th, but my frozen nose and throbbing knees tell me an early frost has crept in during the night. I pull the duvet over my head and give up any idea of walking down the aisle gracefully.

Now I wish I hadn't told my son, Timothy Jr., to clean out the furnace. I thought I'd be well on my honeymoon and the house empty before this chill came in. I pull my right leg up to my chest and massage the knee.

"Whoever heard of a bride creaking her way to matrimony? And whose crazy idea is this anyway? I'm too old to do this all over again. And so is he."

The darkened room doesn't answer. That's fine with me; no one to argue back.

I switch knees.

"How'd I let him talk me into this? I should've run when I first saw him coming."

Nerves are winning the battle for rational thinking and sleep is elusive, but finally the warmth of the duvet settles over me and I close my eyes.

Something is humming. And who is whistling at this hour?

It stops. I want to fall back asleep. *Wait! I can't sleep. Today is my wedding day.* I check for the clock. No clock. It's packed. I fumble for the nightstand. All I hit is air. It was sold last week in the yard sale.

The humming and whistling starts up again, but this time my hand instinctively reaches under the pillow. I feel something hard. It stops vibrating. Slowly the fog of sleep lifts, and I pull my cell phone out and flip it open. Instantly I'm blinded by the eerie blue glow so I have to squint to see the time.

*

6:59 a.m.

My feet hit the floor. I scream, "Cold...cold...cold..." and dance a jig on my way to the bathroom. I don't understand why I can't find my slippers. The bathroom floor is even colder so I keep up the jig while I start my bath water and throw a towel on the floor. I keep the jig going until steam rises from the tub and warms the cozy space.

"Ahh!"

The phone sings from back in the bedroom. It's Celine Deon's "A New Day Has Come." That's my sister's ring. I jig back across the bedroom floor, grab the phone, and jig back to the steamy bathroom.

"Hi Sis." I put the phone on speaker.

"You're up, right?"

I can barely hear her over the filling tub so I turn the water off. Something is missing. "No, I'm talking in my sleep. Call you back in a minute." I turn the water back on. "Bubbles."

"Wait...what?"

I flip the phone closed and add plenty of Champagne Rose bubble bath. Within in a few minutes I'm deep in bubbles and hot, soothing water. Finally, my whole body is toasty warm.

Celine sings again. I want to ignore her, but I know she'll just keep singing unless I answer. "Hi, Sis."

"You hung up on me."

"Sorry. I didn't mean to. It's just..."

"And you didn't call me right back."

"I know. I'm just..."

"You're already behind schedule. Aren't you?"

"No, I'm right on time..."

"Well, you better get moving, or you're going to be late to your own wedding."

"I will not be late."

"Of course you will unless you follow my schedule. You have to be at the beauty salon at 10:30 sharp and then dress in the hotel room at 12:30. Then..."

I put the phone on speaker and set it on the edge of the tub.

"Have you got that, Janny?"

"Yep. Got it all down."

A mischievous question invades my mind. What if the phone accidentally slipped into the bath water?

"Now don't forget the limo and I will be at your house at 10:00…"

My sudsy fingers inch toward my phone.

"…though why that doctor of yours insists on a limo, I don't know."

"He's just a nice guy," I shout.

I imagine my phone sinking to the bottom of the tub. It will only take a little nudge.

"Well, he is a very nice guy, and it's obvious he loves you. Wish my Harold would think of stuff like that…"

I hear a crash, but it isn't my phone hitting the bottom of the tub. It's on my sister's end of the line.

"What in the world? Gotta go. 10:00…sharp. Don't be late."

"I will be on time." I hear my sister shout the dog's name, then silence.

I'm still tapping the phone, but decide there's no point in drowning it. She'd find me one way or another. I flip it shut.

I want to slip back into my neck pillow but realize I am indeed behind schedule, and it would be rude to be late for my own wedding. I have one last important task to finish, but first coffee and…

The phone hums and starts a precarious slide off the side of the tub. I catch it just before it crashes to the floor.

"Be careful what you wish for," I say to thin air while hopelessly wiping suds off my phone.

It's a text. I check the time before I flip open the phone.

*

7:33 a.m.

From: Timmy: *r u k? r groom jumpy as rabbit. wants 2 talk 2 u.*

I put the phone down and wipe my hands with the towel on the floor.

I ask the phone, "Why does proper English have to go out the window with each new gadget?"

I'm fine. He can wait until our check-in.

When I hit *Send,* I see I have 10 more unread messages. Didn't anybody sleep in this morning? The bath water is getting cold, and I need coffee in my veins. Messages can wait.

*

7:53 a.m.

Twenty minutes and a dozen cold floor jigs later I'm sitting on a Rubbermaid tub marked *Cookbooks* with a scone and a vanilla mocha sitting across from me on a tub marked *What-nots.* A pair of thick socks from the tub

Winter Clothes keeps my feet toasty. I randomly think of my slippers and still can't remember where I put them. The sapphire ring Nathan gave me when he proposed glistens in the morning sun.

Mrs. Nathan Hawthorne Redbrook.

I mull my future name over several times. I try saying it aloud.

"Hello. My name is Mrs. Nathan Hawthorne Redbrook."

"Silly woman," I scold myself. "Nobody talks like that anymore."

The phone vibrates next to my Styrofoam cup. I pick them both up.

From Kat: *ppl worried bout u. why r u not answering texts.*

It's Timmy's wife. Did everyone forget I asked for this time alone?

I'm fine. Please remind EVERYONE…

I know I'm not supposed to use all caps, but I've got to close the past before I step into this future.

I need this time alone. See you at the salon.

There's an awkward pause. I take a sip of mocha and a bite of scone. Neither tastes as good as I think they should. Did I offend her?

From Kat: *Will do.*

Such a good daughter-in-law.

"Thank you, Kat," I whisper the words as I type the text.

My second cup of coffee is gone, but the scone remains. I decide I'm not hungry so throw it out along with the empty cup.

*

8:05 a.m.

I walk into the library. The floor-to-ceiling bookcase on the back wall stands empty. Its once-bloated contents have been sold or given away. Two crystal chandeliers glisten in the morning sun and bounce light off the freshly polished hardwood floors. A familiar whinny drifts through the lock of the French door leading to the back deck as the wind picks up outside. I cinch my bathrobe tighter and pull up the winter socks. I sure wish I could remember where my slippers are.

I cross over to the middle of the room where a sturdy RCA Stereo box with layers of old box tape wrapped all around it sits alone in the giant room. The faded words *This Side Up* are stenciled on the top and sides. I sit cross-legged on the floor and caress the large black initials carefully printed on a top flap: *T.S.M.*

"I still love you, Timothy Samuel McClary." My whisper echoes in the empty room.

I wonder if that is wrong and if the loving will go away now that I'm finally in love again. On top of the box lay an old Scofield Bible. Its black leather is dry and cracked, and its pages are worn with reading.

"This was your treasure, was it not, Mr. McClary?" I say in my best cockney voice, though I don't have an ounce of the blarney in me.

I trace the gold embossed letters, *H...O...L...Y...*

"And I will always miss you...your cockney laugh and baritone songs." A tear slips down my cheek, and I'm vaguely aware to be grateful my makeup hasn't been applied yet. "But most of all, I miss you being with me."

I open his Bible where the ribbon has remained these 20 years. Timothy's handwritten note is faded in the margin, but it doesn't matter. I have it memorized: *I must love my Janet as much as Christ loves me.*

"I didn't plan to love again, Timothy. It never seemed to be the right time. I was too busy with going back to school and raising our Timmy. And then there's this."

I close my eyes. The smell of books mixed with leather and Murphy's Oil Soap fills my heart and stirs my soul. I whisper what only I know. "Our bed and breakfast. Our dream."

A familiar piece of wide margin notebook paper slips out of the pages and onto the floor. I pick it up and spread it across my lap.

"This is your room. Just the way you designed it on our honeymoon." I smile. "You were so insistent on having a library. I thought you were crazy, but it's been the favorite room of our guests." A laugh escapes from deep within me. "Oh, how I hate it when you're right."

Some time passes. I don't know how long. I'm in my own thoughts; my own memories. Something buzzes. It must be another text.

From Nathan: *Are you okay? You missed our check-in?*

What time is it?

*

8:35 a.m.

I'm only five minutes late. He shouldn't worry about me, but it's sweet.

Sorry. Lost track of time. I'm fine. Just last-minute details. How are you?

From Nathan: *Anxious to see you walk toward me.*

I'm anxious too, but not for the same reason. An old worry rears its ugly head. My OB/GYN, my sister, and best friend all tell me I have nothing to worry about. But I haven't even kissed a man in two decades, let alone...

"Good grief, Janet!" I give myself a self-chiding tap on the cheek. "You're going on your honeymoon, not to prison!"

I need to reassure my future husband and me.

And I can't wait to be in your arms. XOXO

I mean that. Nathan makes me feel loved and special. It took me a long time to let him do that for me—to let him take care of me. It was his patience in that lengthy process that finally won my heart.

From Nathan: *Maybe we can cut out of the reception early☺.*

I smile. Deep down, I wouldn't mind cutting out early, even with all the nerves. I'm ready to be married again; to be loved like that again. But I still need to completely close a door.

I'm going to be late to my own wedding if you don't let me get ready!

From Nathan: *You won't be late. You're always right on time.*

Gotta go.

From Nathan: *K. Love you so much.*

Love you. Now go get ready!

From Nathan: *Yes, ma'am.*

*

8:47 a.m.

I open the box that sits in the middle of my favorite room and kneel beside it. "God's ways are not our ways are they, my dear Timothy? Only He could orchestrate your old college roommate and me running into each other. I hardly recognized him."

Another laugh escapes from deep within me. It feels good to laugh and really mean it. "You wouldn't have, either. He's as bald as a bowling ball."

I place the Bible on top of a faded Navy uniform.

"Do you remember how we always teased Nathan about his unruly curls?"

I close the box and pick up the tape gun. As usual, the tape gets all twisted between my fingers and I waste at least a yard getting it all untangled.

"Nothing changes," I whisper. "But everything does."

The tape and I finally quit wrestling and I secure the last piece of tape down the center of the box and give the T.S.M. a final caress.

"Only the Lord could have brought you into my life, my dear Timothy. I also know it was only the Lord who took you home to Him long before I was ready."

I stand and fumble in my pocket for the iPod my grandson gave me for my birthday. "And only a gracious creative God could unite two unlikely people today. Strangers…yet old friends."

I hope I remember the instructions on how to use this newfangled gadget. Was he able to find all the songs on my list? I hope so.

*

9:10 a.m.

I'm dancing on the smooth floor of the library designed and dedicated to my first husband. He died before I was ready to let him go, but it was right on time in God's plan. The iPod plays all his favorite songs: "Oh, Danny Boy" and "409" and "How Great Thou Art." They saturate deep within my heart and soul.

The music stops and so do I. I should be exhausted, but instead I'm refreshed and peaceful. My knees don't even hurt when I bend down to pick up the box full of my Timothy.

"Maybe there's hope for a graceful walk down that aisle after all."

I walk across the room and pull the door shut behind me. I pause, but only for a moment. "I'm ready." I take a deep breath. "It is the right time."

The box marked *T.S.M.* is placed next to a box marked *Glass Stemware. Fragile!*

I check the time.

*

9:33 a.m.

If I hurry, I'll be waiting outside for that limo. Just change and finish packing.

"Paris, here we come," I shout, taking two steps at a time.

I congratulate myself. "Not bad for an old woman, Janet."

*

10:05 a.m.

The limousine driver opens the door for me. I poke my head inside.

"Hi, Sis."

"You're late," she scolds.

"I'm not late. God and I are right on time."

ELAINE BALDWIN, a published author with articles in *The Christian Post, EFCA Magazine*, and *Justice Initiatives Newsletters*, is a bi-weekly contributor to Pens and Prayers. Elaine has completed her first novel—an epic fantasy, *If One Falls*.

www.OneAnotherLiving.com

I'll Take Romance

* * *

Kathryn Hartman

"What if?" The two words teetered like cliffhangers on Emma's brain. While her eyes were fixed on the setting sun, she felt her life was also descending. Curling a ringlet of hair around her pinkie finger, she then twisted it into the crease of her mouth.

"Maybe a do-over," she muttered as saliva slid and mixed with the tears dripping down her chin.

The chime of the phone interrupted her pity party.

*

Six weeks earlier

Yoga class was the same old, same old when Emma decided she needed a change. "How do you meet a man at yoga?" she asked Tracy as they wrapped themselves in fleece sweatshirts and circled through the revolving door leading to the plaza.

Tracy shifted her body toward her friend. "So, do you think a dance class would be a step up?"

Emma winced. "Oh, come on! Remember Ms. Corcoran, who invaded Mt. Carmel in eighth grade?"

"I remember the infamous box step. Oh, my goodness, how clumsy the boys were!" Tracy laughed.

"No, something truly romantic," Emma said, eyes glazing over.

"H-e-l-l-o, come on, Emma, you look like Cinderella ready to twirl in your mouse-made gown. The most popular sport is bar-hopping, but what if you ran into Pastor Luke witnessing outside? Plus it's not romantic when a guy sizes you up over a beer, then chooses the beer."

Crinkling her nose as if it activated her brain, Emma had an outburst. "I know, I know. Listen to this!"

Tracy froze, more in anticipation than from Emma's frenzy.

"Golf," she bellowed, romantically hugging her waist. "Think of lessons: his arms wrapping the small of my back, teaching me the perfect swing."

Tracy pushed her tongue against the back of her teeth in hesitation. But after a few seconds of thinking, she nodded, tapping her cheek with one finger. "I think you need a man who will cherish you for the beautiful, manipulative women you are."

"Old friends are the best." Emma glowed, delighted with her plan.

*

"Twin Circle Country Club, how may I help you?"

"I'm interested in taking golf lessons, but I've never picked up a club, unless miniature golf counts." Emma released a nervous laugh.

The silence on the other end of the line was deafening.

She heard the woman clear her throat and resume speaking. "Yes, well, we have two outstanding teachers, Chris and Blake."

"Oh, how old is Chris?" she asked, a bit of an edge rising in her voice.

The next silence was met with a stern sound of its own. "Why is her age important to you?"

"Her? I don't want a her; I want a him. I mean, I think I'd do best with someone my own age," she quickly added.

"Oh, I see, and may I ask your age, please?"

Emma spoke precisely. "Twenty-eight."

The woman spoke tersely. "Oh, well, you sounded older."

Emma almost grunted as her jowls stiffened, and her mouth turned to cement.

"Chris is 38, but super fit. However, I would suggest Blake. He's your age and really patient with *beginners* and a *man,* like you requested."

"Fine. When do I begin?"

"Friday, be here at six p.m. for your sign-up, payment, and first lesson. Four classes, one a week, one hour each session."

*

The following 48 hours dragged for Emma.

"How long do I have to wait before I get engaged, married, have three children, and live happily ever after?" she asked Tracy.

"Girl, you're rushing this. Slow down. Your prince will come along. Just be patient."

After reviewing her looks in the rearview mirror, Emma slowly exited the car and dropped her purse. As she bent to retrieve it, she inadvertently wrapped her left foot in the handle.

"Need help?" a deep male voice echoed from the next row of cars. He appeared to her upside down.

Moving her head from between her knees to attain a standing position, she froze and realized it was him—her soul mate. His mouth was curved like cupids, his hair was sun-bleached, and his abs buckled under a blue-collared golf shirt. She staggered, sputtered, and finally smiled, tossing her hair in the slight breeze.

Mr. Right sauntered over, offered his hand to steady her as she untwined the purse, caught in the tie of her running shoe. As he slipped his arm around her waist, her toes tingled. When she finally got a hold of both emotions and stance, she said, "Hi, I'm Emma Martin."

His face lost the pink tone and, as his mouth slightly opened, it showed beautifully aligned teeth. "You've got to be pulling my chain?" A dimple appeared. "Hi, I'm Blake, Blake Martin."

She turned her head and whispered into the breeze, "Great! I won't have to change my last name." Returning her attention to him, she said, "Now you're pulling my chain!"

As if they had known each other since Ms. Corcoran's dance class, they simultaneously laughed, gently touching each other's shoulder.

"Well, now that we're introduced, let's go to the clubhouse. You register while I grab some clubs and balls."

They chatted like old friends while walking the red brick path.

Quickly she filled out the simple form—name, phone number—and paid in cash. Swiveling, she found him staring at her. Blushing was always hard to conceal. The lesson lasted one hour but ended way too soon.

When the fourth and final session finished, Blake spoke the words she had been dreaming of for four weeks: "Want to go for coffee? I'm no longer your instructor...."

*

"Tracy, it was magical!"

"Did he hold your hand?"

"He gently put his arm around my waist as he led me though the café door. I felt an electrical shock; a bolt went straight to my heart. We talked and laughed for five hours!"

"Did he kiss you good night?"

"No, that was strange. He looked like he wanted to but backed down. When I got in my car I checked my teeth in the mirror for a piece of bagel the coffee didn't wash out, but there wasn't any. He did ask if he could call me."

"And?"

Emma gently blew air out of her lips. "Do I look foolish? I said, 'Certainly,' as I batted my lashes ever so softly."

*

Two weeks later

The cell phone felt like lead in her hand as she answered it. "Hi, Tracy." She sighed.

"What's happening?"

"Well, I'm having a pity party watching the sun set, witnessing my life sinking in the west. Thinking, if I'd told Blake how much I enjoyed being with him, maybe he would have contacted me." Another sigh. "It's been two weeks since he asked if he could call."

"Yes, that's how some guys are. They feel compelled to give you hope, so they don't look like a smuck."

"He didn't act like a smuck. I don't understand; I thought he enjoyed my company. We laughed and had so much in common; our faith and values are mirrored.... Hey, Tracy, I've got another call coming in. I'll answer it, then go back to my pity party, if you don't mind."

"Okay, girl. Hang in there; someday you'll make a beautiful bride. And I'll be your maid-of-honor, like we practiced in kindergarten at Mt. Carmel."

"Sure friend, 'bye."

She quickly hit the call waiting. "Hello," she said half-heartedly.

"Emma, I'm so glad you answered. This is Blake."

She almost choked on her words. "Blake, Blake Martin?"

His laugh embarrassed her. "Yes, is this Emma Martin?" he teased.

As in their first meeting, they simultaneously laughed. Her whole being crumbled in delight, like a chocolate chip cookie melts in your mouth.

"Emma, I hope you're not upset over not hearing from me, but I have the strangest story to tell you."

Momentarily Emma heard Tracy say, *"And I have a bridge to sell you."*

"It's only 7:30. How about going for coffee? I promise I'll show up."

Erasing Tracy's imaginary words, without hesitation she said, "I'd love to."

His sigh came across as priceless. "I'm so lucky. Is half an hour enough time for you to get your natural look on?"

She laughed. "I'm ready now."

"All right, 15 minutes then?"

"Sure, I can't wait to hear your story."

"I can't wait to tell it; it's so bizarre.

"Good-bye, Mr. Martin."

"Good-bye, Ms. Martin."

She hurried to apply makeup, just completing her eye shadow when the doorbell rang.

He was drop-dead handsome as he said, "Gosh, you are gorgeous!"

"And you are quite attractive yourself."

At the Java Café, just like the first time, he put his hand around her waist and led her toward their booth.

After the coffee arrived, he took one long sip, rested his mug on the blue-and-white checkered mat, and inhaled deeply. As if he were blowing out his regrets, he began. "Here goes, and I hope you believe me. I was berating myself for not giving you a good-night kiss. I didn't want you to think I was pushing your buttons, you know…"

Emma just smiled.

"My pastor recently gave a message about abstinence, and I do believe in it, so…"

She smiled again and took his hand in hers as he continued.

"I barely slept the night we parted and couldn't wait to get into work to get the phone number off the application." His blush enhanced the boyish grin. "I kind of cheated and arrived early to avoid Gert, our receptionist, the owner's mother. She's kind of PMS every day."

Emma laughed, nodding in agreement.

"I quickly found your file—easy to remember your last name—and jotted your number on my right palm."

She remembered he was left-handed. During lessons, when he snuggled against her, he had to adjust for her right-handed swing.

"I was bummed out when I called and reached the recording that said the number had been disconnected."

She shrugged shoulders and eyebrows and shifted in the seat.

"I kept thinking, what if I had let you know how much I liked being together? Then maybe I would have found out your address."

"My turn." Emma shifted her position in order to continue holding his hand; she felt him relax. "I too was hounded by what-ifs. What if I had smiled more or given you extra signals, showing I wanted to know you better? The connection between us was instant—at least that's what I felt."

He squeezed her hand, and his dimple widened.

Then she frowned. "I've never had a land line, so I don't understand the recorded message, 'out of order.'"

When Blake tightened his grip, she jumped. "Wait. There's more to our story, the miraculous part."

"Really? I can't wait."

"Yesterday, I went to the altar for prayer from Pastor Jeff. He's a young guy so he understood. I told him I was sure I'd found my soul mate. He corrected me and said. 'Be equally yoked; don't lead with your heart. Ask God that, if this romance is true, to lead you, give you a sign. A soul mate is from the heart; a life mate is from God.' I accepted his words, went home, and prayed."

His hand was so warm and comfortable in hers, like a cozy security blanket. "Would you believe, this morning the miracle happened? I was at the same spot where you parked. When I got out of my car, I saw something sparkly in the base of a shrub, at the curb. I'm a neat-nick, so I bent down to retrieve the card. My eyes darted, my mouth gapped and my spirit leapt."

Hearing that story, Emma's spirit also leapt, and she jumped to a standing position. "My girlie card! You found my glitzy card?"

"Yes, in the stem of a bush; an angel must have tucked it into the plant after it fell out of your upturned purse when you wavered."

Emma was in heavenly awe. Sure, her purse flipped when she tripped so the card could have flown. But the telephone number...what about that? May I see the number you called, please?"

"My, you are polite." He tugged his wallet from the back of his skinny jeans, located the small note, and gently placed it in her hand.

She made sure her hand met his as she slowly grasped the paper and looked—224-2411. "Oh man," she said as she lightly slapped the side of her head. "I was in such a hurry to write my name and number that I forgot to hook the 7's. It's 2477!" she shrieked.

"What if?" both said together, and then laughed as their eyes made contact with their souls.

With a tilt of his head and an awesome smile he said, "Can we have a do-over and start our story again?"

"Our story, hmm I like that...lots," she said.

*

Seven months later

As the music increased in volume, Tracy walked in on Emma, who was stripped to her underwear. "Emma, you're not ready?"

"I'm waiting for you, friend. Since kindergarten we've planned for our weddings. Button my gown, please."

If only her parents were alive to witness her special day...if only the driver of the other car hadn't spent hours drinking, they'd be walking her down the aisle. Emma knew they'd love Blake as she did. She was certain they were watching from their heavenly balcony.

Blake was stunningly handsome in his black tuxedo as he took his place at the altar. The wedding march music wrapped its pure sounds around the pillars of the country church. Scents of roses filled the sanctuary. He glanced to the side, and inhaled the sight of his angel, his life mate from God, his bride. Their eyes locked and their smiles matched as did their last name, forever.

KATHRYN HARTMAN is a daughter of a King, wife of a prince, mother of three sons, and grandmother of ten. Her passions are writing and photography. Over five decades, she has published a children's book, written a novel, and poetry. Kathryn is published in the OakTara anthology *Falling in Love with You* and won an award for "Best Poetry" at the Florida Christian Writers' Conference. She speaks to women's groups about following your dreams, no matter your age.

To email her: **bernie30@aol.com.**

A Friend of Mine

* * *

Lynn Gipson

The homeless man stood on the corner of Main and Second Streets. His clothes were dirty and tattered, and his eyes were blank and staring. He seemed lost, although he had walked these streets many times in the past three years and knew them well. He knew every proprietor willing to give him food and a little change from time to time. He knew every "crazy" on the streets to stay away from.

Jenny Baylor was waiting at this very corner one Monday morning for the walk signal to come. She was in a hurry, for she was late for court again. The judge had admonished her the last time for keeping her client and the whole courtroom waiting. Seeing no cars were coming, she stepped out with the signal still flashing *Don't Walk*.

Suddenly, a car horn blasted, and someone yanked at her. She hit the pavement just as the car rounded the corner, missing her by inches. Then she felt herself being pulled up by someone and gently deposited on the curb. Sitting there for a few seconds, she realized she was all right and turned to look at the person who had saved her life.

"Are you okay?" the man asked.

Jenny heard a voice she hadn't heard in years. It had to be Gary, her high school boyfriend. When she turned toward him, she instantly saw it was indeed Garu. What in the world had happened to him?

"Gary? Gary Saunders? Is that you?"

The man looked at her, tears welling in his eyes, then hurried away. Jenny called after him, but he disappeared into an alley behind Albert's Restaurant. Just like that, he was gone.

Jenny gathered herself together and continued on her way to the courthouse, thinking about what had happened and the man she'd just seen. Gary Saunders had been the most popular boy in her high school—the captain of the football team and class valedictorian. She was so proud to have been his girlfriend for two years. They were as crazy about each other as teenagers can be. He'd told her more than once, "I'm gonna marry you one day." Jenny would smile and say that sounded like a wonderful dream.

After graduation, however, they had sadly parted ways. She went off to Harvard, and he entered the Air Force Academy. They wrote each other for a while, but as other relationships developed in their lives, they slowly lost touch. Jenny became an attorney, and Gary was sent to Afghanistan as a pilot. Ten years had passed since their last meeting, but Jenny had never forgotten him.

Jenny worked for Legal Aid. She'd heard the calling while in law school. Corporate law didn't appeal to her in the least, and she'd never felt the need to become wealthy. She always was that kind of girl, pulling for the underdog. Several of her clients were homeless, but none had the background of Gary Saunders. Most came from poverty and broken homes. Some were mentally ill. Those who wanted it got counseling from a social worker Jenny became good friends with.

After that first encounter, Jenny went to the corner of Main and Second Street every morning for two weeks looking for Gary. She'd wait there for awhile and then walk up and down Main and even through the alley behind Albert's Restaurant. She had to find him and help him if she could. She asked other homeless people, but no one seemed to know him.

One Saturday morning Jenny got up early, intending to search all day until she found where Gary was staying. Someone, somewhere in the downtown area had to know something about him.

She went door to door of the businesses downtown. Some people remembered seeing a man of his description around but did not know his name or where he slept at night. Finally a man at one of the restaurants said he knew him. He usually slept in the alley just behind his restaurant, and the man said he'd given him food on many occasions.

"But be careful now. Some of the alley people ain't too friendly," he said.

Jenny searched the alley and found a man asleep on the ground next to a dumpster. She called out to him gently, intending to ask about Gary. He woke and regarded her through bleary, bloodshot eyes that gazed directly toward her purse. Rising to his feet, he grabbed the strap, knocking her off balance and onto the ground.

Suddenly there were shouts and wrestling and then, once again, Gary was pulling her to her feet. She was okay—just a bruised shoulder where the man had tugged at her purse strap.

"What are you doing here, Jenny?" Gary asked in a stern voice.

"Looking for you! I've been looking for you for two weeks. Where have you been?"

"Around. You shouldn't be here. What do you want with me?"

"I want to help you. Please, let me help you." Tears rolled down her face.

"You can't help me. No one can. Besides, I'm fine."

"You're not fine. Why are you living this way? What happened to you?"

"A war happened, Jenny, a war."

Jenny understood now. One of her clients was a homeless veteran with post-traumatic stress disorder. He chose to live on the streets rather than burden his family with his mental illness. The only way he could live with himself, he said, was alone. Severe flashbacks of the conditions of war caused him to become erratic at times and a danger to his loved ones. He was now getting counseling and medication, had found a job, and a room to live in. He was slowly getting back on his feet, thanks to his attorney.

"Gary, you just saved my life for the second time in two weeks. I at least owe you a lunch. I won't take no for an answer. Besides, we have some catching up to do."

"I hate for you to see me this way. I am so ashamed."

"Don't be. I've seen people a lot worse looking than you." She smiled.

They went into a nearby restaurant amid stares of the other customers. Jenny spoke quietly to the waiter, who seemed aghast at Gary's attire. "He's a friend of mine."

The waiter then showed them to a table in the far back. As they finished ordering, Jenny decided it was truth-telling time. "This is me, Gary. I know you better than you know yourself. I loved you for two years, and we talked about everything. You know things about me I've never told anyone. So shoot!" she said, using a term they often used with each other in their teenage years.

"I was on a mission in Afghanistan with Jeremy Johnson. Remember Jeremy?"

Jenny nodded. Jeremy was a friend of theirs who went into the academy with Gary. Jenny remembered someone saying he had died in Afghanistan.

"We bombed a village where some members of Al-Qaeda were supposed to be hiding. Both of our planes were shot down. We were taken hostage." At this point Gary was almost sobbing. "We were tortured for information. Jeremy broke and told them what they wanted to know; then they beheaded him. I was returned to my cell for further questioning the next day. That night, our own recognizance forces came in and killed most of them, and rescued me." Gary stopped, no longer coherent.

"It's okay, Gary. You don't have to tell me anymore. What about your family? Do they know where you are?"

"I call them once in a while to let them know I'm okay, but no, they don't know how I'm living. I had a wife, Marie, and a daughter, Jenny. Marie left me five years ago because I couldn't be a husband or father when I got back. She's now remarried. I named my daughter after you," he said with a hint of a smile.

Jenny sat quietly for a minute, taking all of this in. *A wife and daughter...* She herself was still single. She'd been so busy saving the world she never had time to become serious about anyone. Most men were intimidated by her dedication to her career anyway. A few thought she was crazy to waste her law degree on the kind of people she defended.

"Gary, you've got to come home with me. I mean it. I inherited my grandmother's big estate house. You remember it. There's a cottage out back. You can stay there and have all the privacy you need. It's sitting there, empty. Please. I live at the place alone, and I could use a man on the grounds."

*

Something inside Gary made him agree with her offer. He'd been praying continuously for help of some kind because he really didn't know what to do about his life and the way it was. He knew Jenny well. She'd never been the kind of person to judge anyone by their circumstances.

So Gary moved into Jenny's small cottage behind the main house. The entire back wall of the den was lined with a library of books.

Jenny insisted on paying him a salary to become her security guard and look after the gardens out back. She had intended to hire someone for this anyway, she told him.

Gary settled into his new life slowly. He kept watch over Jenny and her home and enjoyed working in the flower gardens. After a while, the nightmares stopped coming, and he began to feel more like himself. It was good to have a home again, and with his salary he was able to buy some decent clothes. He got a haircut but kept his beard. Jenny said it made him look quite handsome, so he wore it neatly trimmed.

He started reading some of the books from the back wall and ran across one on ministering to homeless people. During his captivity, he'd become quite close to God. While taking courses in the Air Force, he'd earned a degree in sociology, so that started him thinking about how he might help street people.

*

Gary and Jenny were now spending a lot of time together. They went out to dinner, and sometimes he had dinner waiting for her when she got home from work. They started attending church together the way they did in high school, and both rededicated their lives to Christ.

Jenny was thrilled to see Gary coming around to the way he was back then. She was also falling in love with him again. She didn't know quite what to do about that.

*

One night at dinner Gary brought up the subject of becoming a minister to the homeless. Jenny was delighted. She told him that was a wonderful idea. Of course, the salary would be almost nonexistent. He didn't care. He had finally applied for his benefits from the government, and they were coming in now. He stopped taking money from Jenny for his so-called security job. He was falling in love with Jenny as well and did not want her supporting him.

So Jenny and Gary began working diligently with the homeless. She would bring him her homeless clients and he would walk the streets talking to the indigent about Jesus. He brought many to Christ, and also counseled the mentally ill and helped get medication for the ones who needed it. They eventually raised enough money from local businesses to open a small shelter at the corner where Gary had saved Jenny from the speeding car.

Finally, Gary asked Jenny to marry him. She jumped up and yelled, "At last! What took you so long?"

Gary replied he didn't have much to offer her in the way of material things, and she told him she had all she had ever wanted.

*

They were married at their shelter for the homeless. Gary's daughter, Jenny, was there after having been happily reunited with her father. Both of their parents were there as well. It was a grand day for all. Gary's best man was a guy he befriended while still on the streets. Jenny's maid-of-honor was her friend, the social worker, who counseled her clients. Other than family, all those in attendance were homeless.

Due to an inheritance from his grandfather, Gary was able to start a small church in one of the old buildings near the homeless shelter. Jenny sold her grandmother's estate home, and they bought and refurbished a loft apartment near their shelter. The rest of their money went into supporting their ministry and the shelter.

*

Gary is back on the streets now, but for an entirely different reason. Jenny still works at Legal Aid helping those who can't afford an attorney. They both work at the shelter and also work diligently to raise funds for Gary's ministry.

Quite recently, their conversation somehow led back to their days in high school together. They fondly remembered him playing football and their night together at prom.

"I told you I was gonna marry you one day," said Gary.

Jenny smiled and kissed her husband. "Sounds like a wonderful dream...and, best of all, it came true."

LYNN GIPSON, a 61-year-old cancer survivor, has one son and two amazing granddaughters. She lives in Mississippi and, after a lifetime of dreaming of being a writer, has become one. She is first and foremost a Christian, and tries to reach people who may be hurting through her articles, short stories—both fiction and nonfiction—and poems.

To Love or Not

* * *

Mary Cantell

A generous canopy of mossy leaves clustered together over the roadway, briefly dispelling the sun. This must have been the tunnel of trees Brent was talking about. The picnic grove wouldn't be far from here; I'd find his car by the bronze statue, he'd said.

My pulse quickened. Twenty minutes to 12. Still, I wasn't sure it was such a good idea to meet again. We'd already discussed our relationship—how it wasn't working out. Just why he'd want to see me again was puzzling. And why I would drive all the way from Osceola to see him even more imponderable. We had amicably agreed to end the relationship months ago. What more was there to say? With second thoughts, I quickly swerved the car over before proceeding any farther.

The morning air smelled sweet, moist, and thick as though tinged with freshly warmed honey. I stepped out of the car. Off in the near distance, not far from the clearing, a little pond nestled unassumingly in the shade. A nearby pinewood bench sat among a cluster of wildflowers that gathered at its base. The brass plaque had an inscription nailed to the back: *In Memory of John and Doris Prescott.* I sat down and began to pray.

A few moments later, my emotions stirred like shards of hot glass. They siphoned through the grit and mire wedged deep down as tears erupted with an urgency I hadn't known before. The pain of each breath ripped inside my chest. With labored breathing, I crouched into a ball, trying to control the spasms while watching my tears, one by one, drip onto the bench. After a minute or so, the avalanche of grief slowed. The burden I'd been carrying was a bit lighter, but still there.

Just below the willow, something stirred on the water. There in the humid shadows, a mute swan rested on the water. Her ethereal grace drew me in. While absorbed in the ambience, the strident call of a blackbird somewhere in the reeds by the pond broke the silence, but this was more of a blessing than an interruption of the peace.

I wondered if Doris and John Price were ever here. Was the old house further back on the property once theirs? A rambling clapboard with black shutters stood stately in the distance among a cluster of pines. The leaves and branches gathered just above the windows like the heads of curious children wanting to reach inside. The house looked vacant, its blue paint chipped and faded. Some of the shutters hung askew. It must have been beautiful once.

"It's so peaceful, isn't it?"

The voice came out of nowhere. Just above a whisper. Startled, I turned to see an elderly lady standing behind me. A little dog idled by her side.

"Yes, it is," I said, wondering where she came from. There had been no car engine or any footsteps. Even her dog kept to himself, as though on cue. His chocolate eyes stared up at me with dog-like sincerity. Could he feel my pain?

"Like nothing bad should ever happen here..." Her voice trailed as she spoke her thoughts out loud.

She sat on the other side of the bench while her dog placed himself at her feet. We sat together gazing out onto the pond where several geese and mallards now gathered. The silence drew us in. The serene water splayed like a clear green coin. I imagined myself floating down to the bottom, allowing my cares and worries to slough away clean before rising back to the surface. We sat for a while, soothed by its tranquil powers before her dog began to get restless. He yelped softly and stood, distracted by something across the water.

"Shhh, Toby," she said with mock indignation as the dog settled down once again.

A few minutes later, she stood. "Come on, Toby." The obedient dog followed at her heels. "Have a nice day, miss," she called while moving away as silently as she'd arrived. When I turned again, she had disappeared.

Soon a young couple appeared on the other side of the pond. They must have come from the path leading from the woods. Their frames came together, and I quickly averted my eyes. Watching an infatuated couple was the last thing I wanted to see right now.

Thoughts of Brent, never far away, gripped me once more, along with a strange sense of dread. I looked down at my watch. Seven minutes to 12. The heat of the morning sun penetrated my cotton tank top like a heavy hand at my back. Before yesterday, I thought things were settled between us. Why did he have to stir me up all over again? I'd made peace with the situation, and I thought we'd reached an agreement. While we surely once loved each other, the relationship was just not the same. Something was driving us apart, and it had been apparent to both of us. Getting back together with him would be like trying to repair a broken muffler with a Band-Aid. It would hold for a while, but how long would it be before it would burn away? My head spun with indecision.

Brent's face and his words floated in my mind. Like a favorite tape, I replayed it over and over...memorizing the sparkle in his eye, trying to read the true meaning behind his last words to me before we broke up....

"Laura, I..." His voice faltered. *"I want you to know something."* His eyes fixed on mine. *"Laura, I never lied to you. It's true about Maryann. I did go back to see her the weekend you went away, but I only went there to tell her one thing. It was important enough to tell her face-to-face. I needed to talk to her...about you."*

He had seemed so sincere. How does one look you in the eye, so lovingly, and lie? Was he lying? His expression resembled a little boy whose bike had just been stolen.

"I went to Tampa to tell Maryann that I'd have to break things off with her. I went there to tell her I'd found someone—someone I was in love with. I thought it best to tell her in person. It was the right thing to do...something I had to do."

What he had to do? That wasn't what I'd heard. The story on the street was that he'd gone back to his old girlfriend—to rekindle their romance. My heart broke that night. I had felt two-timed, used. That wasn't love. It felt good to get rid of him. If honesty wasn't part of his makeup, then he wasn't the right one for me. But when would the loneliness stop?

"You don't love yourself, Laura...why do you reach for tinsel instead of gold?"

Professor Bradley's words resounded in my head. He'd often told me that I didn't love myself. I'd never understood it, even after months of counseling. Who doesn't love themselves? It's a natural thing. I tried to process the point he was making. I knew that often I'd been lied to and deceived by people, especially men. Not having spent quality time with my own father, nor having him to guide me or rely on may have been part of why I set myself up for troubled relationships where I'd depend too much on them. I'd taken enough psychology courses to understand a woman's weaknesses that come with not having a father figure early on. But when Brent spoke or even looked at me, my heart softened. I felt that whatever he could offer would be better than no love at all. I'd been tired of looking for the right kind of love. Where would that be? My father had been the right kind of love, but he died. Where would I find another? There would be no one who could fill his place, nor be as loving as my own daddy. Dr. Bradley would never understand.

While the pain of losing Brent had once singed like fire, now a numbing comfort set in like a healing panacea. But had I been too abrupt with him? Too harsh? There was a chance that he had been telling the truth. Hindsight has a way of turning things around, especially when the pain has eased.

The sun's warmth crept over my whole body now, sending a wave of perspiration across my neck and brow. I moved toward the shade trees. Walking in the lush stillness, I felt like I'd been here before. It felt so familiar…like a slow, dizzying ride with nothing to stop it.

Brent's words popped into my mind once more…

"Laura, I believe God brought us together. I've been smitten by you since the first day I saw you at the swimming pool."

He believed God brought us together? I wanted to believe that, but…

"When I first saw you talking to those other guys, you know, back before we officially met, I was…well, jealous, wishing you'd talk to me the way you did to them. Can you understand how much I love you? Now and forever, I want to be with you."

His words drifted in and out…*"I love you"*…

I had wanted to hear these words for so long. Were they real? Was I in love with the words or with him?

Three minutes to noon. I could leave now and be safely back on the road for home. Isn't that where I should be? Yet it would be so easy to see him just one more time. One more look in his eyes, the way they shone like blue-black lakes. Maybe this time I wouldn't drown in them. Oh, how ridiculous.

I went back to the car and started the engine. As I pulled onto the main road, I stopped—again, not knowing which direction to take. One way, I'd be going back to my past, to Brent. The life I wasn't sure was right for me. The opposite way would lead back to Osceola. Back home. One direction would be safe, yet lonely. The other direction would bring me back to life, or, at least, a semblance of feeling alive but without any assurances; A possible dead end.

I pressed the pedal and hoped I was moving in the right direction.

MARY CANTELL is a professional journalist and multi-published freelance writer with a 15-year career as a broadcast news reporter in Philadelphia. She enjoys chocolate, playing chess, and lively discussions on history, politics, and the Bible. She is hoping to see her first novel, *Her Glass Heart,* published soon.

www.marycantell.com

Tehya and Rode

* * *

M.E. Born

"Who is he, Tehya-Rose?"

She hung her coat on the hook, sighing as a puddle formed on the tiles below.

"Is he from school?"

She'd seen her father watching them from the window of his study. The rain had made it impossible to read the expression he wore then, but there was no mistaking it now.

"No… he works. Down by Jessip."

"A tradesman?"

Carpenter, bricklayer—she knew not which. He'd been on site since the laying of the first foundation.

"What were you doing with a tradesman? On a motorcycle?"

The way he spat "tradesman," it was clear the motorcycle was not what bothered him.

"He offered me a ride. It was pouring. You weren't there to pick me up."

"I only now returned from a meeting. You could have phoned me from the school surely?"

Tehya let her bag slide from her shoulder and walked to her father, kissing him on the cheek as she did every night. "I'm sorry, Father, I didn't want to burden you."

"Does the tradesman at least have a name?"

Tehya scraped damp hair from her cheeks. She knew it wasn't to express gratitude that her father wanted him identified, but it wouldn't have made any difference. "I don't know his name…exactly." She'd heard the men on site address him. They called him Rode.

"When your mother took the notion to homeschool, I worried you would be overly sheltered, but I thought she had at least instilled you with common sense."

Tehya tried to meet her father's eyes, but faltered.

The heavy rain had stung against her skin, and she hadn't thought twice about accepting the ride. But he *was* a stranger. She knew nothing of him, except that he'd silenced his workmate's degrading wolf-whistles the first day she passed by the building site. He'd smiled an apology to her that day and she'd looked for that smile amongst the posts and rafters of the building frames every day since.

But weeks of exchanged glances wouldn't pass as evidence of an acquaintance, and neither could her daily observance of his diligence with a hammer and trowel be considered any proof of his honesty.

Father was right. She'd been foolish to accept a ride from a stranger, especially one who seemed already to know so much about her....

*

"How did you know where I lived?"

He was bent over, a water hose in hand, washing mud and mortar from a wheelbarrow load of tools. He glanced up before turning back to pressurize the stream onto a stubborn clod of cement mix.

"I know quite a bit about you Tehya-Rose."

If common sense was an immovable lump at her throat, she felt it now. She'd thought he had said her name as he kicked his bike into gear outside her house, but she'd hoped it was imagined.

"How...do you know my name?"

He glanced again, the smile gone from his eyes. "I guess some of us have better memories than others." He moved the wheelbarrow beneath the shelter of the house's garage.

Tehya followed, stumbling and regaining her footing on the uneven mounds of earth.

He dropped tools from the wheelbarrow into a tray, mousy hair blowing back from his eyes as he removed his baseball cap and set it to hang on the handle.

Although she'd clung to him on the motorbike, he'd worn a full-face helmet and she'd not seen him this close. She swallowed hard against the lump that wasn't commonsense, but disbelief.

"Broden?" The easy smile she'd sought daily waxed again behind his lips. How could she not have recognized those same blue eyes and pronounced cheekbones he'd had, even as a boy? "You've grown up."

"So have you, Tehya-Rose." Heat flooded her cheeks as his eyes swept over her.

Had she? She felt as a little girl standing beside his matured frame. "You knew it was me all along?"

He nodded.

"Even the day you pitched the muddy rag at the other builder?"

"The guys whistle at passing women all the time: I don't condone it, but I'd never get any work done if I defended them all that way."

"Why didn't you say something—let me know it was you?"

"I thought you already knew." He dusted a rag over his forearms. "I didn't speak because it's been the pattern of our families for the past eight years. I didn't know if you wanted it."

"The pattern?"

"A worn-out pattern. Can I give you another lift home?"

Tehya hesitated, looking at her watch. Even her father, immersed in business as he always was, would be wondering where she was by now.

"I'm in the truck this time, if it's the murder-cycle that worries you."

"It's another lecture from my father that worries me. But you're no stranger. Maybe…you could come in; let him remember who you are?"

Broden frowned as he closed the passenger door behind her and slid behind the wheel. "Your dad would probably prefer stranger to Matthews."

*

Tehya was silent as Broden took each undirected turn to her house. What could she say to a best friend she hadn't seen in nearly a decade? A friend whom, as a ten-year-old, she'd promised to marry?

"How've you been Tehya-Rose?" His voice betrayed no unease. Their one-year age difference had grown wider with the passing of years. "I was sorry to hear about your mom."

Tears stung her eyes. She couldn't speak of her mother or the sickness of heart that ended her life.

"My dad went to her funeral. I don't know if you saw him there?"

Tehya shook her head. She hadn't seen Sol Matthews, but she had seen her father scratch his name from the funeral attendance book.

She swept tears from their hold under her lashes. "I'd be okay except Father wouldn't continue home study and enrolled me in private school."

They pulled to the curb outside her house. Broden's gaze skimmed her school uniform before settling on her face. Unbuckling his seatbelt, he caught a tear from her cheek with work-toughened fingers that snagged on wisps of her hair. "Did you never think of me, Tehya?"

"All the time for the first couple of years. I begged Mother and Father to let me see you, but they said our educational philosophy differed too much."

Broden took her hand, holding it between his own. "Tehya, I want to take up where we left off."

"Left off? We were children. Do you really believe what we played at counts now?"

"That kind of affection doesn't disappear."

Tehya's foot knocked against the motorcycle helmet he'd bidden her to wear the night before. "Do you often take girls for rides on the back of your bike? You keep an extra helmet handy."

"The helmet is for my brother. I pick him up from practice. But I guess you're really asking if I've been faithful to childhood promises?"

Tehya nodded, although *faithful* was an embellished word. He'd been bound to her by nothing but memories.

"My parents told me I wouldn't see you again. I held onto a vague hope that they were wrong, but when I heard nothing from you, I dismissed it all as child's play. I had a girlfriend the first day you passed by the site, but once I realized I found more joy in your daily far-off smiles than I did in her company, I ended the relationship. Childish as they may have been, my feelings for you are still there, Tehya-Rose."

*

Broden stood motionless and frowning. "Then I'll pursue friendship with Tehya until you believe she's old enough for more."

"You'd only be wasting your time, Mr. Matthews. Now, please see yourself out and try not to brush past the furniture on your way."

Tehya stood, mouth agape, as the front door closed behind him. "Mother may not have taught me commonsense, but she taught me common courtesy, and I'm beyond embarrassed by what you did, Father."

"I'm sure your mother would be just as dismayed to see you invite someone so soiled into this house. I'll have to pay for an extra cleaning. And what do you mean by encouraging him to ask for permission that you knew I would refuse?"

"You refused on account of my age. I'm 18, Father—an adult!"

"A naïve adult. We did right in removing you from that boy's company, and it's nothing but a shame that your paths have crossed again. He can offer you nothing. His presence would be an ill-fitting distraction in your otherwise promising future. Do you desire to be pregnant before you even graduate, bound to a man so lust-filled and chauvinistic that you're forced to abandon all ambition and bear a horde of unruly children? That was the life Solomon Matthews gave to his wife. She was run ragged and used and died before 35. Is that what you want, Tehya-Rose?"

"She died?"

"Several years ago. And his father has drowned in the bottle while his tribe of offspring have run wild ever since. But I expected you knew all this, considering you sought permission to take up a relationship with the boy."

"I didn't know. He offered me condolence but didn't say anything about his own mother."

"Honesty has never been a Matthews' trait."

"You can't hold a father's faults against the son. Broden is…good."

"You knew him as a 10-year-old, Tehya-Rose. That boy is like his father, even in his looks. But looks are all he has. If he'd done anything besides follow his father into trade, I would have given him the benefit of the doubt."

"His father runs the construction company. Broden works alongside him, managing men twice his age."

"It is still naught but dirty, dead-end trade."

*

Broden was waiting, his arms folded over his chest, as he rested against the unfinished wall. He smiled when he saw her, and suddenly she was overcome by a desire to return to when the boy was still a memory and the anonymous smiles of a twelfth-grade girl and a tradesman were all either of them expected. But her smiles had never been anonymous to him, and now their withdrawal must also be personal.

At least Father had organized a ride home from now on, sparing her from what might replace the smile in Broden's eyes.

He reached for her hand, drawing her close. "Tehya, I'm a God-fearing guy, and I know the fourth commandment, but you're 18…" He smoothed a hand over her hair where the wind had blown it in wild directions. "You must see that your dad is unjustly prejudiced against me. I know it'd be difficult to defy him while under his roof, but once you've graduated high school—"

"Broden—stop!" Her eyes flooded and the confusion in his expression blurred through tears. "My father is prejudiced. But he's also right. I'm not ready for a relationship."

"Tehya, can't you see?" He traced his finger along the curve of her jaw. "You're not a little girl anymore. You're a woman." He cupped his hand to her chin. "I cherished the little girl, and I'm falling in love with the woman." His mouth sought hers and, for a moment, there was nothing but the warmth of his hands in her hair, his breath at her lips.

"No." She pushed away. "I'll never be ready for a relationship with you.

Not because I'm a little girl, but because I'm a woman who wants more than to be the weary wife of a tradesman."

He stepped back. "As opposed to the weary wife of a man in some other profession?"

"I know what happened to your mother. How marriage to your father caused her to sacrifice and die young."

"Loving my dad led her to sacrifice, but that's what love does, Tehya. Just as love led her to sacrifice her life to the cancer rather than harm the baby in her womb. Mom regretted neither sacrifice."

"But if your father hadn't been just a tradesman—"

"Trade wasn't below Christ. Is your ambition merely wealth that you think it so below you?"

"My father—"

Broden's eyes flashed with fury. "Your father hates mine, not because of his trade, but because my mom chose him. Your family left the co-op disgraced because your father tried to persuade my mom to infidelity. It was your mom who lost ambition and life to a loveless marriage. "

"You lie!"

"Your father doesn't know love, Tehya, and you'll never know it either if you continue to judge me and the world as he does."

*

Rain streamed against her window. It had been a week since she'd spoken to Broden, and her world was already a colder place.

She wanted to see him, to know again the love she'd felt in his kiss, but she'd hurt him and he'd retaliated with accusations that she couldn't bring herself to believe…until now.

She heard the front door slam, signaling her father's return. Descending the stairs, she greeted him with a kiss. "I was looking through an album of Mother's. Did you know she and Mrs. Matthews were friends in college?"

"Yes." He looked up from sieving through the day's mail. "We were all three friends."

"Did you wish Mrs. Matthews to be more than a friend?"

"For a time."

"And you resented Broden's father because she chose him instead?"

"Tehya-Rose, where are these questions headed? I believed we were through hearing about that family."

"You lied to make me turn from Broden."

"I turned you against him for your own good, and fate has it that I've spared you any heartache you would've felt now."

"What do you mean now?"

"It's been all over the news for a week, Tehya-Rose."

"What has?"

"The accident on Jessip."

"No—" She swayed, her mind collapsing under images of the boy, then the man. *Broden...*

*

The silence of the room was broken only by the beep of the monitors.

Tehya sat by the bed, her arms outstretched to hold his hand. The painkillers had kept him sleeping most of the day. A single tear ran down her cheek when, still asleep, Broden tore his hand from her grasp and attempted to soothe the arm that was not there. He woke as his fingers grasped against the empty bed sheet. His chest heaved when he saw her.

"Tehya." He reached his only hand to her face. "Have you been here all day again?"

She nodded, smoothing the ripples from the sheet.

"You can't stay with me all the time."

"Time's precious and fleeting, Broden."

"I know. But I'm of little use now, even as a tradesman. I'll be a burden, and I want you to have every opportunity to live."

"Loving is sacrificing, remember? Besides…" Tehya stood, placing a kiss on his forehead. "Now I've found the one I love, there's nothing worth doing without you."

M.E. BORN lives in Australia with her American husband and their four children. After completing a Bachelor of Arts, she spent time in research at her university before becoming a home educator. She is currently working on an inspirational romance series for young adults.

http://meborn.blogspot.com.au/

A Kiss on Michigan Avenue

* * *

Dicky To

Rachel Wellington's pulse beat like a war drum as she gazed at Jacob Peterson sitting at a table along the opposite wall. Why did she have such strong feelings for him? Was it love? She hoped he'd return her affection tonight.

The chandeliers illuminated the State Ballroom, reflecting the hall in a radiance of gold. Jacob's black tie attire added to his already handsome looks—brown wavy hair, broad shoulders, and eyes that sparkled like sapphires.

The boisterous chattering faded as the world around Rachel became still, immersing her in a deep fantasy. She imagined Jacob entwining his fingers with hers and placing his other hand on the small of her back, waltzing her around the dance floor....

Let her lose herself to his tenderness. Let him hold her tight. Would anything else be better than a moment of closeness?

Jacob caught her eye. They waved at each other. Rachel reached up to touch her right cheek that burned hotter than an iron. She swallowed hard when a curvy blonde strolled over to him and pulled up a chair. He whispered to the girl. She smiled at Rachel and chitchatted with Jacob.

Were they talking about her? Rachel glanced back and forth between them, wishing to be within earshot. Jacob looked at her and rose. Was he coming to ask for a dance? She diverted her gaze and clamped her right palm over her chest, willing her rocketing heartbeat to calm.

Footsteps approached, then stopped. A shadow fell across her. It must be Jacob. She waited for his invitation as the pianist played "Someday My Prince Will Come."

"Excuse me, may I have this dance?" An unfamiliar male voice settled over her.

Rachel angled her head to find a stranger's eyes on her. Her shoulders sagged, and she threw a glance at Jacob's table. He was leading the blonde to the dance floor. Her dream shattered like glass crashing on the ground, shards scattering in all directions. Why had Jacob asked her to attend this party in the first place? Why had he dated her?

Abby Wong gently tugged at Rachel's sleeve and leaned in. "Hey, the gentleman is asking you for a dance."

Rachel faced the man. "I'm sorry. I'm not in the mood."

He gave her a small bow and left.

"Are you mad or something?" Abby poked at Rachel's back.

"I'm fine." Rachel watched Jacob and his girlfriend step in rhythm to the music. How intimate and romantic, but she wasn't the girl he'd chosen. She scowled at them, then remembered the Bible had taught her not to covet. Otherwise resentment would crawl into her mind, and she'd toss about on her bed all night long. Rachel took a deep breath and let the air carry her anger away.

The blonde twisted her body toward Rachel, then back to Jacob. She laughed as he spoke to her.

They must be teasing me. Pouting, Rachel started to leave.

"The party just began. Where are you going?" Abby reached for Rachel's wrist.

"I need some fresh air. Don't worry about me." Rachel scurried down the aisle between two rows of tables. From the fringe of her vision, she noticed many people staring at her. Keeping her head low, she quickened her pace, her gown swishing around her ankles.

She pushed open the door and stepped out of the ballroom. Hastening to the elevator, she descended to the lobby. Spotting three empty armchairs surrounding a rectangular glass table in the corner, she walked over and slumped onto the seat with her back to the lounge.

Were Jacob and his girlfriend laughing about her freckles, flat nose, or small eyes? She didn't deserve their insults, even if she wasn't attractive. Rachel looked at her left hand, deformed with thin fingers curved inward like claws. She recalled the night a robber had beat her on her way to the train station near her college campus and dragged her into the bushes. Thank the Lord a campus guard heard her screams and rescued her. Otherwise she'd have been violated, too.

Was she wallowing in self-pity? Didn't First Peter 3 state that a woman shouldn't care about her outward appearance? That it was her inner beauty that mattered. And that her loving, caring heart was precious in God's sight?

"Hey, Rachel." Jacob tapped her chair.

She jumped and forced a smile. "Hi." Her dull voice matched her bad mood.

"May I talk with you?"

"What for?"

He lowered himself onto the seat beside her. "I was searching everywhere for you. Why did you leave the party?"

Didn't he realize he'd neglected and mocked her? She compressed her lips.

"I guess you're mad because I…" He scratched his temple. "I let you sit there by yourself. Sorry."

She heaved a sigh, trying to untangle her jangled nerves.

"We've dated before, but I didn't know why I got nervous when I saw you tonight." He cracked his knuckles.

At his mention of their dates, she was determined to get things straight. "Why didn't you tell me you are already in a relationship?"

"It isn't what you probably thought. Emily is my younger sister, a student at UCLA. I might've mentioned her to you. She flew to Chicago for our dad's sixtieth birthday, and I asked her to accompany me to this Valentine's party. She'll return to California tomorrow after the Sunday worship service. I'm sorry I didn't introduce her to you before the party began. If you'd come with us tonight, instead of meeting me here, you would've already met her.

"I hadn't danced for a while, so I asked her to practice the waltz with me before I asked you. She urged me to ask you for the next dance when she saw a man standing beside you. I chickened out, so she laughed at me. When I finally overcame my fear, you'd disappeared."

The Jacob she knew wasn't someone who would play games with her. She and many friends had admired him for his integrity. Oh, why had she let her emotions take hold of her? She'd made a fool out of herself. "I misunderstood—actually, I didn't think it through. Sorry."

"It's my fault." He paused. "I told her something I'd like to share with you."

"What?"

"I have feelings for you."

The subsiding heat in her cheeks built up again.

"We had fun doing things in the city a couple of times. Would you like to go out with me again? Maybe catch a movie?"

Rachel's pulse accelerated, and she gazed down. A new thought struck fear in her chest. He'd dated her. Why hadn't he minded her impairment?

Jacob held her hand in place as she tried to withdraw it midway. "I know what you're thinking, but no one is perfect. I have a scar at my left temple." He pointed at his mark. "You see?"

"I noticed that. How did it happen?"

"When I was a little kid, I bumped into the corner of a wall." He checked his watch. "Let me take you someplace."

"Where?"

"Do you trust me?"

Did he really have a heart for her? She wasn't sure she could take the risk. "I'd better go see how my friend's doing," she simply said and hurried back to the party.

*

The next day Rachel pivoted at the click from the doorknob and saw Jacob's worried face peeking through the window in the door. Her heart fluttered as he walked in. She fiddled with the books on the shelf.

He trudged to her, his snow boots clacking across the floor. "Do you have a minute?"

"I'm busy preparing for Sunday school. Actually, the kids will be coming in very soon."

"I won't keep you long." He feigned a cough. "Why did you return to the party last night? Did I say something that—"

"It's not you. It's me." She whirled toward him.

"What's on your mind?"

She gulped down a lump in her throat. "I don't understand why you like me."

"Last quarter, I substituted for Paul and partnered with you to teach the first-grade Sunday school class. Your actions touched me. When the little kids smiled, you smiled. When they cried, you cried with them and embraced them. You put yourself in their shoes and let them experience God's love. I admire these qualities in you."

"But…" Rachel stamped her foot. "I don't know what to say. I shouldn't have dreamed of having you as my boyfriend." The instant the words came, she clapped her hand over her mouth. She couldn't believe she'd voiced her thoughts.

"You like me too, don't you? I knew it when you were upset thinking Emily was my girlfriend."

She spun to face the wall. Was his affection for her out of pity? "There are plenty of beautiful girls out there for you."

He edged to her side. "You're concerned about your outward appearance, aren't you? The Bible talks about a woman's beauty. First Peter—"

"Yes, I know." She glanced at him. The realization that he took the words out of her mouth made her smile.

"Looks like you're feeling better now."

"Mmm-hmm."

"And…" Unsaid words dangled off his tongue.

"What?"

"I hope you won't mind if I tell you this: Your long hair is beautiful like satin, and your eyes are like emeralds." He breathed out. "There—I finally said it out loud."

No man had ever complimented her.

Jacob gently grasped her arms. "Will you give me a chance?"

*

Vehicles whizzed on Michigan Avenue in Chicago. Their headlamps, city lampposts, and storefront lights lit up the neighborhood. Pedestrians bustled from store to store.

Rachel clutched her coat collar tighter as she ambled beside Jacob down the sidewalk. Instantly another coat draped over her shoulders, its weight pulling her downward. As Jacob smiled affectionately, she wished he would kiss her.

"I'm sorry I couldn't find a parking space closer to where we're going." Puffs of air formed in front of him.

"That's okay. Aren't you cold?"

"I'm well built." He bent his elbow and patted his upper arm with his mini umbrella.

A giggle trickled past her lips. "Where are you taking me?"

"You'll know in a sec. So, you've mentioned you'd like to be a nurse after graduating from college?"

"Yup, to take care of the patients. And you? A policeman, if I remember right."

"Correct. To serve and protect the citizens."

"How nice."

Rain fell and dampened her cheeks. Rachel scrunched up her face and wiped it with her sleeve. Jacob unfolded his umbrella, raised it over their heads, and tilted it more toward her. The rain pattered against the nylon shade. Its noise mingled with the booming of her heart when Jacob wrapped his arm around her, drawing her closer. Despite the winter chill, his gesture warmed every inch of her. If only the moment could last forever….

The rain stopped as they reached Water Tower Place. After folding his umbrella, Jacob turned toward Pearson Street, keeping his sight on a white carriage. "Great." His grin reminded her of a crescent moon. "I was afraid they might have left due to the rain."

"You mean the carriage? That's on your mind?"

"Mmm-hmm. I was supposed to bring you here the other night, but…well, here we are for our first Valentine's Day."

Jacob offered his elbow and ushered Rachel to the carriage. The white horse nodded at her as if welcoming her.

"Good evening. Would you care for a ride?" The coachman tipped his black top hat to Jacob.

"Yes."

"Thirty minutes or one hour?"

"One hour."

"Sure. It'll run down Michigan Avenue, circle around, and return here. My name is Jim." He opened the door and beckoned for them to step inside.

Jacob helped Rachel into the carriage and climbed in.

"Let me take a picture of you." Jim took his camera from his coat pocket. "Sit closer, please."

Rachel and Jacob shifted in their seats until their hips touched. Before Jim had finished counting to three, Jacob bent his head and pressed his lips on Rachel's. She leaned in, shivers rippling through her.

A few seconds passed as they waited for the Polaroid. Jim slid the photo into a white paper frame, gave it to Jacob, and shut the door.

"Perfect." Jacob handed it to her.

*

Rachel peered at the glossy photo, skimming her fingers over the smooth surface. She folded her arms on the desk and rested her chin atop her elbow, smiling at Jacob's image. Her prince.

The doorbell chimed. Rachel replaced the photo in her wooden keepsake box, slid her chair back, and rose. She strode out of the bedroom, reached the door, and lifted the corner of the panel curtain to peek out. Jacob. Her heart leapt. She smoothed her flowing skirt. "Good morning."

"How are you?" Dressed in a dark blue suit, he moseyed in and gave her a bouquet of red roses in a pink sleeve.

"So pretty." She strolled across the foyer and set the bouquet on the kitchen counter.

"Are your parents at home?"

"They went grocery shopping." She filled the vase with water and arranged the flowers. "Have a seat."

Jacob tenderly clasped her hand as she was edging to the sofa in the adjacent family room. He drew her closer, cupped her face, and brought his lips to hers. The kiss increased in pressure as the scent of his cologne billowed up to her nostrils. Sinking into his softness, she envisioned them snuggling inside the same carriage, tasting that romantic moment afresh.

He eased away. "You're beautiful." He turned to her skirt. "Ah, the navy blue is similar to the color of your ball gown."

"Yup. You look very handsome in your suit, too—actually you always look good." She adjusted his burgundy tie.

He dug in his pants pocket for a CD. "My buddy is a photographer. He just gave me this CD yesterday. He recorded the carriages near the Water Tower the same night we had the ride about four months ago. That's a day to treasure. My love for you will never end, just as Christ's love will last forever."

"I thank God for bringing you into my life." She blinked to hold off her tears. "I wonder if your friend saw us?"

He shrugged.

Rachel walked to the entertainment shelf and inserted the disc into the CD player. Moving to the couch, she sat beside Jacob. Hooking her arm around his, she watched the white carriages trotting down Michigan Avenue.

DICKY TO has published a Christian romance story in *Harpstring* Magazine and has also completed a romance radio series based on the lives of the biblical patriarchs for Christ to the World Ministries. He is a member of American Christian Fiction Writers.

http://dickyto.com

Angel on Fourth Street

* * *

Susan M. Baganz

Top-secret missions were never all the movies make them out to be. He was glad this would be his last.

Sean stepped out of his black Ultima and moved to the sidewalk on the dark street. The Bottoms Up bar was around the corner on Fourth. Its neon sign swung out over the concrete as he walked toward the building. His palms were sweaty. It had been 18 long months since he'd seen or even spoken to his bride. The months in between had been torture for him, literally. He could still feel the vestiges of continued healing in his body. All he'd wanted for the past few hectic weeks was to surprise Jessi by coming home on their anniversary. She still lived in their apartment. His key had worked in the lock, but she hadn't been home when he arrived. He had looked around a bit before finding her calendar with this place written on it. It also had a heart with their names on it. He smiled to himself.

Now he was downtown, hoping to surprise her, although this was not quite the romantic location he would have chosen. As he drew nearer, there was a commotion at the door. A woman with her coat half on stumbled out onto the pavement. The heavy bass of a country tune followed. He caught her before she could fall. She looked up at him with a blank stare and a silly grin.

Jessica? Recognition slammed him in the gut.

A burly man followed, coming to an abrupt halt before Sean. "Let her go, man. She's with me." The brute was dressed in dirty ripped jeans, construction-style boots, and a wife-beater T-shirt that said, *Give blood—play rugby.* He reeked of beer and sweat.

The girl in Sean's arms stiffened as she turned to look at the loser. "I am most certainly *not* with you," she spat out.

Sean's years of military training brought him to high alert at the man's threatening stance and tone. He'd hoped to live a peaceful life now and had left any weapons of his past occupation back at the base. In comparison to this man before him, he probably looked soft, wearing dress pants, a crisp white dress shirt, suit coat, and tie. He glanced down at his disheveled wife. Her blonde hair was pulled into a ponytail, and her blue eyes appeared glassy as she gazed up at him. Whatever it took, he would protect her.

"I know you, don't I?" Her eyes squinted. She'd obviously forgone her contacts, but where were her glasses? She looked adorable in her confusion.

"Come on, Jessica, you promised me," the bully said as he flexed his muscles in an attempt to intimidate and reached a hand out for her.

But Jessica continued to gaze at Sean. Slowly she turned to glare at the loser, her speech slurred. "I promised you nothing, Artie. You can leave now. I'm with him." She placed a hand on Sean's chest, and his heart flipped.

Sean wrapped an arm around her waist and pulled her close as they faced Artie. "You heard the lady. You will leave *now*." Sean spoke low, but his voice was edged with titanium. He had no weapons, but even with his hands and feet he was a highly trained killer. He could feel adrenaline pump through his veins as his body prepared for a possible fight. This certainly wasn't how he'd hoped to spend his anniversary. But then, in the past 18 months, when had anything ever happened like it was supposed to?

Artie's eyes darted nervously between Sean and Jessica. He shifted on his feet, clenching and unclenching his fists. Sean stared him down. The man finally turned and walked back into the bar, leaving them alone on the dark sidewalk with only the neon lights from the bar sign providing illumination.

Sean relaxed and let out a breath of air he didn't know he'd been holding. He turned Jessica toward him, pulled her coat up over her shoulders, and held her gently by her upper arms as he bent to look in her eyes.

Jessica stared at him, and her head wobbled. "You're cute. You remind me of…" And with that, her eyes closed and she fell limp.

Sean swept her up and took her to his car. Maneuvering her into the front seat, he reclined it back and buckled her in. He tried to wake her up, but she didn't respond. Her pulse was slow and weak. Saying a quick prayer, he drove her to the emergency room. She couldn't be drunk. She hated beer.

A short while later, Sean sat in the hospital room, his shirt unbuttoned, his tie loosened, and his sleeves rolled up. His jacket lay over the arm of the recliner. His suspicion had been right. The date rape drug had been slipped into her drink. Her blood-alcohol level had been so low it was almost nonexistent, whereas the amount of the tranquilizer was enough to have killed her. Sean thanked God for bringing him to her when she needed him most.

Needed *him* most? She'd needed him over the past 18 months, and he hadn't been there. He'd been listed as missing in action and had suffered severe injuries in Iraq. If not for the kind ministrations of a missionary family, he would have died. When he recovered, he completed his secret mission for the government...and returned home to find his bride in serious trouble.

Why would she ever go to a bar? It wasn't her style. But she had no way of knowing he was alive and well. The military had been unwilling to tell her, due to the sensitive nature of his mission. Could that have driven her to this? He shook his head. That part of his life was over now. Over for good. He was here in the States to stay. He hoped. But there were never any guarantees for career military personnel.

He watched Jessica hooked up to the monitors but breathing, thankfully, on her own. His heart ached for the pain his service to their country had cost her. Tonight could have turned out tragically different. The weight of that settled around him like a wet woolen blanket, suffocating him in guilt. He should have been here.

But his country had needed him too. His injuries had complicated things. She didn't even recognize him with his slighter weight and different haircut. New scars littered his body. Would she find those repulsive? He cried out to God as he held his head in his hands and wept for all the should-have-beens.

Deep in his spirit he was reminded that God was a God of grace and mercy, and He had brought Sean back in time to protect his wife. God had seen him through the war and the trials in a foreign land. God saw and knew the pain of both of their hearts. If God could bring him here to this moment in time, he could certainly trust God for their future. The weight lifted, and he settled back into the leather recliner and slept....

A warning prickled the back of his neck. Someone was staring at him. He could feel it on the edges of sleep. He tensed. Where was he again? He inhaled slowly. Wherever he was smelled funny, and he could hear a steady beeping. Then it came back to him. He wasn't in Iraq, but in a hospital room in the States. He let himself relax. Opening his eyes, he saw white everywhere with soft blue walls as a backdrop. Jessica was lying there, squinting, watching him. He rose, went to her purse, and dug for her glasses. Gently placing them on her face, he moved a strand of hair off her cheek.

Her eyes focused, but he could tell she still didn't recognize him. He reached down with his left hand to clasp her left hand. There was a white line where her wedding ring had been, and his heart cracked a bit that she had removed it. He had saved two years for that ring, starting after their first date, certain she would be his. Her hand warmed at his touch.

He gazed into her eyes. "Jessie...did you doubt I would return for you?" He croaked the words out. The man who could speak with authority to soldiers in battle was struggling when faced with his wife. Uncertainty filled his heart. What if she didn't want him? The thought was devastating.

Her eyes widened as she glanced from their joined hands to his wide gold wedding band and then up to his face. "Sean?" Tears began to stream down her cheeks.

Reaching for a tissue with his free hand, he wiped the tears, then held the tissue for her to blow her nose. She did so noisily, like a foghorn…something he'd always teased her about but secretly loved. He smiled at her and tossed the tissue to the can by the side of the bed.

Her eyes closed, and her grip loosened in his hand.

"Jessi?"

She didn't respond, so he sat back down to wait and pray as she slept.

Awhile later he returned from the snack room with a cup of instant coffee that tasted like heaven compared to what he got in the field. Entering the room, he saw her eyes open. She seemed startled when he turned the corner by her hospital bed. Little lines appeared on her forehead and between her eyes. He came to set the coffee down and put her glasses back on her face.

"You were listed as missing," she whispered. "It was after a horrible attack, and so many died. But they couldn't find you. They told me you were probably dead."

He gave her half a grin. "Not happy to see me, Jess?"

"How are you here?"

"Later, Sweetheart. I'm sorry you had to go through all you endured in my absence. I'm home now and hope to make it up to you somehow."

"Make it up? How can you make up the past year and a half? You waltz back into my life and want to pick up as if nothing happened?" He could hear the pain and loneliness in her voice. She never was one for surprises.

"You were drugged last night, Jess. If I hadn't 'waltzed in' when I did, you would likely have been raped and dead by now." His voice was soft, trying to take the hardness out of the reality.

She gasped. Her eyes held his as if to test the veracity of his words. "I don't remember much. Only that you were like a guardian angel. I felt safe in your arms."

"I told you I would come back to you."

"Pretty words, Sean, but you're human, and I thought you had died. I thought God had taken my best friend from me." Tears began again and Sean wiped them away with his thumb. She brushed his hand aside. "You couldn't have called or emailed or Skyped to tell me you were well?"

"I was alive—but not well—and in enemy territory. Knowing you were waiting for me back home was the only thing that kept me fighting to come back from the hell I was in. I had no way to contact you. I can explain more later. I feel awful that you suffered so in my absence."

Her body shuddered as she fought back more tears. Sean smiled. His redoubtable wife. She was his treasure, a gift from God he would try to never take for granted. He had missed her so much.

"If the doctor will let you come home, we can start fresh, you and I. Would that be okay?"

Jessica nodded. She reached to touch his unshaven chin, and he leaned forward to make it easier for her. Her frown deepened as her hands moved to his head and traced the scars amongst the short hair and along his cheekbone and forehead. "You almost died, didn't you?"

Sean nodded. "But I didn't. I came back for you. I'd hoped to surprise you for our anniversary. I had so many dreams of how wonderful our reunion would be."

Jessica dropped her hand. "I was heartbroken you might never be coming back. Connie, a friend from work, invited me to meet her at the bar to visit and play pool. I didn't want to be in our apartment. Alone. Missing you." She shrugged. "I kept getting hit on and finally decided to leave."

"But someone had other plans for you. I'm glad I came in time, Love. I would have been inconsolable to learn that anything had happened to you."

Jessica smiled. "But you are here now. Thank you, Sean."

"Anytime." He smiled down at her.

The nurse came in to disconnect Jessica from all her apparatus and Sean left so she could dress. When he returned, he held out a bouquet of flowers. "Happy anniversary, Jessi. I'm home."

Jessica walked to him and took the flowers. She brought them to her nose, inhaled, then set them on the bed. Clasping her arms around his neck, she pulled his face down to hers. His arms went around her waist as he waited for her next move.

"Kiss me, Sean. Please? I have so missed your kiss."

He willingly obliged. Her kiss felt like home.

Mission accomplished.

SUSAN M. BAGANZ is a stay-at-home mom who loves going for a cup of chai with a friend or reading a good book while snuggling her dog. Her kids roll their eyes when Mom's in the writing zone, but they give her hugs anyway. She also writes historical and contemporary romances.

www.susanbaganz.com

Heart Choice

* * *

MILLICENT NJUE

The drive to the countryside was fun enough. There was so much to see for one born and brought up in town as the bus made its way through the country road. Even though she'd been down this road several times, she couldn't get enough of the scenic beauty stretching before her. Gulping the fresh air, she thought of the lazy days ahead at her aunt's farm.

Absorbed in the scenery, she didn't notice the man sitting next to her, busily reading a book as they shuttled along. It was only when they made a stop that she glanced at him as he made his way down the aisle to get a cold drink. What struck her most was his kindly face. Soon they were on their way once again, and she lost herself to the scenery once more.

The long drive came to an end six hours later. Tired as she was, Janice was eager to catch a cab to her aunt's home. She smiled when she thought of the warm, inviting kitchen that awaited her at the end of the ride. She was so engrossed in her fantasies she didn't pay much attention to the man joining her in the back seat. He requested to use the same cab as he was going her way, and it was only a 10-minute drive. Soon they parted ways as he was dropped off first, and she headed further on.

Her auntie met her in the driveway as soon as the cab pulled up. Janice always felt welcome here and couldn't wait to enjoy the delicacies lined up in the warm kitchen. Since her uncle was out visiting a friend, and their children were grown up and had homes of their own, the two had the house to themselves for now. Soon Janice and her auntie were chatting and laughing like old friends. It felt good to be away from the city in this quiet neighborhood where everyone knew their neighbors. Janice looked forward to going with her auntie to drop off tea with some neighbors, as was the custom. The next few weeks would be fun—and wonderfully quiet—as she helped around the farm. It was a good way to spend her time off work every year.

Soon Janice fell into the routine of late nights sitting around the fireplace, exchanging stories with the elderly couple. Sipping endless mugs of coffee, they shared jokes and experiences. Janice enjoyed watching the two retire once she managed to wear them down with her tales. Her uncle usually went upstairs first and would soon call to his wife to join him. Janice admired the genuine love the two had that only got more evident with age.

The first Saturday, Janice was all set to visit her aunt's friends. A middle-aged couple, they reared chickens and usually had their hands full. On previous visits she'd walked in to their house to find them in the backyard tending to the chickens.

Driving up in the old car that afternoon, Janice was so busy chatting with her aunt that she didn't notice the tall young man staring at her in the driveway. Looking up as he opened their car door, she stopped in her tracks, noticing the familiar face of the guy she'd shared a cab with on her ride from the city. So this had been his destination. She'd wondered, as he'd offered to be dropped off on the roadside so she could be on her way.

When he held out his hand, she was unsettled by his lingering gaze, even though he quickly averted his eyes. Soon Janice got busy helping out in the chicken coop while trying to shove away any thoughts of the stranger. It was while they were having tea and biscuits later in the afternoon that their bubbly hostess made the introductions of her nephew, Joshua, whom she said was visiting on his return from a trip to faraway lands. When their hands touched during their introductory shake, Janice felt a rush of warmth.

Joshua offered to walk her around the farm as the two women caught up on gossip. She accepted his offer reluctantly, since she'd only just met him. But anything was better than sitting around two older women who obviously could use some time alone. But it was when he reached out a hand to assist her over the hedge that she felt the now-familiar rush of warmth.

The walk turned out to be a good chance to get to know each other better. It was there she learned of his work offering medical services abroad to needy people. She became so engrossed in the stories of his encounters that she didn't notice the approaching darkness until her aunt's voice brought her back to earth with a jolt. They had to be on their way home in time to start the evening meal.

That evening, Janice was more subdued than usual. She kept hearing Joshua's voice as he had recounted the harrowing tales of human suffering he'd dealt with during his work. She remembered the way his eyes lit up each time he shared how he'd managed to ease the suffering of a child. Flashes of his kind eyes and the warmth of his touch flooded back to her.

That night Janice fought hard to find sleep. Never before had she met a man who invoked such feelings. She wrestled with cutting short her stay and fleeing back to the city. Eventually she fell asleep with thoughts of a tall, handsome man with the kindest eyes she'd ever seen....

The following morning Janice woke to laughter coming from the kitchen. It seemed she had overslept, as she could smell coffee brewing as her aunt chatted with her early morning guest. It was one of the many things Janice loved about this place. Every so often neighbors dropped in to chat.

But she wasn't prepared for the person who leaned on the kitchen door, both hands in his pockets. She almost ran back up to her room, but it was too late. Joshua had already seen her. Warmth rushed to her face. He made her discomfiture worse by reaching out his hand. This time she froze; even her aunt's endless chatter faded in the background.

Excusing herself to freshen up, Janice hurried to her room. She slumped on her bed, trying to make out her feelings. It was an attraction she couldn't deny, however much she tried, and she'd made a fool of herself. How could a mere handshake cause her so much panic? At 23 years of age what she felt in his presence was like nothing she'd experienced. How could she feel so much for someone she hardly knew? She was determined not to make a further fool of herself as she went down to breakfast minutes later. How wrong she was.

This time around, her visit to the farm went faster than she expected. With each passing day she and Joshua found excuses to be together, and her feelings deepened. Janice could only think of his declaration of love when they had walked in the fields. It was a moment to treasure for a long time.

On that afternoon, they had sneaked off together, both knowing they had little time left together and determined to make the best of it. At the edge of the property he had taken her into his arms. She hadn't had the strength to resist him and had welcomed his lips. His kiss had only served to heighten their passion as the two young lovers remained entangled in each other's arms. When they finally came up for air, he declared how he felt.

Janice couldn't remember ever feeling so excited. She dreamed of Joshua every night, and her whole being longed for his touch every waking day. She was happiest when she was with him, locked in his arms.

She was convinced that love had come to dock at last.

MILLICENT NJUE has been writing Christian articles for a long time now and delights in bringing out life's emotions through words. She lives in the city of Nairobi in Kenya. Besides her regular job she enjoys time with her husband and her three kids. Millicent has green fingers too and enjoys time at the farm in the countryside.

http://wwwunmeasuredgrace.blogspot.com

The Value of a Penny

* * *

CANDICE SUE PATTERSON

Josie Bennett sighed into the cloud of steam erupting from the coffee mugs. Through the fog, she memorized the strong profile of the handsome man at table four. His denim blue eyes offset his tan skin in perfect harmony. A bell chimed in the rear of the kitchen, reminding her she had a job to do. Cradling the coffee pot onto the warmer, she wiped down the counter where her daydream had provoked an overflow.

"Why don't you take a picture? Then you could swoon anytime you want instead of the short hour he occupies your section every morning."

Josie pulled her eyes away and turned to Marge Sutton, who was as ornery as the curled-up collar on her striped uniform.

"There's no denying he's beautiful enough to paint his portrait in the Sistine Chapel, but you're never going to get anywhere just gaping at him." Marge loaded her tray with French toast and a side of bacon and eggs.

Josie frowned.

"You're not fooling me, Blondie; I see how you look at him."

"Why, Marge, are your cataracts acting up again?" Josie arranged the cups of java on her tray.

Marge scowled, deepening the lines around her eyes and mouth. "I had them removed last year, and you know it. In fact, my eyes are the only things left on this old body that work like they're supposed to. I see how you look at him, and I know what you're thinking, but he may surprise you."

As Josie balanced the tray on her left hand, her gaze wandered back to table four. The man pulled up the sleeve of his button-down shirt, checking the time on a watch that would no doubt take her two paychecks and a month's worth of tips to pay for. What was he doing in a place like this? She sighed. "This isn't a fairy tale, and I'm no Cinderella."

"I don't know about that. You have an evil stepmother, and I bet if we looked hard enough, we could find some mice in this kitchen somewhere." Marge winked and sashayed across the dingy black-and-white tile floor.

Josie weaved through the tables in her corner, reducing her load to the corresponding customers. She delivered Blue Eyes his usual cup of joe, rewarded by his slow, tempting smile.

"Good morning, Josie."

"Morning, Jake. You ordering the usual, or are you going to be brave and step outside of the pancake box?"

He passed her the menu, brushing his fingers across hers in the transfer, spreading fire up her arm. His business attire exuded money, mingled with a spicy cologne she couldn't decipher. Her heart kicked against her ribs as she wished for an opportunity to snuggle closer and detect the scent's undertones.

"I stick with what I know. I'll have the usual."

She nodded at her serving tray. The very reason she'd never bothered to get to know him in his three months as a faithful customer—other than the way he liked his coffee, where he'd grown up, and the fact he didn't like to chat much on a Monday morning…

"I'll get the order in right away." Josie dragged her heavy heart back to the kitchen. She'd been a fool to entertain the notion there could ever be something between them. Opposites didn't attract when they lived on opposite ends of the money spectrum. Men of his stature desired a trophy wife, not a waitress in a run-down diner who could barely make ends meet.

That's what she needed to be focused on—a way to make some extra cash. At least that would put to rest any fear of losing her apartment this month. Hard telling what would happen to her job once the new owner revealed himself. They'd all be fortunate not to show up one day to find the place bulldozed over with the frame of a high-rise erected in its place. She'd seen it happen to these old buildings too many times before.

The national news blared across the TV in the corner of the small kitchen. The news anchor interviewed a reality star who gave explicit details of her weekend in Jersey. Josie shook her head. This woman hadn't a financial care in the world while living one never-ending party. Josie worked two jobs just to afford her groceries.

God will provide. He always does. Besides, the woman's lifestyle was proof she lacked the most important thing in life: a peace that money can't buy and that passes all understanding. *Being in the center of God's will is more important than money.* And she knew this was where God wanted her to be—a testimony to these strangers. The bell sounded, and Josie loaded her tray with buttermilk pancakes and a carafé of maple syrup.

Jake folded his newspaper when she approached. "So how long have you worked here, Josie?"

She plunked the golden stack in front of him. "About five years now."

His brows arched. "Five years? That's a long time to stay in a place like this. What keeps you here?"

Josie shifted her weight to the foot that wasn't complaining in her worn tennis shoes. As she topped his coffee, the cold winter morning she'd first set foot in this room flooded her memory. The Davises not only gave her a much-needed job but a Bible, sharing with her the gift of God's love. "The owners were always good to me."

"Were?" He raised the mug to his lips.

She stomped the idea of imagining what it would be like on the receiving end and focused on the chipped corner of the red Formica tabletop. "The diner's been sold to some starched-collar entrepreneur. Rumor has it he's got big plans for this place that don't include the food industry. So enjoy those pancakes while you can. Once Scrooge gets his affairs in order, you'll be going elsewhere for a good meal."

Jake's body shot forward, and he set down his mug, coughing forcefully into his napkin. He pulled it away from his mouth and chuckled. "Is that so?"

She twisted her apron string around her index finger. Had she said something funny? She laid his ticket at the edge of the table. "Let me know if there's anything else I can get you."

Josie returned to the muggy kitchen. Through the cook's window, she watched Jake bow his head to give thanks for his meal—a rare quality to find in public nowadays. This man not only made logical sense but confused the daylights out of her. Could he really be different? She found it hard to abandon her instinctual roots after being snubbed by folks with money her whole life.

As the breakfast crowd transpired, Josie cleared the dishes from Jake's deserted table. A lonesome penny mocked her as a thank-you for her labor. She ran her thumb over the copper image of Abraham Lincoln, the rent issue resurfacing in her mind. She must've offended him, because he always left her a decent tip. Josie's hopes plunged. He wasn't so different after all.

*

Jake Waters left the comfort of the diner and hustled down the snow-dusted sidewalk toward his office. The wind nipped his ears and the tip of his nose, but the image of Josie in her pink-striped uniform kept him warm. She'd probably breathe fire when she cleared his table. Her efforts were worth far more than a penny, but what she wouldn't realize was the value of it.

As a young boy, his father scolded him for plucking pennies off the ground. "Don't waste your time on pocket change, son. It isn't worth anything, and it only weighs you down. Set your sights on greater things, make wise investments, and triple your money. That's the only way to get somewhere in life. Money makes the world go round."

His father's deep, aristocratic voice gravitated toward bad advice, but that day had been the worst. Jake had obeyed, following in his father's footsteps—until the day he chanced upon a worn penny on the doorstep of Joe's Diner. He recognized the nostalgic building as the one his real-estate competitor had their eye on. Though Jake didn't buy into superstition, he'd found the coin Lincoln-side up and took it as a good sign nonetheless.

He'd tucked himself at a table for one in the back corner of the room. What he expected was a bad cup of coffee in a noisy atmosphere of sassy waitresses. What he didn't expect was a curvy blonde with glossy red lips and a sense of humor to boot. He couldn't take his eyes off Josie. She joked with the customers, listened to the ones who clearly needed a friend, quieted a screaming toddler with a pack of crackers and a pat on the head. She had a way with people he'd never seen. Centripetal force set his heart in motion, transporting him back every morning like a hungry bear to a campsite.

Jake smiled at the memory, entering the warm confines of his office. "Mr. Davis, I apologize for my tardiness." He extended his hand, greeting his guest. "Breakfast was exceptionally amusing this morning."

"Please, call me Joe, and you needn't apologize on my account." He settled into the black leather chair, resting his hands around his thick, gray scalp. "I'm not in any hurry. I'm retired now."

Jake returned the man's carefree grin and clasped the cold metal keys Joe had deposited on his desk.

"She's all yours now. Take good care of her."

The key ring jangled to the bottom of Jake's pocket. "You have my word."

Joe raised his unruly eyebrows and blew out a loud breath. He stood and made his way toward the door, his dark eyes flashing with uncertainty. "What on earth are you going to do with a diner?"

Jake chuckled. "I have no idea. But if I didn't buy it, my competitor would, and I hated to see those good people lose their jobs."

Joe nodded. "It's mighty honorable of you to care. God bless you, son."

The door clicked shut and Jake stared at its dark finish. The word *son* had never held such warmth from his father. That restaurant felt like home more than any estate he'd ever lived in and, though he didn't even know her last name, Josie somehow felt like family.

It was her testimony, after all, that led him to Christ. He'd overheard her invite a customer to evening services during breakfast that morning and found himself on the back pew. After a thought-provoking message by a visiting missionary, he watched her dig through her purse as the offering plate approached. Though Josie never changed her expression, he could see the layers of worry in her eyes along with her threadbare coat. Like the widow in the Bible who gave her last mite.

Josie's hidden vulnerability brought out a protective streak he didn't know he possessed. He wanted to shelter her from life's hardships, be the reason for that smile on her pixie face. But how would she react when she discovered he was her new boss?

*

Josie stifled a yawn as the last drips of coffee gurgled from the reservoir into the carafé. She poured a cup and settled onto a chair in the dining room. The staff had been instructed to start their shift a half-hour early to meet the new owner. Tension gripped the room with icy fingers as all awaited their doom.

The bell above the front door jingled, and in stepped the famous blue eyes that haunted her every night. Didn't Jake realize they weren't open yet? He shed his charcoal dress coat and made his way to the front of the crowd. A knot formed in Josie's gut as he made himself at home like he belonged here.

"I'm looking forward to getting to know all of you. I'm Jake Waters, the new owner. My friends call me Scrooge." He winked at Josie.

She winced. Her face burned 10 degrees hotter, and she concentrated on the frayed end of her apron string.

"Let's hope he's only stingy with his money," Marge said in a stage whisper, directed to Josie's ear. The cantankerous woman elbowed her ribs.

If Josie had the option of crawling under the table and disappearing from existence, she would have.

Jake slid his hands into his pockets and the room held its breath. "I hate to admit that I don't know the first thing about running a diner—or cooking for that matter—but I'm willing to learn. That being said, I'm sure you're wondering why I'd purchase this place. Truth is, an investment firm wanted the property for reasons other than customer service, and I hated to see the place go. There's one minor change I'd like to make right away, but other than that, keep up the good work and have a great day."

Josie felt the strong brew making its way back up her throat. Her position opening for employment would no doubt be the first change after the way she'd spoken yesterday. Now what would she do? Tears stung the back of her eyelids, and she blinked them away.

Jake sauntered up to her with a cocky grin. "I told the dry-cleaner not to starch my collar this time."

She steeled herself against what would inevitably come next, twisting an apron string around her finger until it throbbed. "Why didn't you tell me who you were?"

"If I'd have revealed myself too soon, I may not have been able to witness everyone's true colors. Now about that change…"

Her feet filled with lead as she stepped away. "I'll get my things."

He lightly grabbed her wrist. "Where are you going?"

"I'm fired. I get it."

"Fired? Why would I fire you?"

Josie's mouth lined with cotton. "I assumed—"

Jake shook his head. He relayed the details of how he'd acquired the place and the way her testimony had affected his life. "The only change I'm worried about making is converting table four into a table for two."

The tenderness in his gaze embraced her, and she wished his arms would follow suit. Her heart sped like a racehorse at the Kentucky Derby.

His lips twisted into a sideways grin. "I'm tired of sitting alone."

She willed the butterflies in her stomach to cease flight. "That depends."

"On what?"

Reaching into her apron pocket, she tossed him a penny. "You're going to have to start leaving better tips." She grinned and pulled up an extra chair to table four.

"Never underestimate the value of a penny." He pressed the coin into her palm.

Josie tugged his tie, pulling him closer. His lips brushed hers, as soft as a summer breeze. She'd never felt so rich.

CANDICE SUE PATTERSON studied at The Institute of Children's Literature and is a member of American Christian Fiction Writers. She loves to bake in her spare time and shares her passion with others on her blog, "Candi Cakes—Baking & Cake Design."

http://candicakes-bakingdesign.blogspot.com

The Unfinished Story

* * *

KRISTINA STORER

The blue and white china clinked together as Roberta angled the small cup out of the glass-fronted cabinet doors. She waited patiently at the small round table as the coffee pot on the counter percolated. Her thoughts wandered back in time to days when the delicate cups held the thick, dark coffee for two, not one. Right there at that worn blue table, too. The table had been just the right size for her and Dempsey. Oh, it did fill up most of their small country kitchen, causing a bit of commotion as one reached to load the dishwasher and the other shuffled around, gathering the milk and cereal to start breakfast. But as they settled down with their little china cups and bran cereal, it brought them close enough for the intimate conversations she looked forward to every morning.

The chairs had seen better days. Through the years, large pieces had chipped off of the arms or the backs, a result of Dempsey shoving the chair back as he finished the last drops of his black coffee. Those chairs almost always managed to catch on the striped Berber rug and fall backward, their frail frames unable to stand the impact. Andrew had faithfully super-glued, hot-glued, or wood-glued them back together, though.

Andrew, their firstborn grandchild, was more like a son than a grandson to Roberta and Dempsey. His parents had taught him the value of God, family, and respect for his elders. He was always bursting at the seams to help with any little repairs around the house, and these days it seemed there was always more than enough to keep him busy in that department. He absolutely soaked up any words of advice or suggestions that Dempsey had to offer him. In Andrew's eyes, Dempsey was the leading authority on fishing, repairing tractors, hunting, and even girls. Girls! Dempsey was already in his early 70s when most of that advice was given!

Roberta felt a little leap in her heart just thinking about Dempsey's advice to Andrew on girls. And she had to admit, Dempsey certainly knew a thing or two about charming women. Well, this woman anyway. He'd held her interest, along with her heart, for 65 precious years. They had been inseparable. She had worn his engagement ring on the finger of her youthful, tanned hand at the age of 21. She had held his feeble, shaking hand with her soft and age-spotted one at the age of 86. Dempsey had spoiled her, no doubt about it. It was a wonder she could do anything on her own. But the love they had felt was profound and reciprocal. As much as he lavished her with little gifts on her birthday, opened every single door, or chauffeured her around town, she built him up with words of encouragement and praise for being the incredible husband, father, and grandfather that he was.

She took another sip of coffee, running her finger across the wood grain on the top of the table. She thought about Sundays with Dempsey. He would open the passenger door of their white Buick and hold her steady as she lowered herself down into the bucket seat. At that stage in their life, they always arrived everywhere at least 20 minutes early. Dempsey would pull up to the small covered walkway at the church entrance and shuffle around the car to open her door. He'd patiently steady Roberta as she lifted herself up and then drive off to park the Buick. He wasn't in much better shape than she was in those days, but it was no matter. He would continue to honor her until he was no longer able.

He'd slip his arm through her elbow before she had taken more than a few steps toward the front doors, and she'd pick up two of the morning's bulletins, handing one to him. Their church was small, often struggling to survive, but it was warm and welcoming. Coming to a halt at "their" old wooden pew, Dempsey would step aside, ushering Roberta in first before sidling in close on her left. The familiar hymns were a little harder to hear as the years went on, but the comfort they brought would seep down into the couple's very souls. The church pianist, Mrs. Brown, was on in years herself and one or two notes would often waft through the air, just a bit off-key, but no one seemed to mind.

Roberta would raise her hand when the pastor asked for prayer requests or praise announcements. There was always an engagement or new baby or job promotion to report in their family. "God Be With You Till We Meet Again" would begin playing soon after, and Roberta and Dempsey would begin their slow retreat back to the car. Dempsey usually chose to take Long Leaf Road back to the house because it was peaceful and generally a nice drive.

Roberta drifted back to the present with the thought of Long Leaf. She drove that road now for very different reasons. She took that road because it was a "back road" between her small town and her house, and she was able to avoid the highway. It also led her past the cemetery that she visited almost daily. She had to do a lot of things on her own now. God had blessed her with an uncanny strength to "keep on keeping on," as she liked to say. Not that she didn't reminisce and feel sadness try to tug on the strings of her heart from time to time, but she was filled with a peace that allowed her to handle all those feelings.

Her cup was now half full, and she considered getting a refill to warm up the bit of coffee that was left. The two-cup coffee pot had always seemed to barely hold enough for her and Dempsey to have their morning fill, but now it was often left half full. Light coffee-cup rings could still be seen on the tabletop surface, no matter how hard Roberta had cleaned it through the years. She and Dempsey had entertained so many different types of company at that table.

Early on, they'd visited with town committee members as Dempsey had ran for a small public office or two. Many coworkers had held conversations at the table before leaving for the field with Dempsey to mark trees and work timber. Church members stopped by occasionally, always grateful for the coffee and biscuits Roberta had ready. And in the later years, there were dear widowed friends who stopped in unannounced, yet expected, for the coffee as much as the companionship.

Oh, and the family members who had shared that table! It seemed only yesterday that Joan and James had shared the news that their first child was on the way. A grandchild for Roberta and Dempsey, imagine! Dempsey had slapped the top of the table with his palm in an exclamation of joy. The love they had felt for those grandchildren was beyond their scope of understanding. It was somehow different from the love they felt for their own children, yet deep and wonderful all the same. There had been six more birth announcements through the years after that. They had seven grandchildren in all, each with their own personalities and gifts to offer the world.

Roberta and Dempsey had even had the opportunity to meet all 11 of their great-grandchildren. Their lives had been so blessed and fulfilled to see their grandchildren beginning their families and trying their best to put into practice the values they had been taught. There were sure to be trials and circumstances to push their faith to the limits, but they had a solid foundation to draw from. Their parents had worked tirelessly to instill patience, hope, and love into the lives of their children.

Roberta and Dempsey's love story was not over. Roberta knew it lived on in many ways. It lived in the legacy Dempsey had left to their children and grandchildren in the words of advice on life and love. It lived on in the example he and Roberta had set together. Theirs was a love to aspire to, certainly. Their story was also unfinished in that Roberta had faith that, in this life, it had only taken an intermission. Her heart longed for the chapters she and Dempsey would write when they were united once again.

For now, though, she would look forward to the visits that were sure to come from her children, grandchildren, and great-grandchildren. She would seat the great-grandchildren here at the worn blue table and serve them cookies and crackers from the special drawer near the refrigerator. She would lean back in her blue chair and revel in their laughter as they played with the now-vintage toys she kept in the little basket by the window in the sunroom. And their love would add richness to the part of her soul that was reserved for the rest of her life story.

KRISTINA STORER is an aspiring writer and mother of two. She is blessed to have three grandparents still in her life, and believes there is much to be learned from the love stories of a "seasoned" generation. She's living out her own romance story with her high school sweetheart, Bill.
    http://guitarsfrogsandvisionsofpink.blogspot.com

Young Hearts

* * *

BEVERLY LaHote Schwind

"Mother, are you sure this is what you want?" fretted Maggie. "This is ridiculous!"

Maggie sprayed gravel as she abruptly pulled into a parking space near the entrance of the sprawling brick building.

Mrs. Julia Morgan stepped out of the black Buick sedan, her cane touching the ground first and then her feet. She carried a large quilted purse, and her stylish glasses hung from a chain around her neck. She looked up with approval at the sign in the entrance, *Sunset Ridge Assisted Living Campus.*

"OK, Mother, but when you change your mind, I'll fly here and move you to our home," Maggie conceded.

Julia nodded at Maggie as the two walked through the automatic doors and into the facility.

Stephan Kratz, the director, greeted them. "It's good to see you again, Maggie. We're happy Julia will be a resident here."

Maggie politely smiled, but the crease between her eyes betrayed her protest of her mother's decision.

"I'll show you to the apartment, and you can let me know if all the belongings you sent ahead are in order."

The two followed Mr. Kratz down the wide hallway. A plaque reading *Julia A. Morgan* marked the door of her apartment.

"It's lovely," Julia commented as she gazed at her familiar pictures, now hanging on the wall. "There is my favorite recliner." She pointed to the mauve chair sitting near a reading lamp. "I will do my reading there...and napping." She laughed.

Maggie gave her mother a tearful hug and kiss. "I have to catch a plane, Mother. I'll call you soon. I love you."

"I'll be fine. Now you go and take care of that family."

Maggie began walking down the hall, then turned once again toward Julia, who threw her a kiss. *Lord, let her have peace about my decision...and don't let her feel guilty. Help her to understand. Be with me in this future journey. I'm scared.*

A tap on the door interrupted Julia's prayer, and she called, "Come in."

"Hi, my name is Emily, and I see by the name on the door you are Julia," said the cheerful redhead who strode into the room.

"Yes, I am; glad to meet you."

"Welcome to Sunset. It's almost dinner time, and you can sit at my table," invited Emily,

"Thank you," said Julia as she picked up her cane and started toward the door.

"I have never seen a cane like that," remarked Emily.

Julia stuck the can out in front of her, "I don't need it all the time, but when I'm tired, it's like holding on to another hand. I ordered this cane from Italy because it had the carved doves on it. If I have to carry a cane, I want it to be interesting and attractive. I call it 'Dovie.' Dovie and I have walked many miles together."

Emily pointed toward the table in Julia's dining room. The table was in front of a panoramic view of blooming day lilies and fern hanging baskets. "At night you can see the sunset over that ridge," explained Emily.

Emily's tinted red hair fit her outgoing personality, and she loved sporting an abundance of bright necklaces and bracelets. With Emily's help, Julia programmed herself to the activities and schedules of the facility. Emily knew the events in the facility because she wrote their monthly newsletter. She interviewed all new residents and employees.

Frequently, Julia struggled, missing Maggie and her few friends from church. Several times she called her daughter to say she was ready to leave, but the voice on the other end always seemed to be in a rush to be somewhere, and Julia knew she would be lonely there, too. She recalled what the chaplain said: "Adjusting takes time whenever you make a change." Julia prayed she had made the right choice.

Julia had been at Sunset six months when her life drastically changed. She noticed a new man at the morning Bible study. He was taller than any of the other men and had an abundance of gray, wavy hair. His warm smile was spontaneous.

"Who is the new resident?" she asked Emily.

"That is Samuel Solis," replied Emily. "He's a former tennis coach and comes from East Tennessee. He has diabetes and cut his leg working on a boat...nearly lost the leg. I guess his house was too much for him with his bad leg, so he is here."

Julia digested the information. "You sure know a lot about these people."

"Well, it's my job." Emily laughed. "You know, I have to get all the information I can for my newsletter. Samuel is a nice man, and he likes to play bridge. Maybe he could be our fourth?"

Emily didn't waste any time arranging the bridge game with Samuel. Now twice a week Emily and Julia played bridge with Samuel and Melvin.

*

Maggie called her mother weekly, questioning her on her activities and hoping to hear some loneliness in her mother's voice. But Julia was adjusting.

"I believe I am where I should be, Honey, and I do like it here. I have some friends I want you to meet when you visit. I play bridge quite often."

Maggie couldn't see the twinkle in her mother's eyes or the slight blush that crept up her thin neck as she spoke.

*

Samuel and Julia gradually relived their past lives with one another. They shared their heartaches, scars, and blessings. They held hands as they went to special events, and Julia did not need Dovie as her extra hand. Julia had not met Samuel's son but had seen a picture of him. Julia did not mention Samuel to her daughter; instead, she wanted her to meet him, personally.

No sooner had the Christmas and New Year's decorations vanished than the busy Activities Department asked the residents to begin cutting out decorations for an approaching celebration. Sunset Ridge was celebrating 25 years as an assisted living center. A Homecoming theme had been chosen, and a King and Queen would be picked. The television station had asked if they could do a special and film the gala event, so early preparation was in order. Dignitaries were coming. Sunset Ridge felt privileged their campus was chosen.

One evening, after their bridge game, Julia and Emily went outside to the porch swing. "I'm concerned something is wrong with Samuel," Julia fretted. "He has been very quiet, and I wonder if he's thinking of leaving or if he's ill."

Emily put her hand on Julia's. "Whatever it is, he'll tell us when he is ready."

"I would miss him if he left," whispered Julia. "It wouldn't be the same."

"Why Julia, I think you have a 'bee in your bonnet' for Samuel."

"Nonsense, but I do enjoy his company."

The next day some of the men helped put up the decorations while the ladies arranged flowers for the celebration. Samuel walked with Julia to her apartment after dinner and came in and sat down. He had done that before, but tonight Julia could sense something was different.

"Julia, I don't know where to begin or how to say this, but well...I'll just come out with it." Slowly he looked up and met her eyes. "Would you marry me? I never thought I could care again about another person like I do you. I want to be near you and know you are OK. I want to talk to you without waiting until we are eating or doing some activity."

Julia's heart pounded. The question completely threw her off guard; she had not thought about marriage being a part of her life ever again. There was a long silent pause, then she thoughtfully spoke. "I'm flattered. My...what would our families say?"

"I didn't ask about our families. I asked you. Julia Morgan, I love you. Would you marry me?"

Julia slipped off her glasses and pushed away a tear. "Samuel, I'll have to pray about this. This is a new idea to me."

"I have prayed about it, Julia, and it is right for me, if you will say yes."

"But you don't know my daughter; she wants me to come and live with her. It was a battle for me to come here. She would never agree to me getting married! We need to pray about this together, Samuel."

The couple held hands and prayed. When they said, "Amen," Samuel kissed Julia's folded, quivering hands. She giggled as she watched Samuel walk down the hall. Inside she felt like a giddy teenager. There would be little sleep for her tonight. She knew she'd never marry Samuel unless Maggie agreed, and she couldn't see that happening.

On the big day, television crews invaded the main all-purpose room. The facility was decorated like never before, and the throne for the king and queen looked like true royalty. *25 YEARS* was written in bold letters on a banner.

Julia and Samuel were voted the 25th Homecoming King and Queen. In the excitement, Julia secretly told Emily about Samuel's proposal and that she wanted to say yes.

The television reporters interviewed the residents and the staff. Speaking to Emily, one reporter inquired, "How well do you know the king and queen?"

"Oh, Julia is my dearest friend. We play bridge several times a week with Samuel and Melvin. Julia and I are like sisters, and I know it won't change when they get married."

"Samuel and Julia are getting married? How wonderful! The King and Queen are getting married? A true royal couple." The reporter was writing all the names down.

"Oh dear," Emily lamented, "I was supposed to keep it under my hat.

Well, don't you tell anyone."

When the television camera zoomed in to the crowning of the King and Queen, there were happy tears in many eyes. The Master of Ceremonies congratulated them, then looked at the audience and said, "I have it under good authority that this lovely couple will soon be officially Mr. and Mrs. Samuel Solis." The camera took a close-up shot of the surprised couple, and the audience applauded and cheered.

Samuel and Julia were stunned that their secret now had been shared with a network television audience. Julia looked at Emily, who shrugged and whispered, "Sorry."

When news of the broadcast reached Maggie, Julia received a phone call. "Mother, I'm sure this is just a rumor; tell me you aren't thinking about getting married."

"Well, dear, I was going to have you meet Samuel on your next visit."

"Mother, I'm catching a plane. This is ridiculous." Maggie called the director of Sunset Ridge and told him she'd be there as soon as she could get a flight.

The next day, Samuel called his son, Larry, whom he hadn't seen in 15 years.

The happy occasion had become a teapot of boiling emotions.

Maggie arrived to talk sense into Julia and to evaluate her mother's mental state. Julia was just happy that Maggie was polite to Samuel.

"All I'm asking you to do, Maggie, is pray about my decision. Please talk with the chaplain."

Larry arrived, and the reunion was strained. Samuel loved his son but had carried a hurt for a long time. He had asked his son to come and see him.

Maggie, Julia, Samuel, and Larry met with the chaplain, who began the meeting with a prayer for wisdom.

The chaplain reminded Samuel and Julia how many times parents feel their children are too young to get married. Now it was reversed. The children were saying, "You're too old to get married." All five smiled in understanding. The chaplain continued, "The question remains the same for all couples: Do you love each other? I know you've prayed about this union, but let's pray that all will come to a peaceful agreement as they consider who is involved here. Larry, I'm glad you came to visit with your dad."

Larry cleared his throat. "My dad and I quarreled after Mom died, and I left home. As the years went by, it was harder to call or come home and to say, 'I'm sorry.' Now he loves another person. I feel like it's too late for me."

"Samuel, your son loves you and asks forgiveness. He is afraid, if you marry, the door for him to come back will be forever closed."

Samuel looked at his son with tears pooling in his eyes. "Larry, I love you and want you to be a part of my life and to know Julia. I'm sorry for the wasted years. I've stored up years of love I want to give you. It isn't too late."

"Maggie," the chaplain continued, "I know how much you love your mother. You would like to take her home with you so you can watch over her, probably much like she watched you when you were growing up. She loves you and the family but has decided she wants to live her life also. She refused to move with you to a strange city. She would only have you and the family there, while your life would remain filled with your activities and friends. Julia loves it here and has many friends, and a special one, Samuel. She and Samuel want to be together; can you understand that?"

Maggie gazed at her mother and then at Samuel. "I guess when I stop thinking about me and look at the joy in you two, I can't be negative; your love seems forever young."

Julia nodded. "Yes, Maggie, I'm happy. Samuel likes to read with me, challenges me in games. and squeezes my hand when we walk. I don't need Dovie…I need Samuel. Is it wrong for me to marry Samuel?"

Larry approached his dad. "I'm sorry, Dad. How can I make it up to you for the hurt I caused?"

"You could be my best man." Samuel smiled.

Larry hugged his dad.

The following month, the wedding was held in the beautiful new chapel at Sunset Ridge Assisted Living Campus. The residents, staff, families, and friends were in attendance. Who would miss a royal wedding?

Maggie smiled through her tears as she heard her mother softly answer to Samuel, "I do."

Together they would share their future.

BEVERLY LAHOTE SCHWIND is the author of four books and writes devotionals for David C. Cook and Standard Publishing. Published in *Love is a Verb*, *Angels, Miracles and Supernatural Stories*, and *Mature Living,* Beverly writes a newspaper column *Patches of Life.* She is a retired nurse, television personality, and has been married to Jim for 60 years.

Chosen

* * *

LORI-ANN WHYTE

What on earth had Craig just said? Kandee's eyes went wide as she stared across the table at her best friend. Exactly. Best friend. Heart thumping against her chest, she scanned the other diners. Good. No chance anyone would overhear. Had the lighting been this dim all along, though?

"Why me, Craig?"

His eyebrows flew together, gray eyes narrowing into shadows beneath strong, sculpted brows. He leaned back in his chair and just looked at her. Fab. If he really thought now was the ideal moment for one of his lovely silences, she...tension shot up and down her right leg. No, no, no. She clenched her teeth and clamped her eyes shut. Deep breath.

"Dee?" The familiar warmth of his fingers enveloped hers. The tension got worse, as if her leg itched from inside. Great timing. She pulled her hand away, pushed her chair back, and stood. Better not make any sudden moves.

She eyed Craig. When had he gotten up? Man, he was fast.

"I just need to go to the bathroom." She waved him off.

"Kandee Wynter."

Uh-oh. Craig used her name only when he was serious. Why did his voice have to be so deep anyway, especially when he got all no-nonsense? It did crazy things to her heart.

"Yes, Craig Nielsen?" Forcing her lips into a curve, she gripped the top of the chair—just in case her leg decided she hadn't seen enough floor time recently. "Can't a girl have some privacy in this country?" She took two tiny steps. Nothing. Cool. She turned back to him and winked. "Too much water. Chillax."

Thank God she made it to the stylish bathroom on time. Not like she could have bolted toward it, since she'd told Craig she was quite fine. Knowing her luck, she'd probably have twisted her ankle in these stupid three-inch pumps. Oh, for her precious flip-flops.

She beelined for the first stall and locked the door. Awesome. Her handbag was still at the table. No sanitizer. She rolled off a wad of tissue. That would have to do for—

Her leg slammed against the tiled wall. She moaned and bit down on her lip. A metallic flavor seeped into her mouth. Blech.

The tissue floated to the ground. Oh, well. She used her bare hands to slam the toilet lid closed. Ugh. Sliding down onto the seat, she stretched out her legs.

Why now? She hadn't had a leg tic in ages. Most of the others she could hide, but this one? The only thing that seemed to "work" was lying flat on her bed, so at least she wouldn't hurt herself while her leg did its own jerky dance. Tears burned her eyes, and her throat muscles knitted together. She pulled in her leg just in time to prevent a connection with the base of the metal stall door. Not even skin as dark as hers would've hidden that killer bruise.

God, I'm so tired of this. She hunched over, fists gripping the curls from her twist out. All this dressing up for nothing. Was one normal night too much to ask? Bad enough she had to live with Tourette's every day. Nothing could make her force Craig to endure the same thing.

*

Craig shoved the gearstick into park in front of Kandee's house and sat back, one hand braced against the rim of the steering wheel. That girl was gonna drive him up every wall in Portland—maybe every wall in Oregon. He grabbed his phone from the console and reread her message: *Sorry Craig. Had to go. Cab home. Pick up my bag plz. Can get money for my dinner from it…or when I see you.*

Her sense of timing was astute. He'd been about to hunt her down in the bathroom when his phone had buzzed. *God, give me patience.* He shook his head and laughed. If she thought she could run away from this, she'd better think again.

Wait. She'd had her phone and money for cab fare. How? He smiled. Oh. She only wore clothes with pockets. Ah, Kandee. Who would've guessed that stunning sleeveless pink—Dee had actually worn pink—dress had pockets? And those silver shoes…mercy. Anyway…

He dialed her number and hummed. Three rings. Four. He hung up. One more try. She couldn't ignore him forever.

Seven calls later, he yanked the key out of the ignition and glared towards the tree-lined driveway leading up to the white split-level house. Pity they had an automatic gate and a high-tech security system.

Fine. He could play her game. Since she was so fond of text messages…

Fifteen seconds. Car horn.

He tossed the phone onto the passenger seat. Beep. He snatched up the phone and pressed the green button. *"Oui?"*

"You crazy or something?" Her whispered words came out as a hiss.

"You'll find out in, hmm, about a second or so."

"I swear, I will kill you, Craig Nielsen. If you ever…"

A chuckle rumbled from his throat. "Well, step outside and we can finish our discussion."

"It's late, Craig. I already told Daddy I was going to bed and stuff."

Nice excuse. As if he didn't know about her insomnia. "Fine. I'm kidnapping you after church tomorrow."

"But I—"

"It's either that, or I use my trusty little horn." They could have the discussion now, or tomorrow. End of story. "Beep beep."

"You are such a punk."

"At your service, Miss Wynter. See you tomorrow."

*

Kandee sneaked through the side door as soon as Pastor Beck said, "Amen." Thank God Craig had to sit up top with the rest of the band. She'd go camp out by Dad's car now, or—

"Fancy meeting you here." Craig appeared beside her, bass guitar bag slung over one shoulder. Where had he come from, anyway? Creep. At least his shadow was blocking the sun.

Squeak. Well, he was used to that tic. She whirled and glared at him. "You know being agitated triggers my tics. Wanna"—*squeak*—"guess who's agitating me?" Her neck snapped toward her right shoulder. She clamped her right hand onto it and pushed it back in place. It better stay there.

His hand rested on her shoulder, and he turned her towards him. "Listen, Dee. We really need to talk—and not just 'cuz what you did last night was really uncool."

"Hey, I promised to pay for—?"

"Seriously, Kandee? You know that's not it. Why would I invite you to dinner and expect you to pay?"

Whatever. "Yeah. Why did you invite me to dinner? I thought we were just celebrating your promotion."

"Clearly here's not the best place for this conversation. Everyone's gonna come rushing out any minute." He pointed toward the west end of the parking lot. "I'm parked over there. Can we talk in the car?"

Nuh-uh. She opened her mouth to tell him just that.

"Please, Dee."

"Fine. I'll call Daddy"—*squeak*—"and tell him I'm getting a ride with you."

*

Was she ever gonna stop shooting lasers at him with her eyes? Hmm. Chocolate lasers. Could be kinda interesting.

Dee looked at her watch, then at him. Dirty look number only-God-knew. Oh. He suppressed a chuckle. Dee was most hostile when she was scared. "You don't have to be afraid, you know."

"Aren't you sweet?" She rolled her eyes. "Whatever would I do without—?"

"I wasn't kidding. I love you. And don't pretend you don't know what I mean."

"I can't do this. Not now." She leaned over and fiddled with the passenger AC vents.

"How long have we known each other, Kandee?"

"Freshman year at UP. Ten-ish years?" She sat back. All three vents were at the same angle.

"Right. And you didn't think all this time we've spent together was bound to lead somewhere?"

"Not here, though." She looked across at his vents, her mouth twitching. He could bet she wanted to climb out of her skin, just so she could fix those, too.

"Kandee, what's the real issue?"

Her eyes flew back to him. "Other than the fact that heartbreak doesn't feature on the bucket list I don't even have?"

"Very funny."

"It just wouldn't work out, Craig. We're too…different."

"What the—?" He cleared his throat. "What's that supposed to mean?"

"Just everything. Yeah, we're best buds or whatever, but there are…things we don't have in common."

So the skin color thing was finally an issue? "Oh, so it's okay to be friends, but you can't take the white boy home to Daddy?"

"Seriously?" She reached over and slapped him upside the head. "How many times you been to my house, idiot?"

Fine. He deserved that one. "It's not the same."

"Well, whatever. I just wish…"

"You wish what?"

"Nothing." This wasn't like her at all. Directness was her specialty, even when it rubbed him the wrong way.

"You gonna tell me why you won't even think about this?"

"Who says I won't?" Her hand flew to her mouth.

Aha. His heart soared. "I caught that."

"Ya don't say. Anyway, nothing to talk about. Just wouldn't work. That's it." She put her hands in her lap and stared at…the glove compartment? "Can't we go back to being us, Craig?"

Only the brilliance of God's engineering stopped his heart from plummeting to his feet. "I don't see how one precludes the other, though."

She sighed and moved her hands toward the ashtray. "I'm sorry."

He closed his eyes. If there was one thing Kandee Wynter knew, it was her own mind. What more could he say?

The metallic jingle of coins sliding past each other in the ashtray seemed the only answer he was likely to get. In about another minute, his loose change would be in four perfect rows. If only other things in his life—and heart—were as easy to arrange.

*

Kandee tucked her legs under the piano bench and eased the piano lid closed. Nearly two hours of her favorite classical and contemporary pieces, and no change. Fine, so her tics pretty much disappeared when she played, but she'd take slapping herself in the face over this madness any day.

She wasn't being fair to Craig, but did she really have a choice? This would be so much easier if he'd decide he couldn't be just her friend. But he clearly had no such plans—unless the past six or so weeks meant nothing. He still called and stuff, still picked her up every Saturday for the special needs dance class she taught at the community center. Everything looked the same, but it wasn't.

Craig's eyes couldn't lie, and there was one thing hidden in those stormy depths each time she saw him. The same thing framed by the new lines around his eyes. Pure, potent pain.

*

He was such an idiot—not because he'd risked the most beautiful friendship he could've asked for. Because it had taken him nine whole weeks to figure this out. It was as if God had flicked a switch in his brain. About time. All those prayers.

What was the one thing Kandee had accepted but found most difficult to accept help with? Her Tourette Syndrome. She was cool when it wasn't "tic season," but when they became too bad to control, he had to summon all his persuasive powers to even see her.

Craig rolled over, kicked off his sheet, and stared at the ceiling. Why did she have to be so stubborn, anyway? Had he ever complained about it? He'd told her maybe a million times how proud he was that she'd never let it hold her back. Well, it wasn't gonna hold him back either.

*

Where was everyone? Kandee scanned the empty dance studio. Her kids were never late. They lived for Saturdays.

She walked to the center barre and ran her hand along the smooth surface, a smile blossoming across her face. She missed her classroom, but these kids had really brightened her summer. *Thank you, God. I—*

The door swung open. Finally. Three boys and four girls ran into the room. They moved around each other, a laughing jumble, forming a haphazard line.

"Guys?" She clapped her hands twice. Usually, that would have had them sitting in a circle on the hardwood floor. No such luck. "Really, guys. We're late, and we have to be out of here by—"

They turned to her, huge grins shining. Seriously? Seven pairs of hands flew upwards. Odd. The same black shirts with one word in white writing—not the same word, though. Ooh, she got it.

She walked towards them. "You guys made some kind of team? That's ama—"

Her feet froze. No. Some kind of message?

*BECAUSE...YOU...ARE...MY...*Some-word-starting-with-C?

She leaned in and inclined her head. *BECAUSE YOU ARE MY CHOICE. ENOUGH SAID.*

Her heart galloped. Okay, this was weird. She glanced from one laughing face to another. "All right, guys. Who put you up to—?"

"Beep beep." Craig tapped her on the shoulder—from behind? She spun and flung her arms around him. "You're insane."

"So I've been told. Can we talk now?" His arms came around her, and she rested her head on his chest. Her eyes fluttered closed.

"But the class—" She looked behind her. No children.

"They're watching a movie in the rec room with their parents. Great little co-conspirators." Craig leaned down, the warm breeze of his breath brushing her ear. "Because if I'm gonna get kicked in the stomach while I'm sleeping, I'd rather it be you than anyone else."

Her head snapped back. "Go away." She smacked him on the shoulder.

"Not a chance." Grinning, he pulled her head back to his chest. "I'm serious. No relationship is easy, but we've had a pretty good start. We've fought and made up too many times to count, shared tears and laughter, we've prayed for and with each other." He swayed, the motion calming her racing heart. "Tourette's isn't a death sentence, but the thought of my life without you feels like one."

Wow. Like, wow.

He eased back and cupped her face. "Whadya say we keep doing life together, hmm, for the rest of our lives?" A twinkle lit up his gaze. "I even got your dad's blessing."

Her head moved from side to side. "Yes." Seriously? Of all the times in the world for that tic to show up. Hilarious.

His hands fell from her face and he squeezed his eyes shut. Head still shaking, she pulled his forehead down to hers. "Feel that? Tic. I said yes."

Intense gray stared back at her. "I love you, Kandee Wynter."

To think those very words had terrified her mere months ago. "I love you, too, Craig."

LORI-ANN WHYTE is the youngest of six girls from a Jamaican home. Her family didn't own a TV until she was eight so she prefers reading to other forms of entertainment. She had no plans to become a writer but has developed a deep passion for the art form. To email Lori: **loriann.writes@gmail.com.**

http://whylori.wordpress.com

The Mechanic

* * *

Beatrice Fishback

Her hair was always getting in the way.

She pulled her blond locks out of the hairband and shook her head with a vengeance. As she maneuvered her hair with one hand, her other hand slid off the torque wrench, and she accidentally banged her knuckles on the car's metal frame. "Drats." She lifted her head out of the car's guts, otherwise known as an engine, and rubbed her swollen knuckles. Then she retied her hair.

Her dad lifted his head from the work he was doing. "What happened, honey?" The vehicle he was fixing was a bright shiny Lamborghini, and its ebony skin shone like a black stallion.

"I'm never going to get used to working with these fiddly bits. Give me a hunk of a jeep anytime. These sweet little girls"—she pointed to the small red sports car with a removable hardtop—"require too much attention." Wiping her hands on the rag she grabbed from her back pocket, somehow she managed to get the tip of her nose smeared with grease. Actually, she quite liked sports cars and only recently had a chance to work on a few special models. In the past it had been standard automobiles with predictable problems.

"What in the world?" she hollered over a roar that seemed to come from outer space. She put her tools down and, out of habit, rubbed her hands along her jeans.

Like a plane screaming down a runway, a car screeched around the corner and headed into the garage. She jumped out of the way to keep from being hit. "You idiot! Where did you learn how to drive?" she yelled above the noise, but she knew the driver couldn't hear a word.

The engine was turned off. A lanky, six-foot-plus man with the looks of a young Brad Pitt stepped out of the topaz-colored car. He wore an expensive, tailored suit, and his tie was casually pulled away from his neck. "Sorry, um, if I scared you," he stammered.

She had seen his likes before. These rich guys always thought they were better than anyone else, always thought they could do whatever they wanted and never considered that others without the same financial status as them were human too.

"Watch where you're going, you jerk!" She spun and headed to the office, her hair falling out of the band again.

Stepping inside the small workspace, she overheard the conversation in the garage.

"Never mind her," her dad said. "She gets worked up when someone startles her." Then he asked, "What can I do for you, son?"

"I need to have the radiator checked, please. Seems to be leaking or something."

She peeked around the corner of the office, curiosity getting the better of her. The handsome stranger looked her way, and she pulled her head back in.

"Who is she?" she heard the man ask her dad.

"My daughter, Carole. You have to forgive her for being so rude."

"Don't you dare apologize for me," she said, stepping out and standing with her hands over her hips as if she were getting ready to draw a weapon like a gunman from an old western.

"Whoa." The young man held up his hands in mock surrender. "I was only going to say I'm sorry for driving so fast into the garage. My foot got stuck on the accelerator."

"Likely story," she said under her breath but loud enough for both her father and the man to hear.

"What can I do to show you I'm sincere?" He first eyed her, then her dad.

"You can begin by driving your car out of here!"

Heading back into the office, she plunked down on the torn office chair next to the well-worn desk. A computer sat atop the file cabinet. She had tried desperately to get her father into the 21st century and their business out of the Dark Ages. But he insisted on using the old-fashioned writing tablet given to him by his father, which was the kind used by his father's father. The business had been in the family since the late 19th century, and she grew up knowing and loving the smell of grease, oil, and car fumes…much to the dismay of the men she had tried to date. At 25 years of age she had given up on ever falling in love, marrying, or having a family. She was a part of this old building and everything mechanical that went with it.

Forget men, and forget men who drive like crazy morons.

She popped the metal clip, then sipped the Coke she'd pulled from the small refrigerator, looking at the stack of mail on the desk: bills, bills, and more bills. They were forever in debt, and the money owed to them never seemed to come in like it should. Dad was too generous. His "do unto others" never seemed to work the other way around. He was always saying God was going to provide for their every need. She put his faith down to old-school mentality, but he was one of the most generous, loving men she knew. After her mom died, it had just been the two of them. She knew her dad would always be there for her, and she was very protective of him.

Slapping the desk, she headed out to the garage. The young man was hanging over the open hood, and he and her father were laughing, having too much fun together in her estimation. "Hey, we can't get our work done if you hang around bothering us," she said sarcastically.

"Carole." Her dad wagged his index finger in her direction. "I want you two to meet."

"I don't need to meet anyone who can't drive a car," she grumbled but obeyed her father and headed toward him.

The handsome man held out his hand. "Nice to meet you."

Carole merely nodded. "What's wrong with your car other than how you drive her?"

"Carole, be nice," her father scolded, while his wrinkled brow indicated he was still mentally working out what could be the problem with the vehicle. "We're not sure what's wrong." He wiped his hands and his wrench on the rag draped on the car's side mirror. "But I think you might be interested in knowing who this man is." He winked at her with his I've-got-a-secret look she had known since she could remember.

"I doubt it." She still wasn't sure what to make of this stranger who seemed to have captured her father's attention and respect. She turned to the man. "So, who are you? And what do we care? We've got work to do and a living to make. We don't have the luxury of driving around in a fancy car wearing fancy clothes." She eyed him up and down.

"Carole Ann Marie!" Her dad rarely used her full name and only when he wasn't pleased with her behavior. "You really are being rude. This man has something to say I think you might be interested in."

"Um, I'm sorry." She lowered her eyes and shuffled her feet. Her golden hair hung along her face, trying to hide her shame.

"No need to apologize. I was just telling your dad here how I've been looking at this building of yours with some interest over the past few years. I'm an architect by trade."

She lifted her face. "NO! You can't have this building. It belongs to our family, and it's the only thing we have besides each other!"

"Carole Ann. Listen to what the man is trying to say, will you?"

The young driver said, "This building is a historical site and worthy of having a facelift, to return it to how she used to be." He took a long look around the gray room and glanced at the stucco ceiling. "She's gorgeous."

"Yes, this building is pretty special," she offered hesitantly. "What are you proposing?"

"I want to help you and your father restore this place. To return it to its original splendor and offer specialty cars a classy place to come and have their engines taken care of. You and your dad are the folks who can do it!" He smiled at her dad with affection as if he'd known him for a long time. "Of course, you'll have to get rid of the grease you wear on your nose if you want to impress the clientele who will be coming here from now on." He reached for her nose and wiped the tip of it with a tender gesture.

Her legs melted like butter in a microwave. "What's in it for you?" She tried to speak with self-assurance but the words came out a whisper instead.

"I hope to spend a lot more time with your dad, coming up with ideas on how to update this place. It's an architect's dream." He looked at his feet. "And if it's okay, I'd like to spend more time with you. Maybe we can get to know each other better. I started off on the wrong foot with you, I think. My accelerator foot." He lifted his face. His eyes sparkled like two amethysts, his smile magical.

"I don't even know your name," she said softly.

"Brad Stevens."

"Why am I not surprised your name is Brad?" She smiled.

"Not sure what you mean by that?"

"Nothing." She blushed. "Well, Mr. *Brad* Stevens, it looks like we're going to be spending some time together." She held out her hand to shake his.

He said, "I want to begin by depositing some money into your account so your father can take some time off from working on cars and spend time working on ways to improve this place to its rightful beauty. Of course nothing could compare to the beauty of the lady who runs this place with her dad, though." His words were cliché but sweet, and he seemed genuinely excited to help them make their business a thriving entity.

Brad got into his car, regarding her with wistful hope. "I look forward to getting to know you better, Carole." He winked at her father and said, "Thank you, sir. I'll be back tomorrow so you can finish working on my car, and we can begin our business together."

Her dad put his arm around her waist as they watched the car leave the garage. "See honey, always told you to 'do unto others.' If I had just told him to take his fast car out of here, we wouldn't have had that conversation with him, now would we? Didn't I tell you God would take care of us? Of course Mr. Brad Stevens might not know what he is getting into with a sweet little girl like you." He poked her in the ribs. "He might be better off sticking with his sweet little sports car instead."

"Dad!" She turned serious. "You've always told me God was in control and would help us out when we least expected it by a means we never could imagine. I have to admit you were right on both counts."

He kissed her on the cheek and moved back to the Lamborghini to finish what he had been working on earlier.

She said under her breath, "And I would never have imagined in my wildest dreams that a man named Brad would drive his car into our garage one day and into my heart for perhaps eternity." She smiled demurely, wrapped her hair into a ponytail, and went back to work.

BEATRICE FISHBACK and her husband, Jim, live and work in Great Britain. Beatrice authored *Loving Your Military Man* and co-authored *Defending the Military Marriage* and *Defending the Military Family*. She and her husband help military couples with their unique life challenges. In their free time they enjoy long walks and lattes.

Her Lucky Break

* * *

DAVALYNN SPENCER

Lydia tramped through the fresh snow, fingers fisted deep in her jacket pockets, her breath a cloudy puff. First to tread the smooth, untouched path, she glanced over her shoulder at the single line of footprints. *Single.*

The label nailed her like a trailhead marker: *Loneliness—straight ahead.*

She'd tried to shake it off, but it stuck more stubbornly on days like this when all but the sky was white…even the river sliding by in its frosty coat.

Ice floes jockeyed on the water, like harried commuters on Friday afternoon. The free-floating slabs bumped and jostled and snapped off smaller pieces that escaped downstream.

She continued upriver but slowed at the bend where the trail wandered into a clearing. Reluctant to leave the water so soon, she stopped to watch and listen.

And then she heard it. A weak whimper that turned her head toward a cluster of naked cottonwoods huddling against the cold.

She moved across the path to the shivering trees. Again they cried, pleading to be heard.

"Hello?" Now she talked to trees?

A sad note sounded and she stepped closer, placing one gloved hand on a white trunk, and leaned in.

A doe-eyed dog with enormous ears moaned from a leafy bed. Snow had melted against its body and refrozen in the night, shrouding it in a crusty blanket.

"You poor thing."

The ears laid down at her cooing. The eyes pleaded.

Crouching, she pushed into the tree nest and held a hand near the trembling dog. It sniffed and licked and whimpered its thanks for being found.

"Come on." She slapped her knees. "Come on out."

The deer eyes flicked from face to hands, but the dog didn't move.

She leaned closer.

The dog's short legs were tucked beneath its body except for the left front paw that jutted out at an unnatural angle.

"Are you hurt?" With gloved fingers, she lightly touched the crooked paw. A white bone had punctured the skin, and a quick pink tongue licked the wound.

"Let me help you." She rubbed away the snowy crust. "I'm going to pick you up, okay?"

The dog raised its fawn-colored head and nosed her chin in consent.

Scooting one arm beneath the warm belly, she wrapped the other around, lifted the animal from its frozen bed, and grunted against the weight.

"You're a hefty one, aren't you?"

Retracing her footprints, she doubted she could carry the dog all the way back to her car. After several yards, she found a sheltering evergreen, kicked away the thin snow with her boots, and set the dog down. Pleading eyes searched her face, and the stumpy tail mimicked a wag.

"I'm not leaving you." She pulled off a glove and rubbed the smooth head. "I just need a breather. You're heavy."

Resting in the quilted quiet, she wondered how the dog had survived the night, how he'd broken his leg, and if he'd been abandoned.

Footsteps crunched behind her. Startled, she turned, still kneeling, a hand on the dog's head.

Black boots stopped not two feet away, topped by a bundled man with blue eyes bold as the sky. A wrinkle creased dark brows and a cloud escaped his lips. "Do you need help?"

The Huntsman from *Snow White*—come to slay her. Or save her.

She swallowed her fear. "Yes."

The frown eased, the eyes warmed. The knees bent. "I'm Jon." He touched the dog, rubbed its back, fingered the pitiful leg. "How did this happen?"

A bit of sky flashed her way.

"I don't know. I just found him."

Jon probed ribs and stomach and hind quarters. "Lying here?"

"No, back up the trail a ways. I carried him out but had to stop for a minute. He's heavy."

The smile lit on his face, melting through her wariness and dripping down inside. Cornflower. The man's eyes were cornflower blue.

He nodded. "He *is* big for a corgi."

"A what?"

"He's a Welsh corgi. Cow dogs originally from the British Isles." A white breath haloed the dog as Jon slipped both arms underneath and smoothly stood. He questioned Lydia with a welcoming look. "Want to come along?"

She stared at the woodsman-incarnate, wondering if she'd lost her good sense to avoid strangers in the forest. "Sure."

At the parking area, a white pickup waited next to her shy sedan. Enclosed compartments edged the truck bed, and a red script on the cab said *Timberline Veterinary Clinic.*

Parking lights winked a bright welcome. Jon walked to the passenger side and tilted his capped head at the door. "Think you can hold him on the way?"

Lydia climbed in and settled on the seat before spreading her arms. "Hand him over."

He laid the dog across her lap and glanced up. "Comfortable?"

"Yes. He's fine."

Jon circled the truck, slid behind the wheel, and pulled off his knit cap. "Ready?" Gray nipped at the dark hair above his ears.

An unfamiliar smile crawled out of her heart and reached for her mouth. "Yes, we're ready."

The pickup's engine surged to life, and years of lonely caution washed accusingly over her body. She slipped a hand inside her pocket and checked for keys. How would she get back to her car? Where was Timberline Veterinary Clinic? Who was this man?

"So what's your name?" His friendly baritone mocked her anxiety.

"Lydia."

"Lydia," he repeated, as if testing the name for too much salt. "Lovely. Lydia, will you check his collar to see if he's tagged? He may have an owner searching for him."

Of course. Why hadn't she thought of that? She slid the frayed blue strap around until the buckle lay on top. No name tag, and immunizations were outdated.

"He's had his shots but not in the last three years."

Jon nodded. His right hand let go of the wheel and moved her way.

She squeezed the dog tighter.

He tapped the radio dial.

She exhaled.

A woman sang of God's love for the lost and lonely, the weary and unwanted. Lydia recognized the melody and traitorous tears rushed forward, clawing to be first over the edge. Shocked by her reaction, she blinked hard and looked at the dog resting in her lap, weary and unwanted.

How long had she felt the same?

She glanced sidelong at the stranger behind the wheel and wondered if he had cued a preset CD.

Across town, the clinic sat tight as a miser's fist. Lydia expected as much this early, but Jon had a key. Maybe he really was what he appeared to be.

He parked behind the building, unlocked and propped open the door, then returned to the truck and lifted the corgi. Lydia followed him inside.

Shiny floors and antiseptic perfection greeted her. Jon laid the dog on a stainless steel table and shrugged off his coat.

"Stand near him, will you, Lydia?"

She moved in and Jon reached for her hands. Gentle, yet strong, his fingers enfolded hers and guided them to the corgi's side, pressing them into the deep fur. "Don't let him jump down."

Warmth rushed up her arms from the dog's body. Or Jon's touch. She wasn't sure.

"Have you ever watched a surgical procedure before?" His rich voice rose above running water where he scrubbed his hands and arms over a deep sink.

"No." She stroked the corgi's head. "But I won't faint if that's what you want to know."

Chuckling, he dried his hands, then filled a syringe and came to the table.

"Hold him steady," he said, massaging the dog's neck and parting the thick fur with deft fingers.

*

Jon injected the pre-anesthetic and glanced at the woman he'd just met. Her slender hands held the dog firmly, caressed it lovingly.

"As soon as he closes his eyes, you might want to take off your jacket," he said.

She frowned and dropped her head lower, her nervous tension nearly tangible.

Her acceptance of his offer to ride along had surprised him, and he'd hoped to ease her concern by tuning in to light praise radio. If anything, it had made her more nervous.

The dog sighed low and long, and Jon knew the animal was ready. He lowered his voice, aimed for nonchalance.

"You can hang your coat on the rack in the hall." He pointed toward the end of the surgery. "There's a strip of weathered barn board with hooks on the other side of the door. Would you mind taking mine, too?"

She studied the sleeping corgi for a moment, then slowly lifted her hands.

Without meeting Jon's eyes, she unzipped her gray down jacket, snatched his coat from the floor, and disappeared through the door.

The bell out front announced his niece's arrival. Her cheerful voice flitted down the hallway as she introduced herself and offered coffee if Lydia didn't mind waiting for it to perk.

He smiled to himself. Hopefully Holly's lighthearted manner would help Lydia relax and realize he wasn't a predator stalking women at the river to do them harm.

In fact, Lydia was the first client he'd brought into his new surgery. And the dog didn't even belong to her. It was a strange situation all around.

He'd almost passed on the Riverwalk, but the lure of unmarred snow and crisp morning air had pulled him out. And he knew he'd have few calls so early. Last night's storm had provided a rare opportunity for an unhurried stroll.

Jealousy surged when he first saw the solitary footprints. Someone had beaten him to the trail—someone small, a woman or a child. His would not be the first steps through the glittering carpet. And then he saw her kneeling next to a dark shape in the snow....

The surgery door opened and a happier Lydia entered with two steaming mugs. Relief framed her face like the dark waves of her loose hair. She smiled.

"I'll set this over here for you." She placed a blue mug on the counter beneath overhead cabinets and scooted it back. Then she cupped both hands around her own mug and sipped. "Mmm. Holly makes great coffee."

"She sure does. Don't know what I'd do without her."

Lydia stood across from him and watched as he secured the splint and made the final wrap.

"This guy will be up and feeling like himself in a day or so. Until then, I'll kennel him here."

Her eyes posed the question before she voiced it. "Could I take him home? At least until we find the owner?"

Absolutely. That would ensure another visit, perhaps several. He wanted to know more about this woman with the gentle hands and rare but warming smile.

"I don't see why not," he said. "I scanned him for a microchip and didn't find one."

A frown pulled at her brow. "Microchip?"

"Pet owners often have them implanted in their dogs and cats in case the animal is lost or stolen. The chip has a number that links to an owner-information directory."

"Amazing." She sipped her coffee again.

He let his gaze linger. "Exactly what I was thinking."

She met his eyes and her cheeks flushed.

Easy, Jon. Don't chase her off.

"I'll be right back," he said.

He carried the dog to the kennels down the hall, checked its pulse, and left it snoozing on a soft pad with a little water nearby. When he returned to the surgery, Lydia occupied a lab stool at the counter.

He washed his hands, picked up his waiting mug, and leaned against the table. "Do you walk at the river often?"

She took another drink, her mug a shield over which she peeked. "Almost every day. Do you?"

He sipped, expecting less than his preferred cup of coffee. "Whoa."

She flinched. "That bad?"

"No. It's perfect. I'm just surprised."

"Holly told me how you like it."

"Did she also tell you I'm not a stalker?"

Choking at his abruptness, she covered her mouth, but laughing eyes spilled the truth. "Yes, she did."

"That *doesn't* surprise me. You looked a little worried on the way over here."

Lydia rested the mug on her lap and sat up straighter. "I'm not in the habit of accepting rides from strange men."

"I'd hoped the clinic name on my truck and the music would ease your mind." He stared into his coffee. "I'm not really *that* strange, am I?"

Her laughter rolled out like a song and settled around his heart.

"No, you're not strange. Just a stranger. I don't know you."

He set his mug on the counter, wiped a hand on his jeans. and held it out.

"Hello. I'm Dr. Jon Timber, the new veterinarian in town. I'm originally from Wyoming, but I thought a move south to sunny Colorado might be a nice change. Besides, my kid sister and her family live here, and my niece offered to run the front office if I kept her supplied in lip gloss, Laffy Taffy, and enough money to pay her car insurance."

Lydia's shoulders hunched as she laughed and coffee jumped from her mug to the floor. "Oh—I'm sorry!"

He grabbed a paper towel from the dispenser over the sink and quickly sopped up the spill. "Not a problem. I also do floors." He tossed the wadded paper with a fake three-point flourish and turned back to Lydia. "How about you? What's your story?"

The laughter ebbed and her voice quieted. "I'm Lydia Parker, and I've lived here all my life. My husband died five years ago in a skiing accident, and I work at the city library. Today's my day off."

"I'd like to get to know you better, Lydia Parker."

Her cheeks reddened again. She slid off the stool and walked to the hall door where she turned to face him. "Could you take me back to my car first?"

Relieved that he hadn't pushed her away, he nodded with a smile. "If you'll grab our coats."

*

At the Riverwalk, Jon parked next to an older Honda and turned off the motor.

Lydia jostled her keys. "I'll put an ad in the paper about the corgi."

"You don't sound too happy about that."

"I'm not, but if he has an owner, they should be reunited."

She reached for the door handle but turned her face toward him. "Thank you for the ride back. And for your help."

"Thank you for the coffee."

A soft laugh. "That was Holly's doing."

He cleared his throat. "Speaking of doing, what are you doing tomorrow morning?"

Light sparked in her eyes and she tilted her head. "Walking in the snow."

He liked the way she looked at him. "Mind if I join you?"

She smiled that warm smile. "I'd like that. I'd like that very much."

DAVALYNN SPENCER is an author and speaker who writes inspirational romance, a monthly column for the Fellowship of Christian Cowboys, Inc., and nonfiction for publications such as *Chicken Soup for the Soul* and *American Cowboy Magazine*.

    www.davalynnspencer.com
    www.davalynnspencer.blogspot.com

Not Just Another Casserole Lady

* * *

Christina Ryan Claypool

Trish Delaney didn't know what a Casserole Lady was. It confused her when her best friend, Eve Hughes, accused her of acting like one.

"You're being ridiculous, Trish. Gary Brown's wife died only six months ago, and here you are marching over to his house with your Chicken Alfredo Lasagna. Let's face it; you didn't even use a disposable pan. That kind of says it all." Eve yawned and looked down at her chipped nails, which Trish was busy filing.

Trish's emery board stopped midstroke. "It's been almost a year since Pam Brown died, but that's not the point. I don't understand what you're accusing me of, Eve. What's a Casserole Lady?"

"Seriously! You don't know about the Casserole Ladies?"

Eve stared into her manicurist's bewildered brown eyes. She had forgotten how sheltered her friend's life had been.

Trish's gorgeous good looks defied her true innocence, since she was a dark-haired beauty with big almond eyes. Her almost flawless complexion was still nearly wrinkle-free, despite the fact she turned 49 on her last birthday.

But it was her Barbie doll figure that caused all the trouble. Over the years, the salon owner had exercised and watched her diet to keep in shape. She still wore a size 4—the same size she wore on her wedding day three decades ago.

Her husband, Bill, had been so proud of the girl he married. They'd met in high school when Trish was a sophomore. She was a cheerleader for the Meadow Springs football team when Bill was the star quarterback.

It really was love at first sight for both of them. Although Trish was afraid that Bill was one of those conceited jocks who collected girlfriends for a hobby. It wasn't long before she found out that her "Billy" was a sweet farm boy at heart who hoped to one day become a veterinarian. The two had married a few months after high school graduation, against both their parents' wishes. Trish had studied to become a cosmetologist, supporting Bill as he pursued his dream of becoming a vet. During the long years of his schooling, she'd worked hard to make ends meet, never complaining for all the things they couldn't have.

"Look, Trish, I'm genuinely sorry. I sometimes forget you've lived the love story that most of us have only read about in romance novels." Eve's heart broke for the pain Trish had experienced losing her husband. "I know Bill is the only man you've ever loved, but he's gone now. You've got to learn to protect yourself. It's kind of a crazy world out there."

Trish didn't want Eve to talk about Bill's death. It had been two years since the car accident, but she hadn't even given his clothes to her church's thrift store yet. She meant to, but every time she began going through his belongings, she would start sobbing and put everything back.

Trying to distract Eve from this conversation, Trish held up a couple bottles of nail polish for her to choose from, knowing she'd select the vivid shade of purplish red she always wore.

"Fuchsia on Fire, Silly Girl. You know I never want you to paint my nails with anything else." Thirty-five-year-old Eve had been Trish's customer for almost two decades.

When Trish first opened Style by Design, everyone who was anyone in Meadow Springs had to try it out. After all, by then Bill was a veterinarian practicing on the edge of town. Local ladies thought it prestigious to have their hair done by a doctor's wife, even if Dr. Delaney tended animals instead of people.

The Delaneys had invested a lot of hard-earned cash to make Style by Design resemble a cosmopolitan studio. The salon walls were painted a soft lavender, accented with a hand-painted mural of brilliant hues of wildflowers. Chandeliers with crystal prisms hung from the high ceiling, reflecting light everywhere, and freshly brewed coffee with a plate of homemade chocolates always tempted the clientele.

When Trish and Eve met, Eve was a high school junior wanting to look her best for prom. She'd loved the up-do complete with rhinestone accents that the hairdresser created for her. More than that, despite their age differences, Eve sensed Trish would be her friend for life. And that's exactly what she had become. Right now, Eve decided she better warn her best buddy about keeping her emotions in check.

"I know you miss Bill like crazy, but he's gone now. You have to use a little wisdom, or you'll really turn into a Casserole Lady."

"Will you please just spit it out, Eve? I told you I don't have any idea what a Casserole Lady is." While she spoke, the experienced manicurist carefully painted her friend's nails. Trish was used to talking while she worked, but she had to admit she was starting to get agitated.

"The definition of a Casserole Lady? OK, you know those retirement communities where the women outnumber the men?"

"Not really." Trish put the top back on the nail polish bottle.

"Well, that's not the point anyway. The point is when women are alone and getting older, they are often looking for a good man. And really, you can't blame them. But it's hard for them to find a good catch, because usually men die before their wives. So when an older man is widowed, like my dad was last year when we lost my mother, these desperate females seem to come out of the woodwork offering sympathy, support, and of course, a casserole."

"A casserole?" Trish asked, not understanding what a casserole had to do with anything.

"Often the first plan of attack for these aggressive ladies is to stop by the grieving widower's home with a warm casserole. They know that the way to a man's heart really is through his stomach. My father was vulnerable when Mom died. I'm glad we were there to fend them off for him. The very first week, there was a 60-something blonde with tuna and noodles; a dyed, raven-haired septuagenarian with that green bean and mushroom soup recipe; and a sleek silver-haired number with her signature spaghetti. They usually bring it in a good glass casserole dish. That way the unsuspecting bachelor has to return it. Part two of the attack is getting the dish back."

Suddenly, Trish realized why Eve had been so upset with her for taking Chicken Alfredo Lasagna to Pam Brown's husband last week. "You don't think Gary Brown thinks I'm one of those Casserole Ladies, do you?" Now concerned, Trish subconsciously bit her bottom lip, something that Bill had repeatedly told her to stop doing.

"Oh, honey, don't worry. Gary is probably just like my father. These poor men don't know anything about the Casserole Ladies. They never realize what hit them until it's too late. I was just concerned about you putting yourself out there and getting hurt."

Concentrating on her task, Trish didn't answer. "It's time to put your nails under the lights for a few moments."

Eve's fingernails looked perfect. New tips, new paint, and now they just needed to dry. Obediently Eve placed her hands inside the nail dryer.

Trish set the timer while continuing, "Pam Brown was one of my clients for longer than you have been, Eve." The salon owner's eyes suddenly filled with tears and her voice cracked as she said, "I hate breast cancer. Whenever a woman has it, and let's face it, lots of us get it, I'm the one who has to make it look like they have some hair when it's getting thin from chemotherapy. Before it all falls out, I'm also the one who has to help them find just the right wig, one that fits and matches their hair color."

Now Eve Hughes was the one who looked confused.

"You probably didn't know that about me, did you? I guess you could call it my ministry. I suppose I'm one of those people who go to church on Sunday, and sit in the back and never say much. But there's this passion inside me to help women look the very best they can while they're fighting their way through cancer."

Trish took a sip of cold coffee from her cup that was sitting on the counter. "I've always felt it was something the Good Lord birthed in me. I'm pretty knowledgeable about wigs. I took some classes so I'd be able to offer struggling ladies special assistance. We don't advertise, but there's a room in the back of the shop for cancer patients. Of course, other folks suffer hair loss, too, and I try to help them, but the reason I opened it was for women with cancer."

Eve stared at her stylist like she was seeing her for the very first time. Just then the timer went off, and Trish brightly said, "Your nails are all done."

"They look beautiful, as usual. Thanks so much, Trish." Eve was looking down admiring her nails, when suddenly she looked up into Trish's brown eyes. "Can I ask you a personal question?"

"Oh, please, we've been friends for 20 years. Shoot."

"What's it like for a woman like Pam to lose her breasts, her hair, and then eventually her life? How do you help them?"

"I don't think Pam would mind me telling you the whole truth. She was really beautiful when she was young, and even though she was getting older like all of us, she still had gorgeous, thick, red hair. We went to school together, and that hair was her trademark."

For a moment Trish was grief-stricken. "Her chemo made her hair fall out overnight. Thank God, we had ordered just the right wig a few weeks earlier. We cried together that afternoon. I didn't have any words that would take her hurt away, but I held her. She told me it was easier to lose her breasts than her hair. It's like that for some women."

"What about her husband, Gary? Was he there for her?"

"If he wouldn't have been, I would never tell you, because it would be wrong to judge his motivation. Some men walk away because it breaks their heart into a million pieces. They can't bear not being able to fix it."

Eve handed Trish a check that included a generous tip. She never wanted to take advantage of their friendship.

"Thanks, Eve. As far as Gary Brown, though, the truth is, I never saw a man who was kinder, more patient, or had more faith. That's why I took him the casserole. Gary really thought his wife was going to be the one to get a miracle. Even when the doctors said there was no hope, Gary kept on believing."

"I'm surprised. I never thought he was a very compassionate person. I mean, he's a judge. You just don't expect a judge to be a softie."

"Don't get me wrong. I'm sure when he's Judge Gary Brown, he's a different man, but in the moments I saw him, he was Gary, the husband of a dying woman whom he loved more than his own life. I bumped into him the other day at the high school where our daughters are both seniors. He looked so thin."

"Oh, that's right, I forgot, you and Pam had your girls about the same time. Your Katie is so gorgeous. Funny, neither of you had any other children."

Trish always enjoyed her conversations with Eve, but she realized it was time to get back to work. "Eve, you know I'd love to talk to you all day, but I've got a salon to run. I have a customer coming in for a cut and color soon. I better grab my sandwich out of the refrigerator in the back. I bring a peanut butter and jelly on wheat every day. Bill would have a fit if he knew how rarely I cook since he's been gone. Don't know what I'll do when Katie goes off to college this fall."

"Maybe I could help?" offered a middle-aged man who had just walked into Trish's manicure station. "I hope you don't mind? I told the receptionist we were old friends. Besides, she remembered me from coming in with Pam."

Trish and Eve were both startled as Gary Brown's six-foot presence filled the small space. He was the picture of professionalism dressed in a dark blue pin-stripe suit with a white shirt and burgundy silk tie. In his hands he held an old white and blue Corning Ware casserole dish.

Eve smiled a little too broadly as she stood and picked up her purse. "I'll make another appointment later, Trish. Have to get back to the office before my boss misses me." Then her face softened as she gently said to Gary, "I never had a chance to tell you how very sorry I am about your wife, Judge Brown. She was my nurse when my youngest son was born."

The attractive 50-something man said, "Thank you. I couldn't have made it through without good friends like Trish here."

"She is the best!" Eve agreed as she slowly turned and walked away.

She couldn't help overhearing Gary Brown say, "Thanks for the lasagna, Trish. My daughter said it was the first decent meal she's had in months."

Then he paused like he didn't know how to express what he wanted to say next. Eve also stopped in her tracks waiting for his next remark.

The judge cleared his throat. "Trish, I've never asked a woman to dinner since I met Pam 30 years ago, but I was wondering…" He stopped again, unable to find the words.

Trish could no longer bear the suspense. "Gary, I haven't had dinner with a man other than my Bill for 30 years, either. Yet if you are asking me if I would like to have dinner with you, my answer is, 'A definite yes.'"

The judge grinned from ear to ear, like he was a schoolboy again.

But it was Eve Hughes whose cheeks blushed almost as brightly as her Fuchsia on Fire nails. On the way out of Style by Design, she mumbled to the receptionist, "I guess she's not just another Casserole Lady."

CHRISTINA RYAN CLAYPOOL, a Christian speaker and journalist who was named the 2011 First Place National Amy Writing Awards winner, has been featured on CBN's 700 Club and Joyce Meyer Ministries. Her latest book is *Seeds of Hope for Survivors.*

    www.christinaryanclaypool.com
    www.christinaryanclaypool.com/blog1

A Sunday Kind of Love

* * *

Lynn Gipson

Melanie Lambert spent a lot of time at her desk daydreaming about the man in the office down the hall. She was a sales manager at her company, and the man down the hall was Guy Morgan, a top-notch salesman recently transferred in from Ohio. She felt an attraction to him every time they met to discuss business. He often asked her to lunch. There seemed to be a slight urgency in his voice, but she always declined.

Melanie regretted her refusals, because she really liked this man with the gentle, composed disposition, and sense of humor. She liked the way his eyes smiled at her when they were in a meeting. They seldom talked about personal matters, but her assistant, Jody, told her he was single.

"Hold on now, Melanie. The last thing you need is an office romance, or anything of the sort! Remember Michael?" she chastised herself.

Even though her ex-husband's betrayal had happened two years ago, her eyes still stung with tears when she thought about it. One day she had a husband she loved, who attended church with her every Sunday, and the next he was gone. He told her he'd met someone else. Just like that—after five years.

"I want a divorce. It's over," Michael said, as if he were reading her the newspaper. He'd then taken an overseas assignment as a news correspondent and took his new love with him.

Devastated, Melanie cried herself to sleep every night for six months, then slowly began picking up the pieces of her shattered life. Every day and night she prayed for God to take the pain and emptiness away. She and Michael had no children, agreeing to wait five years before starting a family. Five years turned out to be too late, so now she worked long hours to delay going home to her empty new house.

Melanie knew Jesus well, and it was her relationship with Him that kept her going. Still, something inside her longed for the companionship of a man—just a friend—who shared her Christian beliefs.

At five o'clock one evening Guy walked into her office and sat down. Melanie looked up and smiled, expecting a discussion about a recent sale, and was completely taken aback by his question.

"Melanie, could I go to church with you on Sunday?"

"What did you just...I'm sorry, what?"

"Church, on Sunday, could you take me to yours? If I've overstepped, forgive me, but I haven't found a church here yet, and I've overheard you talk about how wonderful yours is. My wife died two years ago, and I don't know many people here. I don't have a family. I really need the friendship of fellow Christians right now, and I somehow feel a connection with you."

"I've felt it too," Melanie said, before thinking.

*

The following Sunday Guy came by with a bouquet of daisies in hand to pick Melanie up for church. The sermon that day was about Christian relationships and dating.

How fitting, thought Melanie.

Melanie and Guy went to church together every Sunday. They worked together as professionals. They studied the Bible together and learned the meaning of a Christ-filled relationship. Their dates consisted of dinners, movies, and long walks on the beach. He told her of his life, and she told him of hers.

Melanie kept telling herself to slow down and watch it. She was still in great pain from Michael's betrayal. She had loved him deeply, even though she always felt she was the one doing all the giving and getting very little in return. Guy was so gentle and kind and seemed to genuinely care about her, but she couldn't give her heart away that easily.

Several times she backed away from the relationship, telling Guy she needed space. He seemed to understand and didn't push her any further at first.

After several break-ups however, he backed off completely. "Melanie, I've come to love you deeply. This on-again, off-again relationship of ours is driving me crazy. I haven't asked you for anything but your love and respect. If you really don't want to see me anymore, just tell me."

"Guy, I'm sorry I can't give you something I don't have inside. I care about you also, but I can't bring myself to trust again, and without trust we have nothing. I can be your friend, but right now that's all I can give."

"Melanie, I'm not Michael. He was a fool to let you go! I am a man very much in love with a woman who obviously doesn't feel the same way. I'm sorry, too, but this is it. It's over." Tears rolled down Guy's face as he got up from the sofa and walked out the door.

Melanie sat there on the sofa with the lights out for three hours and cried. He was gone, just like Michael, and there was nothing she could do about it. She sobbed until there were no more tears, feeling empty inside.

The next day at work she stayed in her office. She didn't want to face Guy and the other employees' questions. They had all come to know she and Guy were quite the item; their relationship had been fodder for much office gossip. When she didn't see Guy all day, she supposed he was avoiding her as well.

Late that evening, as she was working, Guy came into her office and gave her his two-week notice. "I can't continue working here. It's too painful to see you every day. I love you too much, and I feel I have to move on."

Melanie was stunned. All she could do was nod. Then she told him she wished him well and turned back to her computer to indicate the conversation was over. She wanted him to leave, so he wouldn't see her cry again.

What is wrong with me? Why can't I trust him? Why can't I forget what Michael did to me?

*

The following Sunday the sermon at church was about letting go of the past. She listened to every word the reverend said and knew somehow she had to find a way to get past her feelings of fear if she wanted to have any kind of peace in her life. When she saw Guy after the service, he smiled and hugged her, then walked to his car.

That night she prayed, asking God to let her be free of the past and of Michael. She was ready. She knew it was time to let him go, whether she and Guy were together or not. Suddenly, a weight lifted from her shoulders, and at once she felt free. She knew God had answered her prayers. If only it hadn't happened too late for her to have a future with Guy.

The last week of Guy's employment with the company was hard to take. Melanie wished with all her heart he wouldn't leave. She knew she loved him. She wanted to ask him to stay, but her pride got in the way. She was certain he had made his mind up and was too afraid of his rejection.

On his last day of his employment, Guy walked into her office and sat down once again. He looked devastated.

"I came to say good-bye, Melanie, and wish you all the best in the world. I will always love you, I hope you know that."

As he turned to walk out the door, Melanie stopped him cold.

"I love you too, Guy. I've finally given Michael up. Please don't leave." she said softly.

Guy's face broke out into a wondrous smile as he rushed over to Melanie and put his arms around her. Melanie's tears of joy were all the motivation he needed to ask his next question.

"Melanie, will you marry me?"

"Yes! Yes! Yes!" Melanie cried.

*

One fine Saturday in April, they came together as man and wife in the little white church they both attended. Guy moved into Melanie's larger house, they did some renovations, and when Guy slyly suggested they make one room a nursery, Melanie jumped for joy. She knew she was ready for a child.

*

A year later, their son, Isaiah, was born. As Melanie sat on the back porch one spring day, rocking her beautiful child and watching her beloved husband cooking steaks on the grill and singing lullabies loud enough for the whole neighborhood to hear, the phone rang.

It was Michael. He had just returned to the States and learned of Melanie's wedding.

"Are you happy, Melanie?"

"Very happy."

"I suppose I'm glad for you, then. I'm sorry I hurt you. I made the biggest mistake of my life when I let you go. I know that now," Michael said.

"You are forgiven, Michael, you are forgiven. May God bless you always. Good-bye, Michael."

LYNN GIPSON, a 61-year-old cancer survivor, has one son and two amazing granddaughters. She lives in Mississippi and, after a lifetime of dreaming of being a writer, has become one. She is first and foremost a Christian, and tries to reach people who may be hurting through her articles, short stories—both fiction and nonfiction—and poems.

Cyber Love

* * *

Jude Urbanski

My fingers flew across my computer keyboard, then suddenly froze. *Will he know this email is not my mom's? In all honesty, Mom did try for all of two emails. After that, she said it was up to me.* Oh, well, here goes....

*

Hello, Jon,

How was your week? Did you finish your painting in time for the Art Fair? I know you were working hard to get ready. I used to do some painting in earlier days and loved doing seascapes, which always gave me a sense of serenity. Do you know what I mean? Haven't painted for several years, but want to get back to it sometime. I've been trying my hand at writing. Mostly poetry and mostly to keep myself occupied.

In reality, I stay quite occupied. Chloe and I attended a forum last night at the university. The forum "Censorship in the Arts" was most interesting with several artist panel members. The discussion of the photograph of Piss Christ drew the loudest roar regarding censorship. Most of the audience felt this particular art should not be censored at all; others were appalled at such work. I sided with those appalled. Wish you could have been there for the animated discussion. Art certainly is in the eye of the beholder.

Have you seen this particular picture? Artist Andres Serrano photographed a crucifix of Jesus in a container of urine. I understand a print of this photograph was vandalized at a recent exhibit in France.

It's hard for me to conceive someone would call this art. This is my dear Jesus, my God, and yes, I'm very offended. In fact, I'm heated up again writing this, so I'll change the subject.

Actually, it's late, so I will close for now. Have a good weekend.

Lily

*

I shut off my computer, leaned back, and exhaled a big sigh.

It had been a lark when it began. Three months ago, my mom, a youngish widow, had finally consented to allow me to post her profile on the Mature Christian Dating Network. I'd hassled her for weeks, before convincing her it was an innocent website, simply men her age who wanted to meet someone with whom to share a relationship and see where it went.

Mom hadn't bought into the concept. It was too foreign and too frightening. She had only gotten one hit, but from one hit a stirring correspondence had developed. Correspondence I'd surreptitiously conducted after Mom gave up and a fact I hoped would remain unknown.

Those emails are stuck on my mind's hard drive. I can't quit thinking about them. I rose and began my bedtime routine. I'd prayed this adventure might ramp up Mom's slowly sinking life, but the computer intimated her. Even with help, she was insecure composing and sending email.

She'd soon begged off and told me to write her "cyber friend," as she called him. She'd see how that went before making a final decision. Initially, I typed Mom's two handwritten letters, but then she lost interest. After a couple of weeks, she rarely wanted to write and only sometimes read what Mr. Jon had sent back. I wasn't sure what she was thinking.

She did say she thought he sounded like a nice man, but since he lived four hours away in upstate Maine, she didn't figure she'd ever meet him. Obviously, her heart wasn't into this romance adventure.

My heart, though, was pulled in like a honeybee to the hive. It made no sense why I was so drawn to these letters, because my love life currently sucked, to be blunt. I still smarted. No, I was still bitter about being dropped by Mr. Right a week before we stood at the altar. It had happened eight months ago, but I was still putting myself back together.

Maybe this letter writing gave me reason to shed my cocoon and try my wings again. That's the best explanation I could come up with as to why I continued.

Mr. Jon's chivalrous emails resonated in my bruised, romantic mind like Sir Lancelot of old. Words of tenderness lifted from the computer screen and whispered in my ear, *'If ever I should leave you, it would never be in springtime. No, no, not in springtime....'* Oh, how my heart danced. Only a zombie wouldn't feel this sensation.

No, of course, Mr. Jon never sang nor said those exact words, but his were close enough that I drooled. Honesty compels me to say he didn't say anything remotely similar, but he did allow himself to be transparent. He released a fountain of emotions, thoughts, and opinions on love, politics, and religion. On where he had been and what he wanted. He became a man I admired, respected, and thought I would enjoy knowing.

Mom couldn't see what she was missing. "Pshaw!" she said.

I shook my head, and for some reason quit trying to get her to see how nice Mr. Jon was.

Late every Friday evening, I hastened to the computer. He wrote at the close of the week. As I settled into the old chair in my bedroom, it became easy to imagine him in comfy sweats, slippers, and a dog at his feet. The dog, of course, was a golden retriever. Soft jazz played in the background. He stretched his tall frame and yawned from time to time.

Am I fantasizing?

Yes, without a doubt. I knew I had a *cum laude* degree. I was no dummy, but something unexplainable drew me. *Mom should be here composing. But then, Mom doesn't want to be here. I do. I embrace these exchanges with more exuberance than I've felt in a long time. Mom and I are really different. She is content where she is, maybe only trying to please me by agreeing to this match business. I am not content....*

Mr. Jon had sent Mom a picture revealing a very handsome, 50s-looking guy. It proved a distinct improvement of the one on the match site. He had thick salt and pepper hair, cobalt blue eyes, and a very snappy grin.

Mom laughed when I said, "What's not to like about him?"

"Honey, your dad was even better looking, if you remember."

"Maybe, Mom, but he's not here. Hasn't been for almost four years."

She got that twitchy, sad little look about her she always got when Dad was mentioned. They had loved dearly. Maybe the memory of that love was all she needed for the rest of her life.

"Well, you should at least read the weekly letters he writes. Want me to pull up the last one?"

"No, Chloe, you just send something back. I'll make up my mind soon...."

I opened the email and inhaled deeply as I clicked on the one from Mr. Jon.

*

Dear Lily,

    Your name says hope and springtime to me. Just wanted to tell you.

    Other than the fuzzy picture on our dating page, I have only the small one you sent a few weeks ago. Why don't you send another, for it is not too clear either? I have formed my own image of you from your letters. Here's what I see: a slim woman with dark hair, a beautiful face, and a gorgeous smile, softening my heart completely. A mischievous look from sparkly brown eyes. A fun partner.

How does that sound? You? You don't have to answer.

I'll answer about Piss Christ, which I have seen. I feel the same as you. When I saw the picture, I actually felt an ache in my heart. My, our, precious Jesus. The one who died for all who believe. You did well to voice a complaint at the forum.

Not only did I get my painting into the Art Fair, I won second place. Talk about surprise. My abstract works do the same for me as your seascapes did for you. When I swirl my brush over the canvas, I am one with my Creator. I don't need to tell you the peace flooding my inmost soul. Isn't it wonderful that God gives us such means of healing and such a sense of accomplishment? It appears He knows us quite well, doesn't He? Amazing.

I'd like to hear more about your poetry. Do you enjoy writing on topics or thoughts? Or people? Poetry is one thing I know I don't have in me, except for expressing my love for someone. Is that also poetry? I think I can do that quite well.

Just say the word when you'd like me to drive down the coast to see you. I am willing.

Will talk more next week. In the meantime, know I'm thinking of you, but remember I asked to know your favorite author(s) and favorite book(s). You also haven't told me which political candidate you favor. I'd like to know. It may be important to our future. Never know.

Jon

*

Dear Jon,

I read your email with interest. I don't have all the answers for you now, but can say, the Holy Bible aside, one of my most favorite books is James Michener's *Centennial*. I have so many favorites, though. Do you?

We'd like you to come down for a visit. How about the 23rd? You probably have plans for Christmas Eve and Christmas Day, but if not, consider staying over. Let me know soon. Thanks.

Lily

*

Dear Lily,

Don't worry if you don't have all my answers. We have time to get to know one another. Michener's works are some of my favorites also, and one of his early books, *The Source,* tops my list. Yes, it's hard to nominate one, when there are so many good books. I confess to thoroughly enjoying James Alexander Thom's historical fiction on Native American lore.

On the visit. I would like very much to meet you and your daughter but have one little problem. On December 15th I will be having rotator cuff surgery. Guess I took my tennis partner too competitively. Anyway, by the 23rd I should be good to travel, but would you mind if my son, Gunther, came along as a driver? I don't want to be a one-armed hazard behind the wheel.

I know a nice little bed-and-breakfast in Snowville and will make reservations. As to being busy for Christmas, our travel plans changed because of my surgery, and we'd love to spend the holiday with you and Chloe. Just say the word. Our kids might even find things to talk about, too.

Will close. Early date tomorrow with my coffee klatch buddies. Really looking forward to our meeting.

Jon

*

Dear Jon,

Yes, please come for the holiday and I'm sure Chloe and Gunther can find things to talk about, even if she is a little gunshy of men presently, due to a broken relationship several months ago. She stays busy with her interior design business. What does Gunther do?

We'll give you the tour of Snowville, small as it is. We always attend Christmas Eve service at our Lutheran church. Hope that is okay with you. On Christmas Day, all we do is eat. I usually have a few close friends drop by in the evening for dessert and conversation. How does this sound?

I must confess I'm a little nervous. Are you? This is all so new to me. Chloe keeps cheering me to push forward with my life.

See the two of you soon.

Lily

*

"Mother, they're here!" I let the curtains fall back in place. "How does my hair look?"

Mom rolled her eyes. *"Your* hair? Shouldn't you be asking me?"

We looked at each other, then broke into gales of laughter.

"Yes, I guess I should, but you said he's bringing his son, and I at least want to look presentable."

I bit my lip to keep from saying more. *I'm definitely more edgy than Mom. I want to see this man who writes like a dream.*

"I'll get the door." Mom swung open the door and stood back. "Hello, Jon. Hello, Gunther. Do come in. Meet my daughter, Chloe."

I've never seen two more handsome men!

The visit progressed well and, by the time Christmas night rolled around, I had things figured out. Mom just wasn't *into* Mr. Jon. Oh, they were courteous and respectful, but no zing happened. I could tell.

"I'll be right back. We need more snacks." *I need to take a breather from our dear friends and from Mr. Jon and Gunther. Need to think a little. Kitchen, here I come.*

I glanced up as Gunther slipped into the kitchen and came to my side as I replenished trays. I felt his hand on my arm. "Don't think it's going to work between them, do you?"

I hedged. "Well…uh, seems your dad doesn't like art, reading, or the theater like Mom thought he did."

Embarrassment flooded Gunther's face. He blinked a few times. "Yeah, uh, he says she really got a laugh out of his thinking she liked to whitewater canoe. Now, *I* sure love everything about canoeing, but it's not Dad's thing." He laughed.

I fussed with the tray on the counter to keep from looking at Gunther. My face would give me away. *I distinctly remember writing how much fun it was to do rapids in a canoe, especially a class four. Jon had definitely written about how much he liked it also. Had it been Jon, or had it been Gunther writing the emails? Just as I had written them?*

"Gunther…I—"

"Chloe…uh…." He grabbed my hands, pulled me toward him, and gazed deeply into my eyes. "I'm busted, aren't I?" He tried unsuccessfully to hide his sheepish grin. "I confess. I wrote all the emails." He gently lifted my chin upward. "Just as I think you did. Right or wrong?"

For a moment, I was lost in deep gray eyes. "Right." I withdrew from his embrace. "I'm guilty, too, but want to know the craziest thing?" I stood back. "The moment you came through our door, I felt as if I already knew you. Right then, I wasn't sure you'd written the emails, but as I've watched you these few days, I've had no doubt. You talk like you write and act like that writer would act."

"Well, lady, you're sharper than I am." He leaned against the table. "It took until Christmas Eve for me to put the pieces together. Scrutiny of our folks had already told me it wasn't going to work for them. You know, too, don't you?"

I nodded and smiled at Gunther. "Simply the way things happen sometimes."

He stepped closer. "That doesn't mean it won't work for us, does it?" Again he raised my chin and softly brushed his thumb over my cheek.

I leaned into his hand. "Want to know my political party?"

JUDE URBANSKI writes women's fiction with inspirational romance. She loves to weave stories about strong characters spinning tragedy into triumph. A member of American Christian Fiction Writers and the National League of American Pen Women, Jude has published both fiction and nonfiction.

http://www.judeurbanski.com
http://judeurbanski.blogspot.com

Earned Love

* * *

CHARLOTTE S. SNEAD

The second semester of my senior year in college, I had three men making claims on me and my life. To say I was in a muddle would be an understatement.

First was my high school boyfriend, who'd taken my virginity the spring of our senior year on a dirt road we'd made into lover's lane. In my mind, I was committed then, and when he moved overseas that summer with his family to his father's new job, we promised to be true, as young love does.

And I was. I met Henry the first Friday the upperclassmen returned to college when he picked up the volunteers for the service project I had chosen. We visited children in an emergency foster shelter, playing with them, tutoring them, and being their friend. Henry was an upperclassman, and an officer in the campus YMCA. I liked him, and we spent every Friday afternoon together. While my boyfriend behaved erratically, sometimes writing, more often not, Henry was consistent. *Stolid*—was that a real word? *Stolid?* He became my best friend, and I wished I'd fallen in love with him, but it was too late. I had carelessly thrown away my virginity.

When my boyfriend returned Stateside and transferred to a university near my home, he was changed. Instead of the laughing, playful guy who had taught me more than I'd been ready to know, he was moody and retreated into dark places. But I was liberated and caught up in the romance of it, desperately trying to make this uncommitted relationship more than it was. One moonless night he took me to a place we'd never been before. I was totally lost—but then I have a poor sense of direction, and it didn't take much.

He pulled me across the front seat of the car roughly and put his hands around my neck. "I could snap your pretty little neck right now and leave you here. It'd be months before anyone found you."

The third man who had been making claims to my life jumped suddenly into mind. Jesus. I'd been going to church with my college roommate, and in her evangelical church I heard the words of Christ more clearly than I'd ever heard them in my religious upbringing. This Jesus refused to remain on the stained glass or in the printed pages of my prayer book. He invaded my thoughts, sought my attention, and demanded my allegiance.

I cried out to him then, this Jesus I was only beginning to know, begging his help, and somehow I broke away, opened the car door, and ran into the woods. Maybe I'd be lost, scared, and hungry for the night, but I'd find help. We weren't in the middle of some jungle, for goodness sake; we were in suburban America. But I guess I ran in circles because my boyfriend's voice kept getting closer. Of course, his long athlete's legs were stronger than mine. He was begging for forgiveness, saying he didn't mean to frighten me. It was cold and very dark, and I decided to surrender.

"Promise you'll take me home?" I cried out.

"I will. I didn't mean to hurt you. Honest." I followed him to the car and, true to his word, he took me directly home. But I wouldn't take his calls the couple of days that remained of semester break and went back to college without seeing him again.

Henry picked me up at the airport. Good old Henry, who had applied for graduate school. He wanted to get a PhD in biochemistry and do research—an honorable man, a solid, responsible man. Not gorgeous, not a star athlete, but comfortable, dependable. If only I'd met him first. I thought about telling him of my dilemma, but I was ashamed. He was a virtuous guy, and I, well...

My roommate, who was the choir director in the little church where she took me every Sunday—now I even attended Sunday school—conned me into singing in the Easter pageant. In my confused and guilty state, I needed the comfort of the kind folks there, and I agreed. One of the other choir members, an assistant in the English Department, noticed my changed mood after my frightening experience over the break. He hounded me until he got it out of me, listening with horror to the tale of my terrified run through the woods.

"You have to break it off with him," he counseled me. "He's an unstable guy. Abusive. Maybe he's on drugs."

I felt stuck—I had values, although I had betrayed them, and I felt I'd ruined my life. I couldn't marry. I'd thrown my virginity away to someone who proved to be unworthy, and I'd discovered I couldn't trust my future to that guy. My choir friend was right. My so-called boyfriend was no good, perhaps even dangerous. I knew that now, and with the prayers and support of my fellow choir member, I wrote a letter breaking it off.

My roommate was relieved, and told her boyfriend, who happened to be in the biochemistry class with Henry, and he passed on the news. Henry called me and asked me to go to a sporting event with him. I made excuses. I was confused, but when he was accepted into his graduate program, I heard about it through the same grapevine.

My hand hovered over the phone. Henry was probably my best friend, but I didn't want to send mixed signals. He knew I'd broken up with my boyfriend, but he didn't know I wasn't the sweet girl he thought I was. *Ah, what the heck, I'm taking him to celebrate.*

"Hey, Henry, it's me, Denver," I said.

"I know your voice. I've missed you the last couple of Fridays."

I took a breath. "I've had a lot going on. But I heard you were accepted into grad school, and I want to take you out to celebrate."

"You do?"

"Yeah, what's a good evening for you?"

"How about Friday?"

"Fine. I'll take you to Ivy's. My treat."

"You don't have to do that," Henry said.

"That's the only way it will be. I want to honor your achievement. Please?"

"If that's the only way."

We chatted a bit, he told me he'd pick me up at six, and we went out to dinner a few days later. It was easy after that. Henry was my best friend after all, and we started sharing movies and walks. He happened to be around whenever I needed a ride, and when he called to invite me to a party, I didn't hesitate. This was my friend. I did feel a bit awkward, though—we were going to an event together. I wore a dressy dress, and he cleaned up nicely in a fine suit.

But it was later, in his car behind the dorm when he leaned down and kissed me, that my traitorous body responded, and I had a profound revelation: I'd never really "loved." I'd merely lusted, and those buttons still worked well. The truths I was learning at that little church had increased my conviction about my poor choices. I now knew God's plan for marriage, and sleeping around wasn't part of it. Furthermore, I was leading poor Henry on. Henry was the kind of guy who'd want rings and commitment, and I was not a fit candidate to be anyone's wife.

I was able to avoid him with the press of rehearsals as our Maundy Thursday performance drew closer. In a jumble of emotions, I joined that part of the choir screaming "Crucify him!" and suddenly I realized I had. I had crucified Jesus as surely as if I had hammered the nails in his hands. Sinless, he chose to suffer and die for me, Denver Miller, and it hit me: if I had been the only lost lamb in the world, he would have left heaven just for me.

With tears running down my face, I gave my allegiance to the third man who pursued me that spring, and he gave me new life.

My old boyfriend drove all night one day the next week, catching up with me as I walked back to the dorm. My pulse quickened—was it fear, guilt, maybe even love? But I felt only pity as he swore his love, threatened suicide, and begged me to take him back. "I can't live without you," he pleaded.

With a calmness I knew had to come from heaven and the strength of God's Spirit that he promised now lived in me, I told my former boyfriend that he'd have to learn to live without me, and that the God I had chosen to serve could help him. I turned and walked away. I didn't look back.

Now I had to face the next hurdle. To be true to the God I now served and to myself, but especially to the good man who was coming to love me, I had to tell Henry the whole sordid story. What a weird role reversal this was for the 1950s: the virgin guy and the soiled gal. At my invitation, Henry came over one evening, glad the Easter program was over and the rehearsals before it.

Maybe he thought it a bit crazy when I told him I just wanted to go for a walk, but he agreed. I walked silently, weeping as I tried to work up the courage to tell him. When he saw my tears, he asked what was wrong. I somehow managed to stammer my confession, fully expecting a well-deserved righteous indignation to rise up in him. I couldn't look up.

He raised my chin, making me look into his eyes. "It isn't what's past, Denver. That's over and done. It's what lies ahead. It's you and me, from now on," he said, and he gently kissed me.

I didn't deserve this man, and if my college roommate hadn't been at our wedding six months later, I would've backed out. I wept my grief that I couldn't bring my groom the bride he deserved, and she reminded me that he'd made his choice, fully knowing the mistakes I'd made.

The next day I walked down the aisle and into our life together. Never once in the many years since has Henry ever mentioned what I told him that long-ago night.

I can't say we lived happily ever after. Like every couple, we had our ups and downs—in fact, I remember one day sitting on the front porch of our little rented house. I was working to put him through graduate school. I dragged home from work, cleaned the house, cooked the meals, hauled our dirty clothes to the Laundromat, and brought them home to iron. He studied. I learned that *solid* meant unromantic, and *responsible* meant hard work. That translated into a lack of understanding. Henry never knew I struggled, and he always put work before play. In fact, Henry didn't know how to play.

Sitting there on the porch, I asked God if I had to stay married to this man the rest of my life, and I heard his still, small voice ask me, "Has he been unfaithful?"

"Henry? God, surely you know better! He'd die of embarrassment if another woman saw him naked."

Again God whispered, "Has he abused you, hurt you in any way?"

"Not physically, but he's not always there for me," I murmured.

If we can hear God chuckle, I did, and he said, "I hate divorce because I desire godly seed. Now brush off your hands, roll up your sleeves, and make this thing work. And remember, Denver, I am always there for you."

I prayed to learn to love my good husband the way I should, and God sent Henry off to war, not even knowing he'd planted a seed of life in me. I learned to love him all right, worrying if he'd come home to see the little baby we'd created together, aching when his letters were held up for weeks in the Army mail, and rejoicing when I got eight in a day. I had our baby alone while he was half a world away. I prayed for him to come home and know his son. I sent him pictures and glowing letters describing our baby's little actions—*he rolled over today*—and noises—*he's making hard sounds now*—but the baby didn't become real to him until the night he walked in, handsome in his uniform, and gazed down into the crib at our son's sleeping form.

"He's really real," Henry said.

In the years since, Henry has given me a daughter and another son. They are all grown and gone now, with children of their own, but Henry and I are enjoying the love we've shared and that has grown for over 40 years. It's a solid love that a responsible man gave to me, and I returned to him an earned love.

CHARLOTTE S. SNEAD, the author of the novel *His Brother's Wife* (OakTara), has been married almost 50 years, and she and her husband have five adult children, one adult foster daughter, and five grandsons. They live on 20 beautiful acres in West Virginia. She has served as a "mentor mom" for her church's Mothers of Preschoolers ministry for over a decade and is the former president of West Virginians for Life, the state affiliate of the National Right to Life Committee, serving fifteen years. She founded the Central West Virginia Center for Pregnancy Care in 1985 and still serves on that board.

www.charlottesreaders.com

Please

* * *

JoAnn Durgin

Such a simple word, really. According to Mom, it was my third word. Even early in life, I understood its inherent value. Saying "please" earned favor with teachers. In high school, that one-syllable, six-letter word afforded certain privileges with the opposite sex. Then came law school and beyond. Put it this way: a judge and jury are much more inclined to find for the side of the hard-headed, brash litigator if he exhibits behavior indicative of good breeding. In essence, the word "please" possesses tremendous power, a lesson well-learned. But it's not always enough, especially when your wife blames you for almost losing a child.

So here I stand in front of the full-length bedroom mirror, straightening my tie clip and smoothing the silk necktie with shaky fingers. Not much makes me nervous, but coming up with a plan to convince Jenna—my wife of 12 years and the mother of our three children—not to abandon our marriage gives me pause. Getting Ted Bundy pardoned would have been a cakewalk by comparison. Jenna's the most stubborn woman I've ever met, but that's one of the countless reasons I adore her. Independent and strong, she's a tireless advocate and defender. No cause is more worthy than fighting for the rights of those defenseless to help themselves. When those incredible green eyes light with passion, she's more formidable than my most esteemed courtroom adversary. But somewhere along the way, those eyes began to dim when she looked my way—love and trust transitioning to a wary suspicion.

Employing my courtroom voice, I practice keeping my voice calm and even. Every way I pose my questions with the word *please,* it sounds either desperate or pathetic. Great. Stepping back a few paces, I make an honest assessment of my appearance. Yeah, I look like a ridiculous relic. My hair is longer than usual, but I still have enough on top. Turning my head, I finger the curls on my nape. Jenna always liked it this way, the way I wore it when we started dating as students at Boston University two decades ago. My suit is the first one I bought when I was promoted to junior partner, made by some designer Jenna said would impress the judge and jury. It still fits, in part because I often take the stairs instead of the elevator at the courthouse and up to my 22nd floor office in the downtown Boston high-rise.

The shirt is monogrammed—an unnecessary excess—but no way would I complain because of the memorable way Jenna presented the shirt and cuff links to me. A glance at my wrist makes me smile. Leaning closer to the mirror, I scrutinize every 38-year-old pore. Not bad. Every line etched on my forehead or around my eyes represents victory, not defeat, and certainly not age. Everything is in place, smoothed, shaved, and clipped. I move my eyes down to my shoes—the same black hightops I wore at our wedding. Nostalgia should count for something, and Jenna has the most sentimental soul I've ever known.

Heading out the bedroom door, I'm seized by inspiration. Ducking into the walk-in closet, I dig out my oldest, battered Red Sox cap and stuff it in my back pocket. Ridiculous, yeah, but I'm out to win back my wife. The hat is the same one I wore to Fenway the first time I kissed her. I knew in that moment she was the girl I'd marry.

I've never been one to pray, but I mumble a quiet prayer under my breath as I slide into my vintage Chevy truck.

"God, if you're listening, all I ask is that you soften her heart."

*

My eyes widen as Geoff comes roaring into the school parking lot in Roberta, his beloved old blue and white truck. It's been tucked away in the garage at the back of our house for the past three-plus years, and I'm surprised he's been able to start her. I resist a pointed glance at my watch; he must have rescheduled more than one appointment and an important deposition. Pulling the truck to the curb beside where I stand, he shoves the gear into park and hops out, coming around the front. The devil-may-care cocky grin he'd worn when he turned the corner transitions into one of concern. "What happened?"

"I slipped this morning on the way into the school." My voice chokes on the words. For a former dancer, you'd think I could have exhibited more grace on the rain-slick stone walkway outside the school. Leaning on my crutches, I almost lose my balance, but Geoff puts a supportive hand beneath my arm.

"Lean on me, sweetheart."

I swallow hard, secretly pleased at the endearment. "You look like a trip down memory lane." Drinking in his appearance, I appreciate his efforts. "What's the occasion?" Part-hopping, part-hobbling to avoid putting pressure on my foot, I grimace as I make my way to the truck. Opening the door, he helps me settle inside before storing the crutches on the back seat. My lips curl at the incongruous sight of the frayed BoSox cap sticking out the back pocket of his suit pants. The smell of restored leather mingles with his cologne and the memory of the passionate kisses we've shared in this truck. Kisses I desperately long for again. My heartstrings slowly loosen, the tight knots inside me easing from fear into hope.

"I'm taking my beautiful wife to dinner." He skims over my nondescript, schoolmarm dress as though I'm the most desirable woman in the world. Tucking the bottom of the skirt inside the door, he gives me a wink. Heat coils in my belly and curls upward, and I feel the warmth in my cheeks betray me.

Closing my door, Geoff hurries around and slides into the driver's seat. The truck is made for much shorter men of the late 1950s, not my six-foot-four husband. He turns to me. "Don't know about you, Jen, but I can't take much more of this emotional and physical separation."

"I agree."

He narrows his eyes with obvious surprise. "You don't know how glad I am to hear you say that." His gaze slants to my wrapped left ankle. "Is it more than a nasty sprain?"

My eyes meet his and I nod. "Yes, it's much more."

A question surfaces in the depth of those gorgeous blue eyes. Eyes I couldn't resist the first time he asked to kiss me. The man actually said, "Please." No man had ever asked permission to kiss me; no man had claimed it was an honor. I gave my heart to Geoff in that moment.

Steering the truck out of the parking lot, he pulls off on the nearest, quiet residential street and cuts the engine. When it rumbles and sputters a bit, I can't help but smile. Twisting his body, adjusting his long legs, Geoff reaches for my hands. I give them to him willingly. "Speak to me." Usually so in-control and commanding, his tone is unbearably tender.

Inhaling a deep breath, I run my hand over my dress and look down at my hands now resting in my lap. "All these months since Trevor's accident, I've blamed you."

"Jen—"

I raise my hand and lift my eyes to his. "This needs to be said, Geoff." When I hesitate, he nods for me to continue. The lines on his forehead ease as does the tautness around his mouth. "Slippery rocks in the creek caused our son to lose his footing and fall. Just like I fell on the walkway at the school this morning. Trevor hitting his head was a stupid fluke no one could have foreseen or stopped, but for whatever reason God allowed it to happen. He loves going fishing with you, spending time with you. That's something he'll always remember."

A tear courses down Geoff's cheek. Then another and another until his cheeks are damp with regret and unspoken heartache. When he scoots closer, I'm thankful we're in Roberta and not the Mercedes. Here, there are no barriers between our shared sadness. I lean into him and he moves his arms around me, sheltering me.

My husband holds me as he hasn't for months. For his part, it's guilt, but anger is my biggest stumbling block. It's time to make up for lost moments and let one another back inside. Geoff's let his hair grow longer, and I run my fingers through it, touching the curls at his neck. If only he knew how many nights I wanted to do this but let my hand fall back on the pillow instead. "I'm so sorry I've pushed you away. Forgive me. No more," I murmur.

"No more," he says, his voice whisper soft as he pulls me into his chest. "Forgive *me*." His broken sob breaks the quiet and my heart as he peppers my forehead, my temple, my cheeks with kisses before seeking and finding my lips. My lips quiver beneath his as I wrap one hand around his broad shoulder and rest the other over his chest. Beneath it, I feel the steady rhythm of his heart. My anchor.

His mouth covers mine again and I savor the forgotten familiarity of his touch, his passion. How I love this man. Finally placing his hands on either side of my face, he pulls away; his breath is ragged with the rise and fall of his chest. "I love you, Jenna. That'll never change. And you know what I love? How you speak of Trevor in present tense. Thank you for that. I still believe he'll pull out from wherever he is and come back to us, the same as before."

Leaning his head against the seat, Geoff wipes away another stream of tears with the back of his hand. "I can't believe anything else. He's a fighter, like his mom." He kisses my cheek. "All the courtroom battles in the world could never prepare me for a fight like this. But I need you beside me, sweetheart. We need each other." I snuggle into him and hear him whisper, "God willing, we'll get through it."

"I love you, too, Geoff. Always have, always will."

My cell phone rings, startling us both. I ignore it until Geoff gives me an odd look. "I think you should answer it."

Although I have no idea why, I know he's right. Reaching for my purse where it's slid down on the floorboard, I quickly pull out my phone. My pulse quickens when I look at the screen. *Marcia Bernard, M.D. Mass General.*

My hand trembles. By now, my heart pounds. "Hi, Dr. Bernard." I listen, hearing the words. I nod and tears stream from my eyes, unbidden. They fall on my lap, and I make no move to stop them. Unable to speak, I close the phone and my eyes meet Geoff's.

"Jen? What is it, sweetheart?" Fear widens his eyes. They're brighter than ever.

I tremble and cradle his handsome face between my palms. "It's going to be okay. Our boy is finally awake again."

*

Three hours later, Jenna sits on one side of our son's bed and I keep watch on the other. The crutches rest beside her chair. Careening into the medical center parking lot like a madman in Roberta, I'd jumped out of the truck and scooped her in my arms, carrying her up to Trevor's floor, using the elevator for once. I held her close, enjoying her warmth, the curve of her body next to me.

The initial results are good from the gamut of tests run on our son. For now, we still wait. He'll be okay. Like I told Jenna, I have faith. I can't think otherwise, and I know she shares that belief. We'll do anything it takes to bring Trevor home to join his younger brother and sister. Our family will be whole again. I close my eyes. *Thank you, God.*

"You know, this is one of those days I'll never forget," I say.

The love in my wife's eyes will linger in my soul as Jenna gives me a weary but glorious smile, brighter than the sun's rays. She's never been more beautiful. "Sometimes God whispers in our hearts, and other times, he shouts to grab our attention." Reaching for my hand, she brings it to her lips and plants a soft kiss. "Today, He's done both." With her other hand, she picks up Trevor's so our three hands are joined together. "Would you mind if I say a prayer for all of us?"

I can only nod, overcome again with the emotion and blessings of this day. Finally, I choke out that precious and most powerful word: "Please."

JOANN DURGIN is the author of the popular Lewis Legacy Series (Torn Veil Books). A full-time estate administration paralegal, JoAnn lives with her family in southern Indiana. Writing Christ-honoring fiction is her passion.

www.joanndurgin.com

Thirty Minutes or Less

* * *

Carole Towriss

Nicole Miller never intended to trust another man, because they'd all let her down—her father, stepfather, brother, her boss, and, most of all, her fiancé.

But Brody Whitson? *He* had come every single day for two and a half months.

The day she moved—fled—into the rental house in Barton Beach, he'd found her fighting back tears as she maneuvered her crutches precariously down the five steps of her front porch to get the mail. Since then, every evening he dropped by after he came home from work to see if she needed anything. The cast from toes to mid-thigh meant she needed a lot of things, but she didn't need a nosy neighbor. For the first week she told him no, but he came anyway. He changed light bulbs, fetched groceries, and fixed a leaky faucet. And always brought in the mail.

Sometimes he stayed for a few minutes and talked. She began to stand beside the window—hidden by the partially drawn shades—and watch him leave his house early in the morning. Lately she waited for him to return. The last couple weeks, he often brought a sunflower. Where he got them in a tiny beach town in November she'd never know.

Last night when he brought a flower he said, "What if you came to dinner with me tonight?"

"I don't go out. I don't date. It never ends well."

"Never?"

"Never."

"Then invite me in for pizza. That's not a date."

"Oh, really?"

"Of course not. It's dinner with a friend."

She chuckled. "OK, sure. But not tonight. Tomorrow."

"Tomorrow." He winked as he walked backwards to the edge of the porch.

She gasped, but he spun just in time, almost as if he'd practiced the move to impress her.

And now she sat before the mirror putting on makeup. Why? It wasn't a date. She brushed her auburn hair and applied the lipstick—carefully chosen to look like she wasn't wearing any. What had she gotten herself into? Maybe she should pull her hair up into a ponytail. That would look more casual.

The knock at the front door stirred butterflies in her stomach. Actually, more like rabbits running. She took several calming breaths and moved from her bedroom toward the front door.

Brody smiled as he tipped his head and peered through the sidelights. The rabbits thumped again.

She opened the door and hopped to the side to let him in.

He held out a handful of sunflowers and leaned forward to kiss her on the cheek.

"Is that how one friend greets another?"

"It is when one of them is as lovely as you." He grinned. "How's your leg?"

"Pain's not bad today. Thanks for asking." She added the flowers to the already full vase.

"Should we order? We can talk while we wait."

She shrugged. "OK."

Brody pushed one button, then held his cell phone to his ear. "What kind do you like?"

"Mushrooms. Extra cheese."

"Mushrooms?" He gave an exaggerated shudder. He finished the order, pressed another button, and plopped into her chair like he was her best friend. Putting his feet up on the coffee table, he grinned. "Thirty minutes."

"Thirty minutes? In this little town?"

"Or less. I ordered from Pizza Market."

"That's in the next town over! Why would you do that?"

"One: their pizza's better. Two: Pizza Palace is closed for the season."

"Really? Guess I should have thought of that." She sighed. "Thirty minutes. I'm really hungry. Want an apple or something?"

"Nah, I'm good."

Yes, he was. Dark blond hair, warm chocolate eyes that sparkled when he smiled, and broad shoulders. Shoulders like that had gotten her into trouble more than once. Which was why she had to remember this was nothing more than a thank you for all the help he had given her in the last two months.

He flashed his dimples. "Come on, sit down."

Dimples. Must ignore the dimples. Nicole hobbled to the couch and sank down, then lifted her leg to the table. "You know, you don't have to keep helping me. I can do pretty much everything by myself."

"I know." His gaze scanned the room, landing on the laptop on the kitchen table. "Do you work from here? Telecommute or something?"

"No, I'm not working at the moment."

His brow furrowed. "Oh." He wanted to ask more, she could tell, but he was too much of a gentleman to pry.

"I got this place for a song since it's off season. As you know, I don't eat out or go anywhere, so my expenses are minimal. I'm living off my savings right now until I go back." She made a face. "Which I really don't want to do."

"Why not?" A flash of a smile said something, but she couldn't tell what. Did he want her to stay?

Nicole studied him. How much should she tell him? His dark eyes and soft expression said she could trust him.

She settled back into the cushions. "I was in a horrific car accident. You see what it did to my leg. I was in the hospital for over a month. I had medical leave, but that only guarantees you *a* job when you return, not the same job. My boss gave my job away. To his niece. After *I* built up the client list. He'd been wanting to for a long time. I came out here to get away from everyone and everything."

"What about your family?"

"My parents are both gone."

"Friends?"

"I worked too hard to make any. There's no one else who cares."

"I care." He moved to the couch. Tucking one leg under him, he faced her and rested his arm on the back of the couch.

"What are you going to do now?"

"I don't know. All my plans were…shattered, along with the bones in my leg."

"All of them?"

"Well, I lost my job. I'll probably have to sell my house. My fiancé broke the engagement."

His eyes grew wide. "Because of your leg?"

"I also have some pretty serious internal injuries."

"And…?" He reached over and tucked an errant strand of hair behind her ear.

She fixed her gaze on his. "I won't be able to have children."

He shrugged. "So we'll adopt."

"We?" She chuckled and drew back. "You're awfully cocky."

He laughed. "Just trying to get a reaction. But you could."

She was falling. She knew it. How could she fall for someone on a first date when it wasn't even a date? Because she'd watched him care for her in a thousand ways for two and a half months, without asking for anything in return, more faithfully than any man she'd known.

She shook her head. "No. Men only want their own blood."

"What makes you say that?"

"Personal experience."

"Such as?"

She huffed. "Why am I doing all the sharing?"

"Answer me, then I'll share. Besides, I've been sharing all along. You've rarely said anything about yourself. Time to catch up."

She took a deep breath. "Before I was born, my mother had an affair. She was never sure if my father was my real father. He never really connected with me the way he did with my brother. In fact, when he died, he left everything to him and nothing to me. My stepfather wanted nothing to do with me, only his own kids. My mother was so afraid he'd leave she never called him on it. I left as soon as I turned 18." She watched closely for his reaction.

Brody moved in close. A faint scent of musk surrounded her. He gently wrapped his hand around her neck and brought his mouth to her ear. "Almost any guy can make a baby. It's the sticking around part that makes a father." He stayed close, even when he finished speaking.

She closed her eyes. Man, he smelled good. Heat lingered on her neck, then spread down as he dropped his hand to her shoulder.

He drew back, but not as far as he had been.

"I'd have to see that."

"You've seen my parents when they visit me, right?" A grin crept across his face. "I know you've been watching me."

Blood rushed to her cheeks.

He chuckled. "Do I look anything less than adored?"

"Spoiled rotten is more like it."

"I'm adopted. My sister, too."

"You are not!"

Brody nodded.

She looked everywhere but at him. What did she say to that? He wasn't running. Didn't care that she was a mess. And his fingers played with her hair.

She faced him again. "Why have you been helping me?"

He shrugged. "At first because you needed it."

"At first? And then…?"

"Then because you're cute." He grinned.

Her cheeks flamed again. Suddenly her hands fascinated her.

He tucked his finger under her chin and gently lifted her face. "Then, Nicole, because I couldn't wait to see you every day." His gaze locked with hers for what felt like hours. He dropped his hand and sat back. "Are you Irish?"

Grateful for the change of subject, she chuckled. "Yeah, part. Why do you ask? My red hair?"

"Beautiful dark red hair, green eyes"—he drew a finger lightly from one cheek to the other—"and a smattering of barely visible freckles that I'd bet grow darker in the summer sun."

Her stomach tightened. Oh, good heavens, she was done for. God had allowed Brody to gently, selflessly circle her far more than seven times in the last 10 weeks so that, like Jericho, all the walls she'd built up would come crashing down, and she would fall hopelessly in love in the time it took to deliver a pizza.

"How can I possibly resist?" He leaned in and placed a feather-light kiss on her lips—more of a promise than a kiss. Warmth spread from her mouth to her toes.

As if on cue, the delivery boy knocked on the door.

Brody rose and opened the door. He paid the boy, took the pizza and two-liter bottle of soda, and set them on the coffee table. Nicole sat amazed as he then moved to the kitchen. Cupboard doors opened until he found two glasses. Ice clinked into them. And the whole time he whistled. Whistled. Not huffed, sighed, cursed, or reminded her that she owed him one.

She could get used to this.

He set the glasses on the table and filled them, then handed her one. His eyes twinkled as he checked his watch and held out his wrist, pointing to it. "See? Thirty minutes."

She laughed. "Or less. That's all it took."

CAROLE TOWRISS, the author of the novel *In the Shadow of Sinai*, and her husband live just north of Washington, DC. In between making tacos and telling her children to pick up their shoes, she writes and waits for summertime at the beach.

www. CaroleTowriss.com

The Gingerbread Box
* * *

Janet R. Sady

Wet snowflakes drifted down and began piling up on the sidewalks as Michele hurried along 49th Street toward her apartment. Her long blond hair stuck to her parka where it escaped from under her hood, and her eyes watered from the cold.

Christmas music played on speakers outside department stores. Window displays danced and twinkled with lights. The square had been decorated with the largest spruce she'd ever seen. She barely glanced at it tonight as she trudged on through the darkening evening. She had always loved coming to the city during the holiday season, but somber thoughts kept her from enjoying the scene now that she lived here.

Her stomach growled, reminding her she hadn't eaten since the hamburger and salad at the restaurant on her lunch break. She'd probably just have soup and crackers again tonight. If she ate soup four times a week for her dinner, she could make her waitress pay last through December. She thanked God daily that the restaurant allowed her to eat one meal at work, but they were closed on Christmas. She couldn't even imagine spending her first Christmas without Jeff and her mom and dad.

The landlord had notified her the rent would be going up $50.00 at the beginning of the New Year. The apartment was too expensive for her meager wages. She'd been looking for another apartment in her spare time, but so far no success. She prayed God would give her a Christmas miracle; she needed it soon.

When Michele had moved to New York City after graduating from the Pittsburgh School of Arts and Drama four months ago, she thought work in the theater would be easy to find. Although she appeared at the casting office regularly, she hadn't been able to land a major role. Oh, she'd been offered some parts in some unsavory films, but she'd quickly turned them down.

She'd gotten cast in a couple of crowd scenes, which paid a few dollars, but a waitress job was all the work she could find. The customers were being more generous during the Christmas season, but she still struggled. Her emergency cash was almost depleted, and she still needed to go Christmas shopping for her mom and dad.

She thought of her home in Avalon, near Pittsburgh, and immediately visions of Jeff's face came to her mind. "No," she said out loud. "I will not go there. Why doesn't he at least write?"

Her thoughts wandered to Christmas back home. Since she was an only child, Mom and Dad always made her a very special Christmas tree. Michele imagined she could see the crystal birds, shiny balls, and keepsake ornaments they had accumulated during the years. The Christmas star Dad had made to surprise her when she was 10 would be shining its light from above the garage door.

For the first time in her 21 years, she wouldn't be home for Christmas. The cost of a bus ticket was expensive, and she was embarrassed to tell her parents she didn't have the money. They thought she was working in the theater, and she hadn't told them any different. And Jeff—well, she hadn't talked to him since the night she told him she was moving to New York. It made her heartsick to think about how much she missed hearing his voice.

Dear God, please be with Jeff.

By the time Michele reached her building, she could barely feel her toes in her leather boots, and her socks were soaking wet. She climbed the steps and entered the foyer. Cooking odors permeated the hall, and she brushed back the tears as she thought of her mother's home-cooked meals. She felt blessed that she had food and rationed it carefully, always afraid it wouldn't last until payday.

She shook the snow from her parka and unlocked the apartment door. The gloomy interior never felt inviting. She flipped on all the lights. No Christmas tree or decorations greeted her. The Oriental rug had seen better days, and the sofa felt lumpy. Every time she sat down, she expected a spring to poke through the upholstery and jab her. The furniture came with the apartment. It was a good thing, too, or she would be sleeping on the floor.

As usual, the apartment felt cold, and Michele banged on the radiator with the hopes that it would kick out some heat to dry her boots. She shivered as she hurried to her dresser and pulled out a warm pair of slipper socks and a fleece sweatshirt. If she didn't get herself warmed up, she might get sick. She couldn't allow that to happen. Who would take care of her?

Please, God, don't let me catch a cold. She sighed.

A knock on the door startled her. She didn't know the other residents in the building and wondered who it could be. Peering through the peephole, she recognized the building manager with his head just above a huge box. When she opened the door, he placed the box on the floor and pushed it toward her.

"Here's a package that came for you today. The postman left it with me because someone had to sign. It says *perishable*. Don't make a habit of this."

"Thank you so much. I really appreciate you bringing it to me."

Michele closed the door and stared at the huge box. Who would take the time to send a package? Could it be from Jeff? Her eyes flew to the return address: Mom and Dad.

Michele grabbed a pair of scissors and cut through the packing tape. She stared into the box and couldn't believe her eyes. A little spruce tree with tiny lights and ornaments sat wedged in the middle of the box. Evergreen scent wafted from the box and filled the air. Clear plastic boxes with red bows were stacked in the corners. She took each one out and saw that they were filled with her favorites: cashews, date balls, fudge, and cutout sugar cookies. There was even a box with three red delicious apples and three navel oranges. Six gifts wrapped in candy-cane striped paper lay tucked around the edges, and an envelope protruded from under a red box with a silver bow. Michele sat on the floor, held the envelope against her breast, and sobbed. She lifted the flap and read the note:

> Dad and I send you our love. We are enclosing a bus ticket and a check for $100.00. Anytime you want to come home, we'll be happy to see you. We miss you so much! Christmas will not be the same without you. Please call us after the Candlelight Service on Christmas Eve. We're praying for you. God be with you and keep you safe.
> All our love to our favorite daughter,
>   Mom and Dad

Michele opened the red box, and her tears turned to laughter. Two dozen homemade gingerbread men lay stacked in rows. Each one had either an X or O written in icing on its belly. Every year since she was three years old, she had helped her mom make gingerbread men for Christmas.

Yes, that was just like her mom to think of everything. Placing the tree in its stand, Michele plugged in the lights. The tree began to rotate and play "Silent Night." Michele clapped her hands for joy. She felt like a child again, placing the presents and goodies around the tree. Just when she thought the box was empty, she noticed another card and gift on the bottom. She recognized the writing—Jeff!

She remembered his expression when she'd told him she was moving to New York. He'd had been devastated.

"Michele, you know I love you, and I thought you loved me. I believe God put you in my life. How can you leave? I knew you wanted to act or teach drama. I'd hoped you would set up a little studio around Pittsburgh somewhere. I can't believe you made up your mind to leave without even discussing it with me. But if that's what you want, I won't stand in your way. I'm sorry, but I can't handle a long-distance relationship. It's just too difficult."

Michele had tried to explain, but her words didn't come out right. She thought she was doing what God had created her to do, but why did she feel so terrible then?

Jeff had kissed her good-bye and then left her standing there too stunned to speak. He hadn't called since she had been there, but then again she had allowed her contract to expire for her cell phone. He could have written. She told her mother to give him the address if he asked.

Not a day had passed in the four months she'd been in New York when she didn't think of him. Sometimes she'd see a man in the crowd with brown curly hair and a familiar-looking jacket, and for a moment she'd hope it might be Jeff. Her heart would always quicken until she caught sight of the man's face. The ache in her heart grew every day and she prayed for him, but she had her pride. She wouldn't call him.

Now she was afraid of what the envelope might contain—but there was a gift, too. She slowly opened the letter. Inside was a card:

Michele,
To the one I love at Christmas-time—
My heart overflows with love for you,
Without you beside me, I don't know what to do.
Please come home, and marry me.
We'll be happy, wait and see.
    Love, Jeff

P.S. Please forgive me for being a stubborn jerk. I've asked God to forgive me. Will you?

Michele covered her mouth with her hand as sobs of happiness filled her throat, and tears flowed freely down her cheeks. "Jeff. Oh Jeff. If only you knew how much I miss and love you."

She opened the gift box, and nestled in the velvet lining lay a gold heart-shaped locket with an inscription on the back: *I'll always love you. Jeff.*

Michele's decision was swift and without hesitation. New York was not what she had expected; she would swallow her pride and admit that to Jeff and to herself. Now she knew exactly what she wanted.

"Yes!" Michele shouted out loud. "I'll marry you, Jeff."

Her mind raced with thoughts of what she should do. Tomorrow, she would call Jeff from the restaurant phone. Then she'd give notice. She wouldn't leave them short-handed during the Christmas rush. *I'll use the bus ticket to move back home after New Year's. All the people I treasure and who love me are in Avalon. That's where I belong.*

"Thank you, God, for showing me the answer to my situation."

Michele fastened the locket around her neck and danced around the room. She could almost feel Jeff's arms around her. Christmas wouldn't be so awful after all. Opening the box with the gingerbread cookies, she bit into one with a big pink X on his belly. The little Christmas tree seemed to wink and sparkle as it continued to rotate and play carols. "O Come All Ye Faithful" played as she felt God's presence drawing her back to her loved ones and home.

JANET R. SADY is an award-winning author, poet, story teller, and motivational speaker. She has published in devotional books and other anthologies, newspapers, and magazines, including *Falling in Love with You, Country Woman, Loyalhanna Review, True Story, Alamance.* Janet is the author of *The Great American Dream, God's Lessons from Nature, God's Parables, The Bird Woman,* and two children's books.

jansady422.wordpress.com

Mission of the Heart

* * *

Laura Hodges Poole

Kristi Hartley weaved her way through the crowd in the church's fellowship hall with her best friend, Delia Reynolds, at her side.

"Is he here?" Delia stood on her tiptoes to see past the people gathered for the mission team fundraiser.

Kristi's cheeks grew warm. "Since he's part of the mission team, he should be." She slipped off her wrap and shook the few snowflakes clinging to her hair. "Try to remember why we're here."

Delia's face clouded. "Of course, silly." She giggled and clutched Kristi's arm. "Derek's on the team, so technically he's part of why we're here. How did you manage to snag the most handsome bachelor in the church, anyway?"

"Nobody's been snagged." Kristi laughed. Her friend had tunnel vision where youth counselor Derek Logan was concerned.

"You've been inseparable for months." Delia pretended to pout. "He doesn't notice anyone else when you're around."

"Not inseparable." Kristi draped her wrap over her arm and smoothed her hair. "You just can't help but notice when he's around, so it seems like that."

Delia rolled her eyes. "If you say so."

Determined to redirect her friend's drama, Kristi scanned the hall. "Let's see if we can find a seat."

"Good luck with that."

Kristi pushed up the aisle with Delia close behind. They found an empty row of seats in the center of the hall. The stage overflowed with bikes, antiques, and an assortment of new and used merchandise for auction. Oversized photos of Sudan refugees hung from the walls. Kristi breathed a prayer that enough funds would be raised for the team headed to South Sudan in the spring to help build a new school. Derek would lead the team.

A shiver rippled through her as she thought about their last conversation—the feeling of warmth and security when he'd hugged her good-bye. What would it have been like to linger in Derek's arms a moment longer? And how had she caught his attention when many single women in the church—like Delia—had a crush on him?

Tall and broad-shouldered with sandy blond hair, Derek had an often-unshaven face that lent a rugged look to his handsome features. Kristi had never considered herself overly attractive. Her own light auburn hair wasn't nearly as dazzling as someone like Delia with chestnut-colored hair and matching charcoal eyes that danced with excitement all the time. Delia reminded her of an untamed pony, lively and the center of any social gathering. Kristi couldn't blame men for looking past her and seeing Delia. Yet, despite Delia's best efforts, Derek had asked Kristi out. She shook her head. Men confused her.

Pushing down her feelings, she focused on the list of items for sale. Derek traveled in a different circle from her. If there was a task to be handled, everyone knew to call him. He was comfortable with a microphone in hand.

Kristi preferred the quiet confines of her church pew, where she could quietly slip away after church. Helping out with the senior adults or the downtown soup kitchen was her speed. She was comfortable in the shadows, while he thrived in the spotlight.

She sighed. Was it too much to hope a relationship between such different people would succeed?

A poke in her ribs startled her out of her daydream. "What?"

Delia frowned at Kristi. "I've called your name three times."

"Sorry. I'm awake now. What's up?"

"He's here." Delia waved to attract Derek's attention.

Kristi tugged her friend's sleeve and whispered, "You can stop waving now. He sees you."

When Derek's gaze settled on Kristi and he smiled, her pulse tripped. He jumped off the stage and headed up the aisle toward her. Kristi's mouth went dry, and she fidgeted with the auction list.

Derek came up the row of chairs in front of her and stopped. He turned a chair around and straddled it, facing her. "Good to see you, ladies." He nodded at Delia before turning his attention to Kristi. "See anything you can't live without?"

Delia giggled. Kristi didn't dare scowl at her like she wanted. Instead she forced herself to focus on the list in her hand. "Maybe the day at the spa."

His brows arched. "So you're a spa lady. I would've never figured that."

Kristi shifted and reached for her purse. "Would you get us some drinks, Delia?"

Delia smirked. "How many?"

"Two." Derek crossed his arms on the chair and leaned forward. "I've got auction duty."

When Delia disappeared, Kristi looked up at Derek, his lake blue eyes enticing her, making her mind turn to mush. She finally found her voice. "I hope you'll be safe in Africa."

He stood and slipped into Delia's vacated chair. "You could come with us."

Folding the list, she tucked it into her purse, then faced him. "We've been over this. First of all, it wouldn't be proper." She groaned inwardly as soon the words left her mouth.

"Because of our feelings for each other?"

"And I've never done anything like this. I'd be like a fish out of water."

He chuckled and tilted his head. "Well, you know, there's the snakehead fish that can walk on land."

She burst into laughter. "You're awful."

He lifted her hand between his and gave it a gentle squeeze. "Perhaps. But I'm trying to get you to see that with God anything is possible. Even for a fish out of water."

She withdrew her hand. "God hardwired me to be an introvert. I don't do well with crowds. I don't do well in confined spaces. I could think of nothing more miserable than a 20-hour plane ride." She raised her finger. "Make that several plane rides, and then what? Trucks or walking to remote villages?"

Her stomach knotted as her words reverberated in her ears. She pulled her gaze away from his. She was a huge disappointment. To him and to her.

"You're right. And it's not my place to call you to foreign missions. It's God's." He leaned in and brushed her cheek with a kiss. "But remember, when He calls you, He'll equip you. I'll see you after the auction."

She gulped down tears that choked her throat and threatened to fill her eyes. *Why can't I be like everyone else?*

The man of her dreams was within reach, so why was she holding herself back?

*

Two hours later, the stage stood empty and the church coffers were full with the last amount of money needed to underwrite the mission trip.

Kristi said good-bye to Delia, then lingered in the back of the fellowship hall where she'd helped the older women clean the concession area.

"I don't know what we'd do without you, Kristi." Mrs. Randall, silver hair pulled into a bun, untied her apron and laid it next to her purse. She flitted around, putting the last of the dishes into the cupboards.

"Glad to help out." Kristi stole a glance through the foyer doors at Derek talking with the mission team. Their eyes locked, and he broke away and headed toward the concession area.

"Well, ladies, the tally is official. The entire trip has been underwritten by the generosity of our church family." Derek beamed. "Who wants to go to lunch?"

Mrs. Randall waved aside his words. "You take Ms. Kristi. The rest of us old folks are headed to McDonald's for coffee." Her breath came in spurts as she swiped the dishtowel over the counter a final time.

The other ladies in the group laughed.

Derek looked at Kristi. "Well?"

"What did you have in mind?"

"The Grapevine Deli?"

"Oh, that sounds heavenly. I didn't realize how hungry I was until you mentioned it." She followed Derek out to the parking lot and climbed into her car. "I'll meet you there."

Derek smiled. "See you in a few."

*

Twenty minutes later, Kristi unwrapped her turkey-on-wheat sandwich, opened her bag of chips, and waited for Derek to unwrap his roast beef sandwich. She slipped her small hand into his strong, capable one and bowed her head while he said grace. When he'd finished, Derek squeezed her hand before he released it.

"I'm so excited by the turnout for the auction." Derek took a bite of his sandwich and wiped his mouth.

"I'm thrilled you all raised so much money."

"Couldn't have done it without people like you behind the scenes willing to give their time."

A tingling sensation flowed through her. Derek's approval meant more than anyone else's. "Glad I could help."

"The youth have a camping trip coming up next month. Care to join us?" His eyes twinkled as if extending a dare.

For some reason, his question irritated her. He always tried some roundabout way to get her to join church trips.

She dropped her sandwich onto the wrapper and reached for her tea. "I can't get off work that Friday for an extended weekend, remember?"

Derek's phone chimed and he reached for it. "Hold on. It's the church's number." Color drained from his face as he listened to the person on the other end. He motioned for Kristi to wrap the sandwiches.

She quickly did so as her heart pounded. *Protect whoever it is, God.*

Derek pocketed the phone. "Mrs. Randall had a massive heart attack. She's en route to the hospital."

A cry escaped Kristi's throat as she fell in step beside Derek. Mrs. Randall was the sweetest lady in the church. More than that, she'd been like a mother to Kristi. The mother she'd never really had.

Derek slipped his arm around her side and gave her a quick hug. "Come on."

*

At the hospital, Kristi watched the hallway for the attending physician while Derek paced. Nurses and technicians hustled through the halls, pushing medicine carts and other equipment. The PA system called out pages from time to time.

"When are they coming out?" Derek ran his hand through his hair.

Kristi rubbed his arm. "We've prayed. Now we have to have patience."

A doctor hurried toward them. Kristi stepped aside.

He extended his hand to Derek. "I'm Mrs. Randall's cardiologist. She had a heart attack, but we took her to the cardiac catheterization lab and performed angioplasty. We'll keep her for observation, but once she stabilizes in a couple of days, she can go home."

"Thank you. Can we see her?"

He nodded. "Go ahead. Just don't tire her."

Kristi pushed through the door of Mrs. Randall's room with Derek close behind.

"Kristi!" Mrs. Randall motioned her to the bedside. An IV pole adjacent her bed pumped fluids into her while heart monitors held a steady rhythm.

"Don't excite yourself." Kristi perched on the side of the bed.

"Nonsense. I'm fine." Mrs. Randall winked at Derek. "See you brought the preacher with you."

Derek chuckled. "Good to see you in fine form. Wouldn't do for our prettiest parishioner to stay down long."

She tilted her head toward Kristi. "This is your prettiest parishioner. And besides that, your most devoted."

Derek raised an eyebrow, then nodded.

"Everyone knows they can call Kristi when they need something. Why do you think the hospital tracked y'all down? I knew she was with you." Mrs.

Randall smoothed a wrinkle from her sheet and reached for her water cup.

Derek groaned, but a hint of a smile edged his mouth. "And here I thought you wanted me."

Mrs. Randall shook her head. "And seeing how I nearly died, I'm not holding anything back anymore."

Kristi chuckled. As if the woman ever had.

"Better do something to make the arrangement permanent before someone swoops in and beats you to it."

The floor nurse poked her head into the room. "Time to get some rest."

Kristi patted Mrs. Randall. "You have your orders." She bent down and planted a kiss on the older woman's cheek. "We'll stop by later."

"Thanks for the advice." Derek squeezed Mrs. Randall's hand and followed Kristi out.

*

In the hallway, Derek led Kristi out of the stream of traffic and into an alcove around the corner. "I want to apologize." He reached out and brushed a stray hair from her cheek.

"For what?"

"For trying to drag you into foreign missions." He dropped his gaze, then looked up. "Your work in our church is just as important because you're right where God has called you to be. There's no more important place than the center of God's will. Your talent and calling obviously lies with our seniors. I was wrong if I implied that wasn't good enough."

Kristi stepped toward him and put a finger to his lips. "Shhh. Your heart was in the right place. I doubted myself until just now when I saw Mrs. Randall in the hospital bed. Knowing that she called for me, well, my work behind the scenes matters."

He kissed her finger before she withdrew it. "Yes, it does."

She took a deep breath to steady her nerves and gather her courage. "But I want you to understand I'm open to wherever God leads me. If that's to foreign missions, He'll make it clear, and I'll know it."

He drew her into his arms. "The question is, what if the mission call is domestic? Say, being a pastor's wife?"

She giggled. "I'm definitely open to that."

She allowed herself to be drawn closer as Derek lowered his lips to meet hers.

LAURA HODGES POOLE has published three-dozen articles, devotions, and short stories. A member of American Christian Fiction Writers, she writes Christian romances and is a 2012 *RWA Emily* finalist, winning second place. Her passion is encouraging others through her blog, "A Word of Encouragement," at **laurahodgespoole.blogspot.com.**

Twenty Years of Convenience

* * *

ALETHEIA VON GOTTLIEB

Peg gazed at his outline against the setting sun as he stood on the porch. Other than the few lines added to his face, her faithful companion for 20 years hadn't changed. He was still as handsome and strong as when they married.

"I'm moving to Colorado with Melanie, Hank." She averted her gaze before he could meet her eyes.

"If that's what you want," he murmured in her direction.

Peg nodded and turned to walk into the house.

"It'll be quiet here without you."

She turned back, wondering how it could be any quieter when they never even talked to each other. He was looking away at the sunset once again. "You were a wonderful mother to my boys. I could never repay you for that."

"Melanie needed a father as much as Derek and Dustin needed a mom." She smiled. "We're even. I think it's time."

He nodded. "I'd better close up the barn for the night."

Peg's smile was sad as he left the porch. She went inside the farmhouse that she had made into a home and lovingly touched the large wooden table that had seen countless meals, school projects, and family game nights. She eyed the rocking chair where she had held sick children and the old piano where Melanie had gone from banging "Mary Had a Little Lamb" to Bach. The house was only loneliness now where life and laughter used to be.

Hank was so different from her first husband, Joseph. She had married Joe young, and they had been madly, passionately in love. He had adored her and loved to talk and laugh. Joe's vitality had made Hank's reserve so much harder to bear. Her two short wonderful years with Joe had been dwarfed by the hardship of 20 years with Hank.

Not that Hank was cruel or unkind; he wasn't. In fact, she'd never had a harsh word from him; maybe that was the problem. They didn't fight. They barely interacted now that the children were out of the house. They were roommates, maybe even ghosts, occupying the same space. Why couldn't he fight with her, or even better, for her?

Even now he had come into the house and was shutting the front door and locking it with the same steady rhythm he'd used every night. His motions weren't that of a man upset to hear his wife was leaving him; he was as unruffled as ever. She retreated to the kitchen and clanked dishes as she put them away.

Tears rose, threatening to spill over her lashes. She hurriedly rubbed them away and steeled her heart. It wouldn't do to let him know that she was more upset to leave than he was to see her go.

Hank came to the kitchen door and cleared his throat. "How soon do you expect to go?"

"Tomorrow," Peg answered without turning to look at him.

"I suppose you'll need a ride to the airport."

"If that isn't too much trouble." Peg's heart wrenched as they worked their way through the courtesies.

"When do we need to leave?"

"Flight leaves at 9 a.m."

"Sure don't give a man much notice." He sounded perturbed.

Against her better judgment, Peg swiveled to scrutinize his face. He looked...annoyed. That was unusual.

"You have plans?"

Hank shrugged and shook his head. "Do now, I guess."

"If it's too much trouble..."

His eyes narrowed. "You think I would make you find another ride to the airport?"

Peg couldn't hide a small smile. "Most men aren't asked to assist in their wife leaving them."

"Is that what you're doing? Leaving?"

"Well, I'm not just going to visit."

"Is there anything I can do to make you stay?" His voice was as quiet as usual but softer, more gentle.

Peg's eyes watered again. "I don't think that's a question any woman is supposed to answer. Do you want to make me stay?"

"You're my wife." With that, Hank pivoted and left the room.

Tears spilled over Peg's cheeks. He had asked the right question, so why couldn't he go on to the next step? Try to stop her? He didn't love her. It was undeniable now.

After living 20 years with the man, he didn't feel strong enough about her to try to keep her. The pain grew to a palpable level. To have given her very best to a man and find that she didn't rate as high as the calf he had patiently nursed back to health last month was heartbreaking. He had given that calf all the love and care she yearned for. He was capable of love—she had seen it with Dustin and Derek and even her daughter, Melanie—but he had never shown her anything more than respect and distance.

They had met shortly after the untimely deaths of their spouses in the same car accident. Neither had family but both had young children. She'd needed an income provider as much as he had needed a nurturer. They'd married under an old-fashioned obligation to propriety and raised their children under the facade of marriage. But now the children were gone, and the facade was getting harder and harder to maintain.

She wiped her cheeks with an embarrassed sniff. If she was freeing herself from the bondage of an unhappy marriage, why the tears? *No, not unhappy,* she admitted, *but not a marriage either.*

A sound from the doorway caused her to swing her eyes toward it hurriedly. Hank stood there holding a dark rectangle. The failing light cast shadows in the hallway, obscuring his hands.

"I've never shown you a picture of her, have I?"

She shook her head, surprised he would speak of his first wife after so many years of silence. He turned the picture frame toward her without looking at it, and Peg saw a lovely young woman with Derek's light brown hair and Dustin's dimpled smile.

Peg took the picture from him and held it closer to her face for in-depth study. She had wondered about this woman for so long. She had wanted to ask her how she'd wanted to raise her boys and what she had ever seen in Hank. The lighthearted beauty was not at all the kind of woman Peg had expected to be married to a man like Hank, but tragedy could change a man just as it had changed Peg.

"Thank you. It's nice to see my boys' mama."

"You've always treated them like they were your own."

"I love them just as I love Melanie," Peg handed the picture back to Hank. He accepted it while carefully not looking at the picture.

Then the truth hit Peg like a sack of bricks. Hank wasn't without emotion; rather he felt too deeply. After 20 years he still couldn't look upon his dead wife's picture; it would cause too much pain. A deep resonance reverberated through her—a connection with this man whom she realized now she hardly knew. She felt compassion for a man who was still so in love with his first wife that he was incapable of loving his wife of convenience.

"I don't want you to leave, Peg."

Peg nodded. "I'm sure if you talk to Mrs. Winters she will bring you dinner in exchange for eggs or something."

"I don't want you to stay for your cooking." His voice had the hard quality of steel laced through its softness.

Peg met his eyes. "Why then?"

"I loved Jenny more than life itself." Peg had only heard her name mentioned from the neighbors, but on his tongue it sounded different, unique. "She was as warm as the sun, giving life and bathing everything in her light. But you, Peg..." He took a step closer and her heart began to race as she saw an intensity in his eyes she'd never seen there before. "...you are like the earth. You are the foundation that everything good springs from."

Peg took a step back in shock, and her hips hit the counter behind her as she recognized the spark that had been aflame in Joe's eyes for her. Her heart felt like it would burst from her chest as she found herself the object of a man's affection for the first time in two decades. Hank took a step after her, closing the distance.

"I have hidden my feelings for you for a long time because I know what we agreed to. I didn't want you to feel obligated to act like we were married just because we were." He then seemed to realize how close they were standing, with only inches separating them. Searching her eyes, he gauged her response.

She held his gaze, also searching. As he waited, she watched as the light in his eyes was quenched to a flicker and then squashed entirely. Before her stood the calm, distant man once again. He took a step back.

Had she imagined his passion? Had he merely been saying the right words to try to keep his cook and housekeeper? How could a man be in love for years and never show it?

"I don't want you to stay for me, Peg. I want you to stay because you want to."

"Why would I want to?" The question came out more harshly than she meant it. The hurt on Hank's face was unbearable. "I meant," she made her voice extra soft, "why stay? You've not convinced me yet, Hank."

Hank's eyes smoldered. He crossed the kitchen in two long strides and swept her into his arms.

In that one kiss was 20 years of tightly held passion. It was everything that had been left unsaid and undone. It was heart twisting, toe-curling, un-fake-able attraction and deeply held love. It was convincing.

After a blissful eternity, Hank pulled back, his eyes shining with a love deeper than she had ever dreamed possible. "Will you marry me, Peg? Not because we have three young children to raise, but because there is no one I would rather grow old with."

"We're already married, Hank."

Hank shook his head. "No, I want to do it right this time. For love, not for convenience."

Peg smiled softly. "I will marry you, Hank. Again."

He leaned to kiss her again, and she put her hand on his lips to stop him.

"Don't get any ideas, Mr. Wilson. We're not married yet." Peg laughed softly.

Hank smoldered. "Tomorrow, then."

"Sure don't give a woman much notice. I suppose you'll need a ride to the church. What time do we need to leave?"

"Nine in the morning. Do you have any plans?" His lips quirked into a smile as he bent his head toward hers.

"Nothing." Peg closed her eyes and savored the lips of her husband and husband-to-be.

ALETHEIA VON GOTTLIEB is an accomplished Christian screenwriter of the films *Summertime Christmas* and *Wait Your Turn*. She also writes romance and fantasy fiction squashed in between mothering her newborn, two-year-old, and four-year-old. She loves to bring stories to life that inspire and move her readers (or viewers!).

Aletheiavongottlieb.blogspot.com

The Tea Set

* * *

Elaine Marie Cooper

Lucy Ryan's head throbbed as she closed the apartment building door.

This time her headache was from the crowded streets in the Bronx. Despite its traffic and crowds, however, it was nothing like the migraine-inducing noise from the huge celebration that occurred last month. During that November party in New York City, the end of World War I was loudly celebrated.

But the Armistice did not end the battle within Lucy Ryan. Ever since she was widowed five years ago, she struggled to protect her heart—and determined to keep up every defense necessary.

Despite the fact that it was Christmas Eve, the young widow was not in the mood to celebrate.

Ascending the three flights of stairs in the darkened stairwell, Lucy's swollen ankles rebelled against the effort. *I can't wait to get these pumps off.*

She finally reached her apartment level. The floor creaked beneath her shoes as she crossed the empty hallway. As soon as she opened the splinter-covered door, she was assaulted with the arguing voices of her four-year-old daughter, Abby, and her teenage brother, Peter. Pressing her fingers against her temple, Lucy opened her mouth to quiet them. But Lucy's mother intervened, ambushing the quarrel as she came in from the kitchen and threatening bodily harm with a stew-covered wooden utensil. Both Abby and Peter scattered, their voices ceasing.

"Thanks, Ma." Lucy rubbed her forehead.

Irish-born Mary Rogers put her hands on her hips. "So Mr. Bell could not do without ya on Christmas Eve. Has the man no heart?"

Lucy plopped onto the flattened sofa cushion and unbuttoned her jacket. "He has a heart, Ma. Just lots of phone calls. You know—for the holiday."

"Well, I hope you're plannin' on goin' to church with us tonight. Abby's been lookin' farward to this all day."

Lucy grimaced. "Ma, I forgot. My head is pounding."

Mary's expression softened. "Let me get ya some ice. I think there's still a bit in the ice box." In two minutes, Ma returned with a sizeable chunk—but only after she'd hammered the ice block with some large and very loud tool.

Lucy's head throbbed more than ever. She tried to smile. "Thanks, Ma."

A now-subdued Abby returned to the living room and sank into the cushion next to her mother. "Mama, tomorrow's Christmas. Did you see the tea set in the window at Jernigan's store?" Her eyes lit with childish anticipation.

Inwardly Lucy groaned but forced a smile and hugged her daughter close without speaking. All she could think about was how desperately lonely and poor they were.

Too poor to buy a tea set.

They had always struggled to make ends meet, but since her husband was killed at work, things had become even tougher. When Abby came along, Lucy had sought employment at the phone company. Her mother took care of Abby while Lucy took calls at a huge switchboard.

Abby had never even met her father. Before the child was born, Lucy's husband had gone to work one day on the elevated city train. He'd never come home. They said it was due to change of shift. They didn't know her husband was under the car, working on it. The engineer had started the train...Lucy shook the horrible images out of her mind.

"What's wrong, Mama?" Abby was staring at her with moist eyes.

"Nothing, sweetie."

Abby brightened. "Grandma says the war's over. Maybe Jamie will come home." Her eyes were sparkling, and she wiggled in the chair.

Lucy tried not to dampen her daughter's joy, but she had to make her little girl understand how life really worked. "Abby, we don't know that Jamie...I mean, Mr. Durgin...is coming home. He's been far away. I've not heard from him in a very long time." She didn't want to get the girl's hopes up. Lucy knew all about dashed hopes and dreams.

Abby's eyes narrowed. "But you said the mail is bad. That's prob'ly why he didn't write." She nodded as if encouraging her mother to agree.

Lucy couldn't take away every dream her daughter had. "You're probably right, Abby." The ice cube was melting down her sleeve, soaking her gabardine dress. "Oh, dash." She put the residual chunk in a glass dish on the side table.

Ma walked in, wrapping her wool shawl around her shoulders and pulling on gloves without fingertips. "Abby, get your coat. Lucy, will ya change your mind, lass?"

"No, Ma. You and Abby go. I'll go to church tomorrow."

Maybe.

Peter hurried in, wrapping his scarf around his neck several times. "I'm ready."

Ma suspiciously eyed the teenager. "Are ya, lad? Could it be that Miss Katy Bartlett will be there, all primped for ya?"

Peter blushed. "Come on, ladies, unless you want to walk the streets alone." With a look of disgust aimed at his ma, he held the door open.

Abby ran over and threw herself into her mother's arms. "I'll pray for you, Mama. Tonight I'm gonna finish knitting that scarf for Jamie."

Lucy quelled the tears that arose. "That's nice, sweetie."

Oh, to be four again.

But at 24, Lucy's faith had already been tested. It was apparently lacking, as she had long since given up feeling God's joy and peace. She despaired of ever knowing God's love. This Christmas holiday felt like a joke. Peace, joy, and...death? She knew there were too many new widows whose husbands would never return from the war.

Lucy pushed herself up from the sofa with difficulty. Wincing from her tight shoes, she limped into the small bedroom she shared with Abby. Searching for her shoe hook, she found it—right on the dresser next to the photo of her deceased husband. *Abby looks so much like him.*

Sighing, she sat on the bed and starting unlatching the dozen buttons on her black leather shoes. *It was easier doing this in the morning before my feet swelled.*

Struggling to twist the too-tight boot from her right foot, she sighed with relief and tossed it toward the wall. It landed right near the basket where Abby's knitting lay. The long gray scarf was a mass of imperfect rows of knitted yarn. But Lucy knew the hours of love that had been poured into each row. And Abby loved Jamie.

Do I?

Lucy remembered Jamie's impassioned marriage proposal before he went to war. Despite the earnest look in his green eyes, she had resisted. She would not be widowed twice.

Now Lucy refused to think about him. It was too painful. She knew when he was drafted that she'd never see him again. She couldn't even bring herself to bid farewell to him when the troop transport left dock last spring. It carried him and thousands of other soldiers across the Atlantic...away from her.

Men Lucy cared about always left and never returned. She wouldn't allow herself to care.

After several more minutes, the other shoe was wrestled off. She removed her seamed stockings and rubbed her feet. They were so warm that the cool floorboards felt comforting.

Walking toward the window, she opened it a few inches to breathe in the sweet chill. It soothed her blazing head. In the distance she could hear a few street singers performing Christmas carols. Despite the blockade she had erected in her heart, somehow the holiday songs of her childhood always managed to edge around her fortress, exposing her vulnerability.

"God rest ye merry gentlemen, let nothing you dismay; Remember Christ our Saviour was born on Christmas Day...." The words knocked at the door of her soul.

Before the tears could start, she slammed the window shut. Wiping the dust off her fingers with a slapping motion, she trudged toward the kitchen.

I just need something to eat.

Ladling some stew onto a plate, she ate without enthusiasm, her appetite as dull as her emotions. After washing her plate and spoon, she sauntered toward the living room, slumped onto the sofa, and dozed off....

She startled when she heard something. *A knock? Did I lock the door?*

"Is someone there?"

What if it was a burglar? She inhaled sharply as she tiptoed to the apartment door. City life was fraught with terror.

She swallowed past her dry throat. "Who's there?"

"Lucy, it's me."

Her mouth gaped. "Jamie?" She feared saying his name.

Gripping the knob, she pulled on the door slowly. It opened to reveal a shivering soldier holding a hat in one hand and a duffle bag in the other.

She couldn't read his expression, but his eyes seemed moist from the cold.

He just stared at her. "I-I'm not sure if I'm dreaming." His face seemed thin, and his eyes searched hers for some sign of welcome.

She had convinced herself for so long that Jamie Durgin would never come home that she felt he must be an apparition...until his hand touched her arm.

"Lucy...are you happy to see me?" He looked like he might cry.

But before he could start, Lucy put both hands up to her mouth and sobbed. She let him slowly wrap his arms around her shoulders and hold her closely. Neither spoke for several moments as her body convulsed against his chest.

He stroked her back tenderly as if soothing away every ounce of her fear. "I love you so much, Lucy. I told you I'd come home. Every time...every time

I thought I couldn't go on...I imagined your face. You kept me going." His voice trembled.

Pulling back, she touched his cheek. "Are you really here, Jamie?"

Without saying another word, his lips met hers with a warmth she could feel all the way to her bare feet. When he pulled away, his heavy eyes captured her gaze. "Please...please say you'll marry me?"

"Yes." Her headache was suddenly gone. "Yes, I'll marry you, Jamie Durgin."

A voice from the hallway interrupted their reunion.

"Well, now, are you going to stand in this cold hallway all night?" Her brother grinned at them. "Just to warn you—Ma is on her way up the stairs. You'd best unlock those lips."

Jamie kissed Lucy briefly and laughed. "Can I come inside?"

"Yes." Lucy's voice was breathless. "Yes." Pulling him into the apartment, she giggled. "Hide in the kitchen and surprise them."

He did as instructed. When Lucy's mother and daughter came inside and closed the door shut, he stepped out and grinned. "Merry Christmas."

Abby's screams of joy were only matched by the tears of Mary Rogers as she patted the young man's shoulders and arms. "Are you sound, Jamie? No injuries?" She clucked like a mother hen around a missing chick.

"I'm fine, Mrs. Rogers. Fit as a fiddle, as my father used to say."

Lucy wrapped her arm around his and leaned against his shoulder. "He came home." Her eyes misted as her words emerged in a whisper.

"I prayed he would." Abby grabbed his other side and hugged him tightly. Neither Lucy nor Abby seemed willing to release him now that he had finally arrived. Suddenly Abby chirped with excitement. "Your gift! Jamie, I made you something."

Releasing Jamie, she scurried to the bedroom and then returned with her arms behind her back. "Close your eyes." He did as instructed.

Abby held out her prized gift to the man she had prayed would return.

The faith of a child... Lucy shook her head.

Jamie's eyes widened with pleasure as he reached toward the handmade scarf. He accepted it from the little girl as though it were a treasure. And, indeed, Abby's gift of love to this man was a prized possession.

"Thank you, Abby." He reached his arm out toward her, and she ran into his embrace. "Thank you."

Lucy's hands pressed against her lips. *Thank you, God.*

"I have something for you, too, Abby." Jamie pulled her away and smiled. Reaching for his tan bag, he untied the rope and dug inside the military-issued satchel. His eyes brightened as he very carefully pulled out a cloth-covered parcel. He sat on the sofa and set it on his lap. "Here, Abby." He slowly unwrapped the layers of linen that enveloped a treasure within.

Abby's eyes widened. "A tea set!" She jumped up and down, grinning.

"This isn't just any tea set, Abby. This is from a place far away called Bavaria. Look at the fine paintings on each piece."

Abby pretended to drink from one of the cups.

Lucy inspected the china teapot with awe. She was enthralled with the figures of several children reaching out to each other in a circle. They were simply dressed, perhaps poor. But they were rich with love because they had each other. And their faces reflected that joy.

She blinked back tears. A warm trail of moisture rolled down one cheek, and she felt a finger carefully wipe it away.

"Merry Christmas, Lucy. I-I'm sorry I didn't have enough left to buy you anything…" Jamie's face was filled with love—the same expression she saw painted on the faces of the children on the tea set.

She touched her fingers to his lips to quell his concern. *"You* are my gift."

She joined her hands, one with Abby and the other with Jamie. Gazing at the man she feared would never return, she was finally unafraid to love—to give it as well as receive it. Releasing that fear was her greatest gift from God.

Lucy kissed the back of Jamie's hand. "Merry Christmas, Jamie. I've nothing to give you either."

He leaned toward her, his own tears combining with hers. Kissing her tenderly, he whispered, "You are the gift I prayed for."

ELAINE MARIE COOPER is an award-winning author of historical fiction, including *The Road to Deer Run*, *The Promise of Deer Run* (First Place in Romance at the 2012 Los Angeles Book Festival), and *The Legacy of Deer Run*, and also has a published devotional. She contributes to two blogs:

http://ReflectionsInHindsight.wordpress.com (every Friday).

http://ColonialQuills.blogspot.com (second Wednesday every month).

See also:

http://www.facebook.com/ElaineMarieCooperAuthor

http://DeerRunBooks.com

The Right Partner

* * *

SARA GIPSON

"May I have this dance?" His bass voice floated over my shoulder, low, raspy, James Bond sexy.

I wanted to dance. In fact, at that moment I would have done anything to get away from the table where I sat alone while the younger unattached women from my office monopolized the dance floor. But those bold and beautiful females were destined to charm even though they lacked discrimination. I worked in research, wore outdated glasses, and had no idea how to engage in small talk. My ideal male partner would be like the Good Samarian that Jesus described in one of his parables, and it was unlikely that I'd meet him at a wedding reception where fraternity brothers held beer-chugging competitions.

It didn't take Sherlock to detect the tobacco scent that wafted from this man. As much as I wanted to say yes to his invitation, I couldn't tolerate a smoker. So, even if he had been the last available male in the world, I would've refused to hook up.

Without turning my head, I said, "No." It didn't matter if I felt like the only milk carton left on the grocery shelf after a blizzard. My *use by* date had expired the day I went to work for Dad and found my niche reviewing dusty documents and tomes.

Hearing chair legs scrape the floor, I turned to look. The man hadn't left. Instead, he'd jerked back one of the cloth-draped chairs, causing the fluffy bow to skew off center. Settling beside me, he offered a huge hand. "My name is Mark Castle."

I glanced at him. He wore a tuxedo, which identified him as a member of the wedding party. Instantly, I recognized his name. A couple of my tablemates, Glenna and Sharon, had mentioned the doctor as a target man to meet. Well, they could have him. Tobacco reeked from his rented suit. I couldn't help wrinkling my nose as I waved at imagined smoke and turned away.

Across the room, musicians played. The lead vocalist crooned a romantic ballad with feeling while couples swayed. I watched and ignored Mark until he interrupted the silence again. At that moment, I thought he appeared as dense as the crowd of dancers. Unbelievable, but the man hadn't gotten my message. Instead, he acted as if my rudeness was expected. Leaning close to my ear, he asked, "May I bring you a glass of champagne?"

I stared at the empty flute while my fingers drummed the table. For the toasts, I'd chosen sparkling grape juice. "No, thank you."

"Do you have a name?"

Finally, I relented and faced him. Mark wasn't leaving unless I acted truly nasty. For some reason it struck me as humorous, and I almost let a smile leak. Wouldn't Sharon be upset she'd missed this golden opportunity? "Sorry, I didn't realize we needed to be that personal. My name is Abigail Hardy, Hardy Investigations."

"I know. My brother, Matt, is the groom. He works for your father. By the way, I saw you wince. I don't smoke. At my brother's request, I followed him to the restroom. There, while he sneaked a cigarette, I listened. When we returned to this room, he pointed you out. I apologize for the awful smell. This tuxedo must have absorbed more smoke than I thought."

"So, you really don't smoke?"

"I could never smoke. Too often my patients at the hospital let me see the results of tobacco use. But, no matter what I say, I can't get Matt to quit."

"What does Matt want you to tell me?"

He adjusted his chair and stretched his long legs under the table. For an instant, his knee brushed against mine and transmitted a burst of electricity. Shock flicked in his eyes. Then he said, "Nothing. As much as I detest his nasty habit, I'm glad he shared a bit of brotherly advice. Now, could I convince you to reconsider and dance with me?"

That instant the band kicked up the tempo. Some of the older couples eased off the dance floor. Sharon took advantage of the extra space, separated from her partner, and gyrated to the center of the area. My foot began to tap the beat.

Maybe I felt tired of being me, the office wallflower. I knew I wanted to dance, just once before I left the reception and returned to my apartment to watch television with my cat. And what could have been safer than making a few simple motions in front of a doctor? So I said, "Okay."

Mark smiled. A dimple creased one cheek. He stood, removed his stinky jacket, and helped ease my chair from the table. When I rose, he grasped my hand. Electric waves pulsed into my fingers while he led me to a corner of the hardwood dance floor. In the center, Sharon writhed, slinging her hands up and down. Men gathered to cheer her on. I couldn't determine her partner.

Still holding my hand, Mark nodded toward my coworker. Then he whispered, "They're waiting to see if she does a Janet Jackson peek-a-boo."

Why hadn't I realized that? Sharon wore a bright orange strapless gown which appeared spray painted to her body. She reminded me of a carrot without its green top.

I felt a slight jerk. Mark pulled me close, then spun me away. He repeated the moves a couple more times, before he initiated a double spin.

So much for simple and separate. My heart rate climbed to a dangerous speed. I didn't care. Dancing with Mark felt exhilarating.

But I hadn't danced swing steps since college days. What if I did something wrong, misstepped, lost a shoe, fell? What if I embarrassed him, me, or both of us?

The song ended. I expected Mark to walk me back to the empty table and disappear. Instead, he pulled me towards him until my back met his chest. Then he wrapped both arms around me as if he intended for us to dance the next number. With my hand, I fanned the heat from my face.

Sharon still consumed the male attention. We inched closer, and I noticed her bodice had slipped dangerously low. She tugged, but I saw no change. At least I didn't have to worry about a wardrobe malfunction. I'd chosen a simple, pale blue, long-sleeved sheath with a matching sweater. In fact, I felt much too warm.

The band began "Proud Mary." I watched Sharon begin to wiggle. Mark whispered, "Your friend's in trouble."

Friend? Until tonight, Sharon and Glenna had ignored me. Once I'd overheard Sharon entertaining coworkers in the office break room by making me the butt of her jokes.

Now Sharon's discomfort radiated across the room. I said, "I must help. She'll never live down that sort of embarrassment."

"Follow my lead."

By the time we sidestepped next to Sharon, her flattened palms shielded exposed cleavage while her feet shuffled back and forth off-rhythm. With Mark's guidance, I maneuvered between her and a man whose eyes appeared ready to pop from their sockets.

Wedged between Sharon and the eye-popping man, we stopped dancing. Mark helped me out of my sweater, and I tossed it to Sharon. Fanning my face with my hand, I said, "Dancing with Mark makes me warm to my toes."

Sharon slipped on the garment, fastened buttons, and mouthed, "Thanks."

After that, Mark led me back to our corner. While we wove through dancers, he said, "That was kind. And, I admit, a test."

"A test?"

"I want to raise my future children in a Christian home. With a busy practice and long hours at the hospital, I haven't become active in a church. Since I'm a single man whose friends are more than willing to introduce me to available females, I've developed a screening process to help me avoid women unsuitable for marriage."

"But you didn't cause Sharon's predicament."

"No. But a similar situation would have developed. It always does."

I raised an eyebrow and stared.

"When it happens, I wait to see how the woman reacts."

"And I thought I was the only person who sought a Good Samarian."

"Earlier this evening, Matt advised me to ask you to dance. He said there's nothing better than dancing with the right partner."

"And?"

"I believe I've found mine." Mark winked before he drew me into his arms to begin a slow dance.

The next year, Mark and I danced as bride and groom.

SARA GIPSON, published in several anthologies, has won awards for works in fiction, nonfiction, poetry, photography, and art. In 2011, she received the Euple Riney Memorial Award for The Storyteller Magazine Editor's Choice in Short Story. She is also an active member of All Souls Interdenominational Church in Scott, Arkansas.

A Star-Spangled Courtship

* * *

Gail Kittleson

Claire Hensley had no intention of falling in love. She only intended to serve her country, along with thousands of WACS across the nation in 1942. No one chanted "Make Love, Not War" along the streets in those days. No one held moratoriums on the war, and if they had, Claire would have told them a thing or three.

She had met some young women who'd already joined, and she liked their spiffy uniforms. They had a way about them, she thought. They knew what they were about. In those days, people from all walks of life signed up to give their all for the U.S. of A. Claire said yes to the recruiter with absolutely no doubt she was doing the right thing. Back then, the war made it easier, in a way, to make choices.

Sixty years had not dimmed Claire's memory of her "Decision Day." If anyone had asked her even then, Claire would have made her loyalties clear, along with her determination to remain unattached until after the war.

The day she turned 18, Claire signed up for the WACS. Her friend Helen went along for the ride and ended up signing on the dotted line, as well. When they came home from the county seat to their small Iowa town, Claire led the way.

"Mama, I've decided, and that's all there is to it. I want to be an air-traffic controller. I want to do my part."

A month later, Mama drove Helen and Claire to Fort Des Moines, where they interviewed, received their uniforms, innoculations, and company assignments.

By late afternoon, Mama still waited for the results. She listened, dried her tears, and helped the girls carry their luggage to their newly assigned barracks.

Claire would never forget the look in her mama's eyes as she kissed her good-bye. Such a mixture of grief and pride. If she could have enlisted with them, she probably would have.

*

Owen Bruggemann felt the same intense patriotism on his father's farm in eastern Nebraska. While he made the first crop of hay, he couldn't keep his mind on the work. He eyed his two younger brothers, one just out of high school, one almost 21. "Better that I go than they. And Dad'll be all right with them around to help with all the farm work."

Meeting the woman of his dreams was far from Owen's mind on those brilliant July days when he returned to his barracks in Fort Des Moines after a grueling 16-mile march or a challenging obstacle course. He had one focus: making it through this brutal training to what he assumed would be an even more brutal war. He had just turned 24, and his older brother had already flown secret missions for the British RAF. Owen had no starry dreams of an air command but intended to do his job in the dirt and muck. The infantry called his name.

Mature in many ways, Owen also knew what he wanted in a woman. He had thought it all through, and made a commitment never to put a young wife through a wartime separation such as his sister-in-law had endured.

He didn't wait for the draft. That way, his brothers would stand a better chance of being kept home with a 4-F status. He'd been reared with the mantra of always watching out for "the boys," and this was one way he could fulfill his calling to protect them. He would go anywhere the Army sent him, fight as hard as he could fight.

*

But fate had other ideas for Owen and Claire. Instead of being trained to control air traffic, Claire's group was assigned to the secretarial pool. She flew to Washington, D.C. and spent her days in an office attached to the Pentagon....

"You see how God works in mysterious ways?" Her eyes sparkle as she tells the story to me, an avid listener, years later. "Owen wanted to be a grunt. He was willing to wallow through the worst battle zones, leading men in hand-to-hand combat. But his commanding officer saw a different potential in him. Organization."

He rolls his eyes under brows as white as the snows at Valley Forge. No comment comes forth, but he pats Claire's petite, veined hand and takes a deep breath as if preparing for time travel.

"So he found himself in the last place he'd imagined, Stateside in a command office—a very important one, I must say." She giggles and covers her blue-tinged lips.

"So how did you meet exactly?" I ask.

"Oh, Owen will tell you he saw me first, because we were both at Fort Des Moines at the same time, but I don't think so. One night in Washington, at a show with Bebe Daniels...you've heard of her, haven't you?"

I shake my head no.

This admission ignites Owen into speech. "What a great actress. She was the best of our day, though she maybe wasn't as famous as some others. You'd better find yourself an old reel and give her a watch, young lady."

I promise. But I want more details. "So, you both went to the show?"

"No, that would have been too easy. Owen made it more complicated for me to meet him. He got into some sort of trouble, and he was put on duty that evening cleaning latrines." Her smirk raises her husband's ire.

"I didn't get into trouble, no sirree. But I did end up on cleaning duty. Can you believe my luck?" Owen's brows dance as he straightens out Claire's version.

But she cheerfully takes back the floor.

"I walked home with a couple of the other girls, right past a parking lot where Owen and a couple of his buddies scrubbed rubber shower mats."

"Yep, and that was it for me. They stopped to talk with us. Time passed, and pretty soon everyone else left, so Claire and I talked some more, and I knew right then." He glances down at Claire. "Right, Babe?"

"Right. I knew, too. It sounds so spontaneous, so...so impulsive."

"I have to agree. Did you have a first date?"

Owen guffaws. "Doesn't that count? Does a man have to spend his hard-earned paycheck for something to qualify as a date?"

"Well, no, but..."

"We did have a proper first date, now, Owen. Be nice to this lady. Tell her where you took me."

"It turned out that Bebe Daniels got held over, something about her plane being rescheduled, so the show was repeated the next day, a Sunday afternoon. I took it as a sign from heaven. I found Claire's billet, threw a stone up to what I figured was her window. Somebody found her, and I asked her from the ground."

I turn to Claire. "You said yes?"

"Absolutely. We had some kind of mutual magnetism, I'd say. Sitting beside Owen that day seemed so right. Suddenly, he became the center of my world. I wrote to Mama about him, and she wrote back, 'You say he's a farm boy too, from Nebraska? Then he must be from good stock.' We saw each other as often as possible after that night."

Claire's gray-blue eyes take on a dreamy look. "He took me sightseeing, to the Washington Monument, the Lincoln, the Jefferson. He took me out to eat at the cutest little hamburger joint. It became our place. We had so many Cokes and malts together at the USO station, I'm surprised they didn't throw us out. Three weeks after the day we met, I said yes to Owen's marriage proposal."

Owen can't hide his lopsided grin. "I was a sucker for love, I guess. Or maybe the good Lord was watching out for me. I still say I glimpsed you at Fort Des Moines back in the summer, old girl."

Claire turns to her beloved with a stoic face. "And I still say you didn't."

GAIL KITTLESON, a former writing and ESL instructor, now makes writing her priority, along with her grandchildren. She has completed a three-book historical women's fiction series and a WWII series. Her heroines always travel the road to empowerment. Gail's husband served two wartime deployments.

Something More

* * *

Tricia Saxby

The hallways of Argyle High School were deserted. The quiet mumble from behind the closed classroom doors offered a sense of being amongst a crowd without all the congestion.

Amy glanced at the clock, and a nervous rumble settled in her stomach. She had no business being on this end of the school, darting by classroom doors so the teachers inside wouldn't see her. She'd left class early with the excuse of an upset stomach—well, it hadn't exactly been a lie. The real reason she wanted to leave was to "accidentally" run into Eric McMain, a grade-11 student who consumed her thoughts to such an extent that sitting in her English 12 class discussing poetry seemed like a waste of time.

Friends since grade 9, she and Eric had hung out with the same group of friends. They had a lot in common and participated in many of the same extracurricular activities. His dark good looks and blue eyes had most girls making fools of themselves, and she had a wonderful time bugging him about it. Yet Eric took it all in good fun and didn't string them along…for too long.

Amy knew there was an attraction between them. She could feel it each time she approached him, but once either of them opened their mouths, the tension disappeared and laughter filled the air. She used to like this arrangement. It made things simple and didn't complicate their friendship. But she knew, deep down, that if Eric ever started seriously dating one of the many girls who swooned over him, she would not be happy. She used to classify this as protectiveness, a good friend looking out for another, but lately she wondered if it could be more.

She had made it down to the end of the hallway and now stood beside the row of lockers across from the chemistry room. As soon as Eric walked out the door, he'd see her and walk her to choir practice.

Then it hit her. What excuse could she give him for being here, when she had English on the other side of the school? Panic consumed her and the knots in her stomach grew. Suddenly not feeling well, Amy pushed away from the lockers and headed for the closest girls' washroom. *What was I thinking?*

Just then the bell shrilled in the hallways. Classroom doors swung open, and students shot out, talking and laughing. Squished in the traffic, she felt her progress to the washroom come to a halt. Turning her head as the chemistry door opened, she watched student after student leave the room. Where was Eric? She had talked to him first thing this morning. He didn't say anything about having to leave.

Amy's temper started to rise as students continued to push her up against the lockers in her attempt to get to the chemistry room. "Excuse me!" she shouted, and most of the students around her moved to let her by. "Finally," she mumbled under her breath as she reached the door.

Inside, she saw Eric talking animatedly to a girl with long blond hair. Amy waved, but his attention seemed to be wholly on the other girl. He grabbed the girl's books from the desk with such a besotted expression that Amy had to turn away. The pain in her stomach intensified at the realization he'd fallen for one of those silly girls. A familiar high-pitched flirty laugh pierced the air. Amy couldn't believe it. The blond girl who had stolen Eric's heart was one of her friends...one of Eric's friends...Tamara Howey.

The walls of the classroom seemed to close in around her. Desperate to escape, she hugged her books closer to her chest and left as fast as the crowded hallway would allow. The thought of eating lunch almost made her nauseous, but even worse was the thought of having to watch Eric and Tamara walk into the auditorium together all lovey-dovey. Her friends would question her strange behavior, and Amy didn't want to explain her turbulent feelings to anyone at the moment.

"Hey, Amy! Wait up."

Amy whipped her head around and saw Eric and Tamara waving at her. She picked up her pace and ducked into the stairwell that lead up to the second floor. Instead of going up, where she knew they would follow, she went out the exit and into the warm summer sunshine. An oak tree situated between two ball diamonds came into view, and Amy ran towards it. Placing her books on the ground, she sat beside them and leaned back against the rough bark. The enticing scent of lilacs tantalized her nostrils and she sighed, letting the tears come at last.

"Amy?"

A small squeak escaped as she jumped up in surprise. "Eric! Wh...what are you doing here?" she stammered, dabbing at the tears on her cheeks. How could she forget that this was their favorite homework spot and the first place he would look?

"Why didn't you wait for me and Tamara? Are you crying?" he asked, taking a step closer.

"No! Of course not." Humiliated beyond belief, Amy swiveled away from him and frantically wiped any remaining tears from her cheeks. Then she picked up her books. "We'd better head inside. Choir practice will already have started."

"Okay."

This was something new—uncomfortable tension. She needed to say something. "Where is Tamara?" she asked, not really caring.

"She has a dentist appointment."

Nope...she cared.

Eric didn't elaborate any further, and Amy put a few feet of distance between them as they walked back towards the school. She wanted to say something—maybe yell at him and punch him hard in the arm...anything to let out the jealous monster that consumed her. Crying under a tree sure didn't help.

"Look, Amy. I..."

WHACK! Amy chose the latter and punched him hard in the shoulder, then pushed him. Eric staggered backwards but didn't fall. "What was that for?" he shouted.

Amy dropped her books and stood with her feet shoulder-width apart, hands in fists by her side, and her jaw clenched. "What is going on with you and Tamara?"

"Nothing!" he said, but too quickly.

"I would call gazing at her lovingly and carrying her books for her more than nothing," Amy spat out.

"You saw that?" Eric asked, his face coloring a light shade of red.

"And why didn't you tell me that you had *feelings* for her? I thought we told each other everything."

"We do...I don't know. I..."

As Amy watched the struggle of emotions playing across his face, her anger simmered away into nothing. She closed the gap between them. When Eric flinched, she laughed. "I'm not going to hit you again."

"Good," he said, rubbing his arm.

Amy decided to be honest with him. He didn't need to deal with her yo-yo emotions. If her feelings wouldn't be returned from him in the way she so desperately wanted, then she needed to deal with it, because their friendship was too important. "You got a glimpse of my little green monster," she started. "And I'm not proud of it."

"Little green monster?" he repeated with a hint of sarcasm.

"I'm sorry!"

Eric surprised her by showing a bit of his grin.

This gave her the courage to continue. "I'm usually okay with you being surrounded by girls. I bug you about it all the time."

Eric nodded.

"But lately it hasn't been okay, and when I saw you looking at Tamara like that in the chemistry room, I was shocked and angry." She paused. "I was hurt."

Eric stepped a bit closer. "Why are you feeling this way?"

Amy was not going to answer that. Not when he obviously had feelings for another girl. "Because you kept it a secret," she said instead.

Eric sighed and rubbed his face with his hands. "I'll be honest with you."

"I wish you would."

"I only like her as a friend. That look you saw was my reaction to what she told me."

Amy snorted her disbelief.

"She actually said there was someone else I should have my eye on. Someone, if I was honest with myself, who had my heart right from the beginning."

Amy could feel the color draining from her face. "What?"

"Don't you mean who?" He took another step closer, so they were only inches apart.

"Who?" she asked, her gaze straying to his lips.

"You," he whispered and placed his lips upon hers for their first kiss.

Something more turned into love at that moment.

TRICIA SAXBY is a romance writer working on her first novel. She is a member of the Interior Authors Group, Federation of BC Writers, and the Romance Writers of America.

triciasax.wordpress.com

More Than Just Another Day

* * *

Diane K. Ellenwood

Alexis hit the snooze button for the last time.

"Mommy, it's time to get up," she heard from the doorway.

"Okay, honey, I'm coming."

It was hard raising the girls alone. Every day seemed exactly like the one before. She wondered what had happened to the plans she and Chuck made before their wedding. They were going to have children, raise them, and grow old together. For a couple of years, they tried to have children; then she sought help through a fertility clinic. Chuck had left soon after the girls were born. She'd blamed herself, until she discovered an email from another woman....

But time was wasting; mornings were always rush hour. She set the girls at the table and poured cereal and milk for them. At first glance you couldn't tell them apart, but Trina had a small strawberry birthmark on her right ear.

After rushing the girls out the door and dropping them off at daycare, Alexis headed for the office, where she processed insurance claims.

"Good morning, Alexis," she heard as soon as she plopped herself in the chair in her cubicle.

She turned to see Mark, the new man at the office, standing at her desk. Six-foot-two, handsome, and blond, with a dimple in his left cheek when he smiled, Mark made her heart race. She hoped it wasn't obvious. After all, she wasn't ready to be involved with anyone yet; the girls were her top priority. Besides, she wasn't sure any man would date her, knowing she had children. "Good morning, Mark. How may I help you?" she answered professionally.

"Would you show me where these are filed?" He held a small stack of manila folders.

"Right over there." She pointed across the room.

Mark didn't seem in a hurry to leave.

"Anything else I can help with?"

"Would you join me for lunch today?"

The phone at Alexis' desk rang. "Excuse me, Mark. Thank you for calling Hillside Insurance. This is Alexis. How may I help you?"

"Alexis, it's Annie. Trish is running a low fever and says her tummy hurts."

As if sensing a personal phone call, Mark retreated to his desk.

"Okay, Annie, I'll pick her up. Thank you."

Both relieved and disappointed, Alexis stopped by Mark's desk to thank him for the invite but said she'd have to take a rain check. Taking an early lunch, she headed for the daycare. Since it was midday, she'd have to take the girls to her mom's house. Next fall they'd be in kindergarten all day.

After dropping off the girls, she ordered a salad through the drive-thru and sat in her car. *Now what do I do? He's going to want to know when he can have that rain check. I should've told him I wasn't interested.*

But she was interested, and now she knew he was interested too.

As she entered the office, he smiled at her, then returned to his work.

At the end of the day, they left at the same time. He held the door for her. "See you in the morning, Alexis. Have a good night."

"Thanks, Mark. You, too."

*

The next day, Alexis put in a little extra effort. Trina, her observant girl, noticed. "Mommy, you look extra pretty today, and you smell pretty too."

"Thank you, sweetie." Alexis grinned. You couldn't get much past Trina's detective-like senses.

Arriving early to work, Alexis turned on her computer to start her day. But today she wasn't the only one here; Mark had come in a little early too.

"Good morning, Alexis," he said, smiling.

"Well, good morning, Mark. You're early." She returned the smile.

"Since no one else is here...," Mark began.

Oh, here we go for the rain check...

He paused.

"...would you like to go to lunch?" Alexis finished the thought for him.

"Well, I was going to say, why don't we get to work," he teased, "but since you brought it up, yes I would like to go to lunch!"

Alexis felt herself blush. "You weren't going to ask me to lunch?"

"Yes, I was." Swiftly he apologized. "I didn't mean to tease you. *Will* you go to lunch with me?"

"Of course. And with that said, I really do need to get to work." She grinned.

Alexis made herself focus on her work until lunchtime. From noon until one, Hillside Insurance closed its doors, so she waited for the others to leave before approaching Mark.

"How about walking to The Café?" Mark suggested.

"A great idea."

Within minutes they were seated at The Café, and the waitress took their order. Conversation flowed easily; they were so relaxed and comfortable.

Can this man be real? Alexis wondered. Was it possible she'd found someone with whom she had so much in common? *And he's a gentleman, too!*

All too soon it was time to return to work.

"Thank you for lunch," Mark said, "I hope we can do this again."

"I'd love to."

"Okay, how about Monday through Friday?" Mark laughed.

She laughed too; she'd been thinking the same thing. On their walk back to the office, their hands brushed a little, and Alexis secretly wished he would hold her hand.

"Would you mind if I asked for your phone number?" Mark finally geared up the nerve to ask. "If you aren't seeing anyone, maybe we can go to dinner."

"I'm not dating anyone, but I do have plans this weekend." Alexis took a small notepad and pen out of her purse and wrote down her phone number.

*

The next morning, her cell phone had a text: *Good morning, Sunshine. Mark.*

Alexis stared at the phone. She could hear his voice in her head. *Good morning, Mark,* she texted back.

May I call you?

Yes, she replied.

A second later, her phone rang. "I just wanted to hear your voice before I started my day. Hope you don't mind."

"Not at all." She couldn't help but smile.

They chatted for a few more minutes before saying their good-byes.

"Who was that, Mommy?" Trisha asked, bringing her back to earth.

"A friend from work, honey."

"Who's your friend?"

"Never mind," she quickly answered.

*

After church on Sunday, Alexis treated her mom and the girls to The Buffet for lunch. She'd also decided something else. In their next conversation, she was going to tell Mark about the girls. She was very proud of her girls, and she wasn't going to ever think twice about telling anyone again.

A quick change of clothes, and they were off to the park. Trisha and Trina headed for the slides, and Alexis sat on a bench to read.

A minute later her phone notified her of a text. *Can I call? Mark.*

Yes, she responded. Her phone rang.

"Hi, did I interrupt anything?" he asked.

"Right now I'm at the park. Want to join me?"

"Sure, which one are you at?"

She told him which one and to meet her at the play area.

Soon a white Mustang convertible pulled up to the parking lot, and Mark got out. Alexis stood and waved.

Trina and Trisha came running over. "Mommy, where are you going?"

"Nowhere, girls. I'm staying right here," she reassured them.

Mark looked at the girls and then at Alexis.

"Trina, Trisha, this is my friend from work, Mark."

The girls giggled.

"Okay, girls, go ahead and play." Alexis wanted Mark's reaction privately. "Well, what do you think?"

"They are every bit as beautiful as their mother."

"You don't mind that I have children?"

"If you don't mind that I don't have children," he teased.

Alexis was sure tomorrow would be more than just another day.

DIANE K. ELLENWOOD resides in southeast Michigan with her husband of 36 years. Together they've raised three sons and enjoy eight grandchildren. Her children's book *The Mis-Adventures of Three Amigos* delights children of all ages. "Oh, Tannenbaum" was published in *Celebrating Christmas,* and "Come and Dine" and "God's Arms" in EACM Ministries' newsletter.

To email the author: **dianeellenwood@gmail.com.**

A Christmas Party

* * *

ANNE-MARIE MOONEY

Glistening snow covered the ground, and icicles hung from the eaves of the few quaint homes scattered about the countryside. Stars shone brightly in the night with only the Christmas lights decorating the small town to equal their beauty. The streets, hidden by a thin layer of ice, were lined by sidewalks where window shoppers enjoyed the quiet evening. Overlooking the frozen pond in the park was a charming bed-and-breakfast, known as Lola's. It was the closest thing to a hotel in an 80-mile radius. The most recent visitor staying there happened to be the owners' daughter. Sitting at the desk overlooking the pond, she watched children ice skating outside her window, then glanced back over the lines of a letter she gently held.

> I can't wait to see you! Definitely want to meet your parents while I'm there. Don't forget about the special surprise I have for you! Been waiting a long time to spring it.
> Sincerely, Nathan

A special surprise. Katherine knew it had to be a proposal. They had been close friends for nearly two years, and even though Nathan wasn't the most affectionate person, he was reliable and trustworthy. And the timing was perfect, with Katherine finally taking her mother's advice about visiting her hometown, Crystal Cove. A quiet village in Vermont, it offered the perfect opportunity to relax and let down her constant guard. Even though she thought it meant she wouldn't be able to see Nathan until the New Year, when mentioning it to him, she was surprised to hear that he thought it was a wonderful idea. Now she was left anticipating his upcoming arrival. *He'll be here just in time for the Christmas party,* she thought.

The Christmas party was an annual event the town had. Everyone was invited, and everyone always went. The stores would close early, and the streets would be bare. Held at the mayor's estate on top of the hill, everyone looked forward to it all year. There would be music, dancing, and a delicious buffet. Katherine was so excited that Nathan would be going with her, she almost couldn't wait.

But soon the day arrived....

The night of the party, Katherine drove her red sports car up the hill to the mayor's estate. The best parking spot she could find was at a bend on one of the steeper portions. Either that, or she'd be walking a long way in the cold. Easing the car into the slippery spot, she turned off the engine and opened her door. As she did so, a male voice from behind said, "Nice car."

She looked over, and once she laid eyes on him, she lost her breath.

With scruffy, dark hair spilling over his forehead, his face was strikingly handsome, having an honest appeal. His tender brown eyes sparkled as he flashed a warm smile. "I'm Cam."

Nervously, she grabbed her purse, then hurried out of the car. "Katherine," she said, finally regaining her composure.

"I've wanted one of those ever since I was old enough to get a ticket," Cam said, studying her car like a piece of artwork. "You new around here?"

As they started walking toward the house, Katherine answered, "I grew up here, but now I live in the city. I'm just visiting for the holidays."

"It's a beautiful little town. I moved here a couple years back."

"Oh really? Well, it's great if you like that whole 'everybody knows everybody' thing."

"And you don't?" he asked curiously.

"I do and I don't," she replied, not really sure what she thought about it anymore. When she was younger, she was definitely ready to move away, but now she found herself missing it more than she imagined possible. "You like my car so much, what do you drive?"

Laughing, he said, "I'm still working on that. I've been doing a lot of walking lately."

"You walked here?"

"It's not that far from my house."

Katherine shook her head. He was so unlike what she was used to, but she couldn't help admiring his optimistic outlook.

When they entered the house, Katherine immediately scanned the room for Nathan but, after a few minutes, realized he wasn't there yet.

"Would you like to dance?"

Katherine was almost startled by his suggestion but was happy he asked. "Of course."

He smiled at her sweetly, his gaze making her knees a little weak. As he slipped his hand into hers, he led her towards the middle of the room and then wrapped his arm around her. They began to slowly move with the music while she rested her head on his shoulder. He held her so close, yet so gently.

"You're a beautiful dancer," Cam said.

She only smiled, too taken by him to reply.

"I'd like some punch. How about you?"

She nodded, and they headed toward the buffet. But before reaching it, Katherine said, "I'll get us something. Could you hold my purse?"

"Sure."

Katherine couldn't admit to herself that the real reason she wanted to get the drinks was so she could start breathing again. She felt almost faint around him. He was so captivating. How could a man like that even exist?

Returning with two glasses of punch, she gave him a cup as he handed back her purse. He took a quick sip as concern crowded his face. "I better head out. My boss'll kill me if I'm late."

"Do you have to?" Katherine asked, not ready to lose him. "I mean, who works during these hours?"

"I do, unfortunately," he explained, looking away for the briefest moment. Then he added, "I'll see you again, though, I hope."

"Right."

She watched him walk out the door, feeling as if her dreams were disappearing before her eyes and wondering if she *would* ever see him again.

Spotting her mother standing among a group of people by the side, Katherine wandered over, hoping to at least find some distraction, if not consolation. Her mother was all excited to see her, but Katherine couldn't concentrate on the conversation.

Glancing back towards the door, Katherine saw Nathan walk in. Reality flooded back. *The proposal.* Thank goodness. He was just in time to wipe away the sad thoughts of her lost "dream come true."

But then she noticed he was with someone—a woman.

"Katherine!" he called vivaciously.

"Nathan! You finally made it."

"Wouldn't miss it."

"Who's this?" Katherine asked, referring to the woman.

"This is my surprise!"

Katherine glanced at the smiling young lady, completely confused. "What do you mean?"

"I told you I had a surprise. This is Ashley—my fiancé."

"Your what?" Shock overtook her. "I didn't know you were engaged."

"That's what makes it a surprise."

Katherine wanted to melt right through the floor. The night had turned into a disaster. "Congratulations! I have to run, though. I'll probably see you tomorrow."

"So soon?"

"Yeah." She walked out of the house, a tear sliding down her cheek. "Wait....where's my car?"

It was gone. Katherine couldn't believe it. Her car was nowhere to be seen. Then it hit her. "That guy! He took it! He was holding my purse and must've taken my keys. He stole my car! How could I have been so naïve! So taken in! He's just like the guys in New York!"

Katherine ran back inside and told her parents what had happened. Then she called the police. A patrol car showed up a couple minutes later, but when Katherine saw who got out, she was dumbfounded. "It's you! What are you doing?"

"I'm here to investigate a missing car."

Katherine just stared at the man standing before her. It was Cam. "But *you* took my car! Did you finally get tired of walking?"

"No, my partner picked me up." He gestured to the other police officer with him. "What's that?" He pointed to the bottom of the hill, where something dark lay under a pile of snow...her car.

It had rolled down the hill while she was at the party. She'd been so flustered when first meeting Cam that she'd left her keys in the ignition and parking brake off.

While the car's snow was being cleared off, Katherine sat alone, struggling to keep from bursting into tears.

A few minutes later, Cam came and sat next to her, looking concerned. "You looked like you were crying when I got here."

At that moment Katherine realized she wasn't crying about the car, or about Nathan's engagement. She gave up on shielding herself, whispering, "I thought I'd never see you again."

He gazed at her, then caressed her hair. "I wouldn't let that happen."

That's when Katherine knew he had stolen her heart—and thankfully not her car.

ANNE-MARIE MOONEY has had two other short stories published and enjoys writing fictional love stories that entertain and inspire others. She lives in South Carolina, where she keeps up with college classes and writes to her heart's content.

You may write her at **storiesfromtheheart@aol.com**.

Don't Miss...

41 REAL LOVE STORIES GUARANTEED FOR A SMILE

COMPILED & EDITED BY
RAMONA TUCKER & JENNIFER WESSNER

Surprised by Love...

Where did you first meet the person you fell in love with? The person with whom you could be totally you? Or do you still dream of that magical moment, when you know you're in head-over-heels, dancing-in-the-rain kind of love?

Fall in love again...or for the first time...with 41 of the sweetest real-life love stories collected from across the globe. They're guaranteed to make you smile.

For other great love stories:
www.oaktara.com

Don't Miss...

42 REAL STORIES OF ENDURING LOVE

COMPILED & EDITED BY
RAMONA TUCKER & JENNIFER WESSNER

Forever Love...

When did you fall in love? And when did you know that love would be a lasting one—celebrating life's joyous moments and walking together, hand-in-hand, through challenging times? Or are you still longing for that person to come into your life, as a side-by-side companion?

Experience "my love to you always" kind of love through 42 of the sweetest, real-life love stories collected from across the globe. They're guaranteed to make you misty eyed and renew your faith in the power of enduring love.

For other great love stories:
www.oaktara.com

About the Compilers/Editors

RAMONA CRAMER TUCKER has been on the cutting-edge of publishing for nearly 30 years, in a wide variety of positions, including: Senior Editor, Tyndale House Publishers; Editorial Director, Harold Shaw Publishers (now WaterBrook); Editor, *Today's Christian Woman* magazine and Executive Editor, *Virtue* magazine (Christianity Today, International); as a freelance writer/editor/project development specialist for Simon & Schuster, Random House, Viking-Penguin, Zondervan, Nelson, Baker/Revell, InterVarsity, Howard, David C. Cook, Barbour, HarperCollins, Summerside/Guideposts, and other publishers. She is Cofounder and Editorial Director of OakTara and Adjunct Faculty for the English Department at Wheaton College.

JENNIFER WESSNER, a Wheaton College graduate with a B.A. in Literature and History and a former journalist, now works as OakTara Publisher's Social Networking Director.

www.oaktara.com
- *Fresh, new authors. Leading-edge established authors.*
- *Inspirational fiction in nearly every genre, from suspense to romance*
- *Mind-stretching, heart-transforming, life-inspiring nonfiction*

CPSIA information can be obtained at www.ICGtesting.com
Printed in the USA
BVOW040858191212

308678BV00002B/492/P